Praise for *How to Disappear*

"What a thrill ride! *How to Disappear* sucks you in from the very first page and never lets you come up for air. It's a game of cat and mouse with an end that will leave you gasping."

—APRIL HENRY,
New York Times bestselling author of *Girl, Stolen*

"*How to Disappear* is a funny, sexy thrill of a book, with two characters who crackle and sparkle on the page, as they struggle to outrun danger and resist their growing attraction. Nicolette and Jack are streetwise yet vulnerable, tough yet broken, old for their years yet entirely teenage in their sensibilities. A delight to read!"

—CARRIE MESROBIAN,
award-winning author of *Sex & Violence*

"A deliciously gritty dive into the dark side of human nature! This book pretty much defines #MorallyComplicatedYA in a beautifully written but fast-paced read that's both twisted and thought-provoking."

—MARTINA BOONE,
award-winning author of the Heirs of Watson Island trilogy

"A high-intensity, cross-country thrill ride that will have you breathlessly turning pages until the very end."

—GRETCHEN McNEIL,
award-winning author of *Ten* and the Don't Get Mad series

Also by
ANN REDISCH STAMPLER

Afterparty
Where It Began

HOW **TO DISA**PPEAR

ANN REDISCH STAMPLER

Simon Pulse

New York   London   Toronto   Sydney   New Delhi

〰〰 SIMON PULSE An imprint of Simon & Schuster Children's Publishing Division | 1230 Avenue of the Americas, New York, NY 10020 | First Simon Pulse paperback edition June 2017 | Text copyright © 2016 by Ann Redisch Stampler | Cover photograph copyright © 2016 by Thinkstock | Also available in a Simon Pulse hardcover edition. | All rights reserved, including the right of reproduction in whole or in part in any form. | SIMON PULSE, logo, and colophon are registered trademarks of Simon & Schuster, Inc. | For information about special discounts for bulk purchases, please contact Simon & Schuster Special Sales at 1-866-506-1949 or business@simonandschuster.com. | The Simon & Schuster Speakers Bureau can bring authors to your live event. For more information or to book an event contact the Simon & Schuster Speakers Bureau at 1-866-248-3049 or visit our website at www.simonspeakers.com. | Cover designed by Regina Flath | Interior designed by Gail Ghezzi | The text of this book was set in Filosofia. | Manufactured in the United States of America | 10 9 8 7 6 5 4 3 2 1 | The Library of Congress has cataloged the hardcover edition as follows: | Name: Stampler, Ann Redisch, author. | Title: How to disappear / by Ann Stampler. | Description: First Simon Pulse hardcover edition. | New York : Simon Pulse, 2016. | Summary: "A sexy road trip thriller, told from alternate perspectives, following a girl on the run after witnessing or committing a murder and the boy who has been sent to kill her"—Provided by publisher. Identifiers: LCCN 2015027340 | ISBN 9781481443937 (hc) | ISBN 9781481443951 (eBook) | Subjects: | CYAC: Mystery and detective stories. | Love—Fiction. | Murder—Fiction. | Organized crime—Fiction. | BISAC: JUVENILE FICTION / Social Issues / Physical & Emotional Abuse (see also Social Issues / Sexual Abuse). | JUVENILE FICTION / Social Issues / Dating & Sex. | Classification: LCC PZ7.S78614 Ho 2016 | DDC [Fic]—dc23 | ISBN 9781481443944 (pbk)

For Rick, Laura, and Michael, as always

Prologue

There is a body in the woods.

The flash of an electric yellow blanket in the moonlight, unfurling as it's dragged along. A glimpse of nylon binding at the edges, sweeping the ground at the corner where the arm has fallen out.

At the end of that limp arm, a hand is trailing through the leaves into the darkness. But I have seen the fingers, curled like talons, the nails all broken, the blue polish chipped away.

Shoes shuffling through the leaves.

And then the digging of the hole.

I'm crouched behind a fallen pine tree, soft leaves and pine needles underfoot, cocooned in darkness. I pause to catch my breath. My heart's banging so hard that it could crack my ribs.

A walk in the woods, that's all it was. That's what I tell myself now, when it's too late to do anything about it, when it's done—when the kind of person I am and will ever be is thrown into unanswerable question.

When all I want is to pretend it never happened.

But how do I forget that there were pine needles stuck in the laces of my sneakers, and that they were wet with blood? How do I pretend I never felt the handle of the knife pressed hard against my palm?

Part 1

1

Cat

I'm not Catherine Davis.

My hair isn't brown.

And I have never lived in Tulsa, Oklahoma. I've never even seen the state of Oklahoma, despite what this convincing but completely fake ID says.

Or, technically, not fake.

Just not *mine*.

Cat Davis.

Born in Oklahoma City (where I wasn't born).

Got so drunk, she didn't even notice when her license was stolen right out of her bag nineteen years later. At a frat party (where I shouldn't have been) in Galkey, Texas (where I didn't want to be).

Stolen by me.

Morally speaking, this wasn't my most glittering moment. But it definitely answered that Sunday School question of whether I'd steal bread if it would keep me from starving.

Yes.

I would.

The license just seemed like one more untrue thing to stuff between me and my past. A tiny piece of laminated plastic I actually thought of as my ticket out of the obituary column.

One more little thing I needed to make it to the age of seventeen alive.

That, and a different-looking face and a different-shaped body and bulletproof skin.

That, and a heart of stone.

2

Jack

I slide the gun into the trunk of Don's shitmobile, between the ruck-sack and the cooler. My gut feels like someone took a Weedwacker to it.

I tell myself, *Man up, the bitch cut Connie Marino*—I have a thing against people who cut other people's throats. They'll convict her as an adult anyway. They'll inject a fatal dose of potassium chloride into her veins if I don't get to her first. I'm doing her a favor. She won't know what hit her.

But I'll know what hit her: me.

I try to think of ways out of it all the time, but I just keep getting pulled in deeper.

Two weeks ago, I was studying for the AP English Lit exam. I was taking notes on the poetry of T. S. Eliot.

This is the way the world ends
This is the way the world ends
This is the way the world ends
Not with a bang but a whimper.

No, T. S. Eliot, *this* is how the world ends: with a bang.

I slide the box of bullets into the compartment where the spare tire goes. The knives are already in there, wrapped in a hand towel, tied with twine.

I can hear my dad's voice when he found me on the floor of his room when I was little, unpacking a cardboard box of bullets. I was trying to get them to stand up on the carpet.

"Don? What did I tell you?"

But when I turned around and he saw that it was me and not my older brother, Don, he shook his head. And in an ice-cold voice, he said, "Jack, what are you doing? Think about it. *Think, Jack.*"

When I remember my dad now, that's always what I hear: him saying, *Think, Jack.* Because I was the one with the brain, the one who could analyze, assess, figure out consequences.

I was the one who said no thank you to my dad's business and his crazy-ass expectations. My career path was not going to be selling secondhand shoulder-mounted rocket launchers, describing tanks as "scrap metal" for the bookkeeper. And the rest of what my dad did for a living—the part of his career that required a silencer, his sideline in ending peoples' lives—was a nonstarter.

I was the one who got out.

And he was fine with my defection. He stopped saying, "You and me, Jack—the same guy in two bodies." He got it.

Don, on the other hand, doesn't get it.

If he had any idea who I am, he wouldn't have asked me to do this thing in the first place. It would have been like every other prison visit—me nodding through his complaints about the food, the exercise equipment, and the fact that his request for early release got turned down.

Instead, Don lays out how "this bitch Nicolette Holland" has to fall off the face of the earth.

At first, I don't get that I'm the person who's supposed to get rid of her. When I do understand, I say no.

It's not as if I've never turned him down before. Being Don's brother is a long string of refusals:

No to being his alibi.

No to being his lowlife friend's alibi.

No to running errands where nothing could go wrong—unless someone shows up with a drug-sniffing dog.

"No."

"You're not listening," Don says, leaning toward me in his orange prison jumpsuit, fuming.

Don is always fuming. He's flunked out of court-ordered anger management half a dozen times. If he'd come to live with me and

Mom instead of choosing Dad when our parents split up, one of us wouldn't have survived childhood.

He says, "This isn't optional, Jack." It's one of my dad's lines. The man's been dead for four years, but I can still hear the way he sounded when he said it. I can still feel the dread.

Don and I are sitting in the visitor's yard at Yucca Valley Men's Correctional Center, wedged between a cluster of tan stucco buildings and a fence with concertina wire looped on top. If you go through the visitor's log, you can see what a dutiful brother I am. I'm the reliable, law-abiding one with the clean record and the .El Pueblo High crew team sweatshirt from the preppy school I've never been expelled from.

But I'm also the guy with the killer pedigree that scares the shit out of people. I'm the one who's been trying to live down our last name since the day I figured out what it meant to be named Manx.

I lean back across the metal picnic table. "Don't try to jerk me around, Don. I'm not in."

Don says, "Then I'm a dead man."

"Shit, Don. *What* did you do?"

I'm slammed with memories of things Don did:

Don pushing me on my two-wheeler without the training wheels. Then he yells, "Die, asshole!" and lets go.

My mom hugging Don, holding on to him in a rib-crushing embrace in the courtroom, the first time he got sentenced to juvie.

My dad slapping him across the face, the ring streaking Don's cheek with a thin red line.

"Stupid," my dad said to no one in particular.

Don's first big fuckup was when he tried to hold up a 7-Eleven that had security cameras and a heavily armed owner behind the counter, his two crime-buster sons mopping the floor. The police gave my mom a security photo of Don, hands up, a hairline fracture in his right wrist from the mop's wooden handle.

My father asked me, "What did he do wrong, Jack?"

I said, "He tried to hold up a 7-Eleven?"

My dad said, "He didn't assess his target. Big mistake."

I was twelve. I was crying because my big brother was going to jail, and even my dad couldn't fix it.

I thought, *I'd be better at this than Don.*

Now I'm eighteen and I'm supposed to figure out how to murder a blood-crazed girl who disappeared. Because if I don't, maybe my brother dies—or worse.

Murder.

Welcome to the family business.

3

Cat

It happened five weeks before I became Cat.

When I ran.

Five weeks and one day before I was Cat, I thought I was Xena, Warrior Princess of Cotter's Mill, Ohio.

Up for anything.

Taker of dares.

Defender of downtrodden victims of mean girls and authority.

Invincible.

It's not that hard to be the slightly wild girl everybody likes when the only dire consequence in sight is when your stepfather tells you not to be reckless and impounds your car keys.

Until that next day, there was no reason not to like me.

The smart kids liked me because I was a fellow smart kid who underachieved. No competition, but got all their jokes.

The football guys liked me because, in eighth, I was the only cooperative girl they could find who was small enough to fit through the Jefferson coach's doggie door and let them into his house so they could hang the traditional COTTER'S MILL RULES, JEFFERSON SUCKS! banner in his living room.

The we–hate–football kids (stuck in track as their mandatory team sport) liked me because I led cross–country off–trail to Taco Bell.

The rich kids liked anyone with a big enough house on Green Lake.

And I owned the churchy girls (this would be half our school) because my best friend was the pastor's foster kid, and it was a (slightly exaggerated) well-known fact that I didn't go all the way despite a lot of opportunities. Also, I accidently dropped a chocolate shake down Matt Wagner's crotch when he dumped Jody Nimiroff for saying no.

As for the populars, I was a cheerleader. I was the girl at the top of the pyramid, hurtling headfirst toward the ground with her ponytail whipping around.

The populars were kind of stuck with me.

Until I ran.

Until I rolled out of Ohio, hidden in a cement pipe on the back of a flatbed truck.

I'd spent the night before huddled in Jody Nimiroff's lakeside tree house under the flannel sleeping bag she's kept up there since we were eight, eating the dregs of last year's Girl Scout cookies.

Every cell of me wanted to go home. I wanted to tell Steve, my stepfather, what happened. I wanted him to pull me into a bear hug, slightly pissed off but more than willing to take care of everything for me. Again.

But he already knew.

It felt like I'd been gutted by a dull knife, every idea of who I was and where I fit into the world pouring out of me like a deer's innards when it gets cut open in hunting season.

I was in wounded-deer survival mode.

Evade hunters.

Run.

Hide.

When they came looking for me along the narrow strip of gritty sand that rims Green Lake, tracing the ground with beams from their flashlights, I was pressed against the back wall of the tree house, chewing a stale Thin Mint.

Everything was so loud.

The chocolate bits between my teeth.

My pulse thundering in my ears.

Their footsteps as they disappeared past the Nimiroffs'

dock, scanning the lake with their puny globes of light. As if they thought I was paddling a canoe through pitch-black tributaries up to Canada.

If I knew how to find true north by looking at the stars— if I'd paid more attention when Steve tried to teach me—I might have been in a canoe. That's how desperate and lacking in judgment I was.

I had to get out of there before first light.

As soon as the men disappeared from sight, I lowered Jody's rope ladder and bolted back into the woods that skirt Lakeshore Road. Sliding between trees in the darkness, listening for footsteps.

By the time I hit the truck stop at Bonnie-Belle Pie, it was almost dawn.

I had nothing to lose.

I climbed onto the flatbed and into the pipe.

4

Jack

Supposedly, Eskimos have fifty words for snow. That's how many ways I keep saying no to Don. Because at first I don't believe him. I've heard too many variations on the threat before. If I don't run his errand, this dealer in Reno or that wannabe gangster from LA or the Russians will off him.

But here he is, alive and hunched over a metal picnic table.

Unfortunately, my dad snapping "Curiosity killed the cat" a hundred times immediately before smacking me when I was a kid didn't have the result he was going for. My curiosity is the peg Don uses to hang me out to dry. Because while I'm saying, "Don't try to jerk me around, no fucking way," Don pulls a white envelope out from under his jumpsuit.

I know it's a mistake before my hand touches the envelope.

I say no but shove it into my jacket in the interest of not getting caught wrestling over something neither one of us should have.

"I knew you'd see reason." Don smirks. "It's all there. Everything about her. Good stuff. It's from somebody's lawyer."

Why do they bother having guards at this place? Things slide in and out as if it were a dry cleaner: drugs, sharp objects, dossiers on girls with targets on their backs.

I say, "Whose lawyer?"

"Need-to-know," he says, as if suddenly he's CIA and not a low-life enforcer. That's what he's locked up for, whaling the crap out of guys who didn't pay back the loan shark he was working for. "You're just the technician."

I'm Don's murder *technician*?

"I know you," Don says. "You're going to look in the envelope. Then you're going to have to win the game. You can't help yourself."

All right, I'm going to look in the envelope. Who wouldn't look?

But how can he think I'm going to do this? It's almost May. AP exams are in a couple of weeks. Then comes Welcome Admitted Students weekend at Mercer College, twenty-five hundred miles east of Nevada, where my future's supposed to take place. I have a life as an upstanding citizen, honor student, and varsity crew captain that I'll be right back into as soon as I peel out of the prison parking lot.

"You know where my stuff is, right? In Mom's garage?"

"I don't care where your stuff is, Don!" You get good at shouting in a very quiet voice if you visit someone in prison enough. "You order me to do it and I do it? Are you kidding me? Do you even know me?"

Don stares out at the bleak landscape of the high desert. "I know what this Nicolette Holland did to Connie Marino," he says. "Doesn't that bother you?"

Of course it bothers me. It makes me sick.

I've known Connie since before my folks broke up. She was a nice girl from a nasty family out of Detroit, a little older than we were, liked to shoot hoops with us when her dad still lived in Vegas.

Connie Marino should *not* have had her throat cut. And if this had anything to do with her dad being a hood, it's flat-out wrong that death should be an occupational hazard that the kids inherit. I grew up with this gnawing at the back of my mind. Someone should do something about it. But it's hard to see how that's connected to me hunting down the girl who stuck it to Connie, this monster girl I'm supposed to find.

I don't say anything. It's my father's trick; it reduces grown men to babbling.

"She might know things she shouldn't know," Don whispers. "You have to get to her before the cops find her."

"What *things* could a sixteen-year-old girl know?"

Don looks away. "She might be Esteban Mendes's bimbo's kid."

"Crap, Don! You want me to piss off a Colombian guy?"

Don's eyes narrow in derision. "He's not *Colombian*," he says, as if this were information everyone with half a brain already knew. "He's *Cuban*. He was Dad's money guy."

"We're connected to her *dad*?" This keeps getting worse. It feels like someone threw a bag over my head and dragged me into a true crime documentary—the true crime documentary I've spent my life trying to avoid.

"He's not her dad. He's not anything to her. What he wants doesn't matter, anyway—he answers to Karl Yeager, and Yeager wants her gone."

"I'd be doing this for *Karl Yeager*?"

Two years ago, the FBI dragged Karl Yeager out of the sleaziest strip club in the city that sleaze built. He was free in two weeks. Every time he gets mentioned on the news, it's "alleged crime boss Karl Yeager" this and "believed Midwestern mob figure Karl Yeager" that. The man's a crime celebrity: "Karl Yeager, also known as 'the Butcher.'"

He's everything Don wants to be.

"Yeager doesn't want cops talking to this girl," Don says. "Do you get what has to happen?"

What I get is that since NO didn't work, I'm going to wait him out. Sometimes leading him on gets you a lot less grief than getting into it with him. Cross him directly, you wake up with his knee on your chest, the grill lighter poised so close, you can feel your eyelashes approach ignition temperature, one by one. But let it slide and, eventually, Don loses interest unless there are explosions involved.

I walk out before he can signal a guard to march him back to his cell. I've never seen the cell, but I can imagine myself in it.

5

Cat

I climb out of the pipe under a white-hot sun.

My skin is slick with perspiration, the palms of my hands burnt from pushing the chains at the mouth of the pipe out of my way. Shoulders scraped raw from my night slamming against the inside of the pipe. Sun beaming fire to my scalp. Dead muscles coming back to life, not that enthused about walking.

I smell like a football player's gym bag.

And this upsets me only because I'm afraid it'll make it hard to hide. That no matter how well hidden I am, someone will smell me.

I'll be betrayed by my BO.

That, and the sound of my stomach demanding nutrition.

This is how far I've come from a life with lavender-scented body wash in it.

Things change so fast.

I tell myself to get a grip.

But my palms are charred and my fingernails broken from *actual* gripping. It seems like God's laughing at me for thinking I could get a grip on any part of this.

I lower myself off the truck and into a field crisscrossed by derelict railroad tracks. A couple of sheds, tin roofs reflecting the relentless sun, not one person in sight. And all over, NO TRESPASSING signs warning of armed patrols and watchdogs.

Oh God, oh God, dogs!

They come from out of nowhere. Small, muscular Dobermans. Clipped ears, clipped tails, and fast.

I run at that fence with a shot of adrenaline so massive, you'd need a horse syringe to hold it. The pain just feels like motivation.

The dogs snarl and jump at my sneakers with what look like werewolf fangs. Do these dogs get to tear trespassers to pieces until someone shows up to view the carcasses and bury what's left?

There are more pressing questions.

Such as, what if they know where I am, and they're on their way here?

How much easier for them could I make it? Hanging off a rickety fence like a midnight dare at cheer camp, a slow-moving target as they reach for their guns.

I know guns; people in Cotter's Mill hunt.

I know that the ones they were waving, silhouetted in the moonlight, are for going after people, not Canada geese.

Steve was always dragging me off into the great outdoors to fish. Or, at least, cook the fish. The worst was hunting season, a buck tied to the hood of the SUV on the way home. But as sexist as he got with me, Steve made sure I knew my way around firearms.

But I don't see any stray rifles lying around. (As if I'd shoot a dog—I wouldn't.) What I see is a flat, wide sky, a blue lid with fat clouds stuffed underneath, pressing down, closing me into a tight Texas box.

A box I have no idea how to get out of.

I could make it over this fence so fast, but there's razor-edged tape up there that could separate your fingers from your hands if you grabbed it.

Watch enough crime shows on TV, and you know this gruesome stuff.

Wake up caked in blood a thousand miles from the scene of the crime, and . . . what? Pray that the pickups driving by aren't *them* is what.

I poke my sneakers into the fence's unforgiving little holes and scramble toward the slim opening of the loosely chained gate. Pull it shut. Walk toward the row of trees that shields the lots behind them from the street.

Trying not to be the out-of-place moving speck that draws the hunter's eye.

Trying to look as inconspicuous as if I were cutting fifth period back home, sneaking under the bleachers and over the fence behind Cotter's Mill Unified High School with Jody Nimiroff and Olivia so we could get Big Macs for lunch and sneak back into school for sixth period.

That's what seemed like life-and-death two days before.

Scarfing down fries in time to sprint back to school unnoticed.

Avoiding Saturday detention.

That life is over.

If I don't stop crying like a helpless baby, so am I.

Over. Done with. Dead.

I have to deal.

I'm dealing.

6

Jack

It takes everything I've got not to gun the car past the prison gates and fishtail out of there.

Don's envelope is pressing against my chest like a dead weight, like a rat corpse you pick up by the tail and chuck into the incinerator. It pokes me through my shirt. I'd reach down and scratch, but I won't risk a move that could make the car jerk and give the Highway Patrol any excuse to stop me. Face it, when those guys see my name on my driver's license, they've been known to come up with a bogus excuse to pat me down.

I don't know what's in this envelope, but I know enough not to let a cop find it on me.

I count the minutes, miles, and tenths of a mile to the first turn-off. I pull into a bar and grill that looks least likely to have electronic surveillance, as if the security cam at the Jack in the Box could see into my car and call me out me for taking step one in Don's deranged plan.

Tearing open the envelope, I have the feeling I get when I'm crouched in the scull at the starting block, just before the starting pistol fires, waiting to pull back on the oars and launch across the water.

Bang. There she is, staring out from under the envelope's flap. A girl with long hair and doe eyes, all narrow shoulders and collarbone and small breasts.

Hello, Nicolette.

I've lost it. I'm seeing thought bubbles over her head that aren't there: "Don't." "You aren't going to, right?" "Guns don't kill people; assholes kill people."

I think, *At least she's got a sense of humor.* Then I think, *Stop hallucinating.*

Her face is heart-shaped, freckles across the nose, and a wide mouth. She's not completely confident when the camera catches her eye, but she gives up the suggestion of a grin. There she is in the next picture, prancing around in a cheerleader uniform. She could be junior varsity, that's how young she looks—young and in-your-face pretty. This girl doesn't even look as if she'd kill a spider.

The Weedwacker that keeps me in line starts up in my gut.

This is fucked. Heavy-duty guys like Karl Yeager aren't supposed to hand small-time hoods at Yucca Valley Correctional school portraits of future dead girls, with the girls' addresses printed on the back. A penciled annotation says it's Esteban Mendes's house—surprise, surprise—with a note to stay away. I'm happy to oblige.

Why go to her house when I've got the address of her school, her Tumblr, her Instagram, her Pinterest board of fancy dresses, and her defunct three-year-old blog where her last entry was about *Twilight*? (She was thirteen. She liked it. She was Team Jacob.) I have her log-in and her password for a dozen different sites: BUTTERcup9. Apparently, no one told her it's smart to change things up.

I unwrap her driver's license. I don't mean a scan of it: *it*. Sixty seconds later, I'm in the men's room at the back of the lounge with my Swiss Army knife, slicing the license into pieces small enough to flush. It's a liability. She's a missing-killer-crazy-girl, and I have her driver's license on me?

Think, Jack.

I pull out the ID my friend Calvin and I trade back and forth for emergencies and buy a beer. I've held on to this ID for most of senior year. My mom won't let me drink, whereas Calvin can take a beer out of the refrigerator in his kitchen. Calvin is the only person I talk to about Don. *His* older brother, Gerhard—the guy with the legitimate claim to the twenty-one-year-old ID—goes to MIT.

I want to call Calvin up, but how would that conversation go? First I'd listen to him moan about how his girlfriend, Monica, might leave him when he takes off for Caltech in August, then he'd listen to me explain how I'm supposed to kill somebody?

Not with a whimper but a bang.

What's wrong with me? Don't say genetic predisposition, I already know that. On one side, we have Art Manx, whose family crest might as well say, *Live by the sword, die by the sword.* On the other side, meet Isabella Rossi Manx, the sweetest insanely strict mother alive, but weak as jelly at the center.

You learn from the Killers-'R'-Us side of the family that weak-as-jelly has its pitfalls. You are never weak as jelly. Then you take the envelope, and you want to bang your head on the bar you shouldn't legally be sitting at.

Don thinks this is happening.

I sit there eating old peanuts, making myself visualize this Nicolette creeping up behind Connie Marino. I imagine the soft skin of Connie's neck peeling open, gaping like a thin-lipped mouth, drooling blood. I picture Connie lying on a linoleum floor, bleeding out while this twisted little cheerleader, this tiny evil Nicolette (5' 2" according to her license) stands over her, laughing.

But the image that keeps interrupting is a cheerleading Nicolette bouncing around with pom-poms, so compact, so deceptively delicate, doing cartwheels in a lit-up stadium during a night game.

I make myself see her kneeling on the linoleum floor next to Connie's corpse, swishing her crazy hands in Connie's blood and laughing, getting blood on her pom-poms. I stalk her, catch her from behind, drag her away.

Shit.

I can't do this. I can't pretend I'm going to do this or let Don think for five more minutes that I'm doing this.

7

Cat

I'm bolt upright on a broken-down lounge chair, with a death grip on a pointy stick. Concealed between old, disgusting mattresses and bloated garbage bags in a vacant lot rimmed with trees.

The stick is for rats (saw them) and snakes (didn't). But it feels like a hundred degrees, and it's Texas, and don't rattlesnakes crawl out of the ground to cool off and bite people in weather like this?

I would.

If Olivia were here, she'd be weaving together strips of plastic bag. Making us a tent and matching shoulder bags. She'd be distracting me with ghost stories. I might be the bouncy one with the pom-poms, but she was the one who was with me

24/7 when my mom died. The picture she drew of my mom with a sparkle-marker halo and wings, sitting on a cloud, looking down at me and waving, had a permanent place under my pillow. Until Steve steamed out the wrinkles and framed it.

I want my friend.

I want my picture.

I want to be home, where I can never go again.

If I were in Cotter's Mill right now, I'd be at Olivia's house, listening to Katy Perry. We'd be copying each other's math.

At twilight, I'd run home along the lake. Yellow light would be pouring out of my house like the steady beam that glows from a lighthouse. Rosalba, who cooks for us, would pile food onto my plate, complaining that I'm too skinny. And when Steve got home late, I'd cut myself a thin, tiny slice of the tres leches cake Rosalba and I baked. Sit with him. Feed Gertie tiny scraps of meat off his plate while Steve pretended not to notice.

I force myself not to let images of home eclipse the landscape where I actually am. This works for about thirty seconds.

Then I start torturing myself with mental tours of Cotter's Mill Unified.

These are the trophies from when cheer squad took second at State twice in a row.

That's the dark stairwell where my first kiss with Connor happened. And happened. And happened.

Here's the principal's office where Steve had to show up

and use the phrases "harmless prank" and "Of course I take this *very* seriously" more than once. While I pretended to be contrite, also more than once.

After we made over Maura Brennan in the locker room and her mom had conniptions that I dyed her hair blue-black and pierced her ears twice each. ("Stop saying how good she looks!" Steve said. "What were you thinking?")

After we cut and went ice-skating on the lake all day. ("So if this Connor does something, *anything*, you do it too?")

And when Mr. Kirkbride decided that doing our math homework together was *plagiarism*??? ("There's going to come a time when I can't fix things for you.")

It's like some part of my mind is stuck, acting as if the worst thing I ever did is make Maura Brennan look good.

As if it didn't happen.

But this is now. It happened. My hair is caked with blood, my stomach screaming for me to put something in it *now*.

And between now and when (if) I come up with a plan more immediately workable than buying a new face and fingerprints and passport (hatched in the cement pipe), I need water and a Hershey bar, a sun hat, and a place to hide.

And as basic as those things are, I have no idea how I'm going to get them.

Steve always says to have faith, and the universe provides. This is what you'd expect from a guy who got from Havana to Miami Beach on a raft that was basically a tabletop.

I used to believe him.

But the obvious fact is, I have to provide for myself. I can't just sit here forever, slamming the ground with a stick whenever I hear the sound of rodents. It's not like I'm going to spear one and eat it for lunch.

I peer out at the street through the wall of trees. Pickups going eighty miles an hour billow dust to waist-high clouds, skidding around curves.

Across the street, there's a Five Star Gas and Mini-Mart.

I run into the street like a crazed squirrel. Trying to make it through the door of Five Star's mini-mart without getting spotted, run over, turned in, or shot.

It seems like a whole lot of trouble for candy. But what's the alternative?

The guy behind the counter takes one look, and the obvious question of how I got this way might as well be printed on his forehead.

I say, "No bike helmet. Stupid, huh?" That's the best I've got. Flirting is out of the question in my current situation. "Could you please tell me how to get to downtown?"

Even though I don't know what town it is yet. I only know it's Texas from the license plates.

The cashier points and tells me only to hitch with the ladies.

I thank him by lifting four supersize Almond Joy bars out of the rack under the register while he's distracted. Proving that old shoplifting skills never die. No matter how sorry you were at the time.

I really was sorry. I was only eight, but I took enough nail polish to open a salon before anybody noticed. And it is like riding a bike—you don't forget how.

At least last time I took things, everybody thought some variation on the theme that I was filling the void after my mom's aneurism. The tiny flaw in her brain that killed her. Everyone except for Steve, who said, "You didn't do this because you're sad, did you?"

I said, "I like nail polish."

Steve patted my shoulder, signifying his recognition that he was stuck dealing with me forever. Or so I thought.

He said, "I'll buy you all the nail polish you want, but don't ever do this again."

I didn't.

Until now.

I have to stop thinking about how nice Steve was to me and how much I want to go home, or I'm not going to make it.

I slide the key off the counter. Drink rusty water out of the sink in the gas station's bathroom until I start gagging on it. Then I stuff a candy bar into my mouth. Oh God, *chocolate* and *coconut* and *almonds*. Which could be fruit and protein if you leeched out all the sugar.

It does feel morally worse than stealing bread probably would, but try sticking a loaf of bread down your yoga pants.

I say thank you to the universe.

I apologize to the universe for caving to despair (big sin) in case any divine forces are watching.

I don't apologize for any necessary thing I did or am about to do.

There's no mirror, but even in the dull reflection of the stainless steel towel dispenser, you can tell my face made contact with a blunt object.

I try to scrape the dried blood off my face and out of my hair with wet paper towels, watching it darken the white washbasin in the already half-dark ladies' room. I wash with the pink soap in the dispenser and dry off with my hoodie.

It's not that I've never had blood in my hair before. I have. A cheerleading move that I might have pushed too far.

Olivia sitting in the ER, holding my hand while the doctor stapled my head shut. "What's wrong with you?" she asked, tears streaming down her face. "Summer said it wasn't even in the choreography. Why do you keep doing this?"

Oh God, Olivia, I don't know. Not then, and not now.

This time it takes me longer to get the dried blood out of my hair than it took to wreck my life.

That took three minutes.

No more than five minutes, tops, and my previous state of oblivious faith and my family and my face gave way to this. A fugitive girl with a forehead caked in blood.

8

Jack

The whole way driving back to the prison, I'm getting angrier and angrier at everything about Don, and about my family, and the fact that I'm saddled with a last name everybody in Nevada recognizes. I'm saddled with the memory of my dad packing his bag with enough firepower to bring down a cartel.

I slam the steering wheel and mentally shout out rhetorical questions for Don:

Like you think I'm going to track down a cheerleader and end her between prom and graduation—are you out of your freaking mind? You tell me to jump, and I jump on someone's neck?

Who does that?

I, of all people, know the answer: bad guys who are nothing like me do that. Vigilantes with no respect for the law or human decency do that. They see blood, and their eyes glaze over as they set off on lethal adventures.

I kissed my dad good-bye when he set out to hunt, waiting for the limo to pull up and take him to the private airport. Because the TSA guys at McCarran International don't like it if you have too many ounces of shampoo or a sniper rifle in your carry-on. I wasn't supposed to notice him packing this rifle, but even disassembled, it was hard to miss.

He was just another guy in shades off to neutralize an irritant, solve the fucking problem, kill his prey. My plan was to ignore hered-ity *and* environment, and become his antithesis. I was the model guy, attending the closest thing to prep school a city that runs on vice can offer, battling Dan Barrons for every honor in the place. I was home on school nights, heating up nutritious dinners my mom left for me as she powered her way through night law school and setting out a striped tie and regulation button-down blue shirt for the next day.

But look at me now.

I've got the shades, and I know where to find Don's gun in Mom's garage. I've got good marksmanship, penmanship, grades, and skills with a bow and arrow, a fencing saber (useful if someone dressed up like Zorro comes at you with a sword), a harpoon, and, right, my bare hands.

I have years of Krav Maga to thank for that—starting at six years old, jamming my fingers into the teacher's eyes, crying because I was afraid that when I pulled my thumbs out, his eyeballs would be stuck on my thumbnails like two candy apples on sticks.

My dad smacked me on the butt. "Don't cry, Jack. That's just stupid."

You want stupid? Stupid was taking the envelope when Don first handed it to me. I wish I'd buried it out in the desert. I lock it in the glove compartment before I pull back into the prison parking lot.

I tell the lady at the sign-in, "I didn't use my time up. Please?"

You have to look pretty pathetic for Yucca Valley Correctional to cut you a break.

They bring Don back out. He has his slack-jawed, superior face on. I hate the part of myself that wants to smash him.

I tell him, "I can't do this."

Don shrugs. "Can't or won't?"

This is another gem from our dad.

"Either way, it's not happening."

Don's eyes get squinty, like on the kind of animal you don't want in your attic. I know his eyes don't glow red in the dark—I've shared a bedroom with the guy—but they look as if they would. He shakes his head, and this time he looks smug.

"It's not just me you have to worry about," he says. "You want to be an orphan? If this girl doesn't disappear, I'm not the only one Yeager's coming after."

What?

I level my gaze into the center of his pinprick pupils. I can't tell if he's lying or juggling half truths, or why this is happening, but I'm shaking like winter in Alaska with no parka.

Dead Don is one thing, but my mom? *Not* my mom.

"Shit, Don. *What did you do to piss off Karl Yeager?*"

Don waves for the guard.

I say, "Stop! What the hell? You can't drop that and disappear. Explain."

I reach for the pocket where I keep my phone, which isn't there because they take electronics away from you on the way in.

"Don't bother calling her," he says. "You know what you have to do to make it right. If you care what happens to her . . ."

In what universe do I salute him and not call her?

I can't get my phone back fast enough. In the corner of the prison parking lot, I'm locked in the car, blasting the air conditioner, radio cranked up, trying to noise-bomb fear so I sound normal enough to call home.

"Mom?"

"You're not holding that cell phone while you're driving, are you, Jackson?"

I'm so relieved to hear her voice, I'm not even annoyed by what the voice is saying.

"No! I'm parked! And it's hands-free. I never do that. It's just . . ." *It's just that Don just threatened your life?* "It's just, I'm leaving Don's late, and hey, is everything okay over there?"

There's a longer than usual silence. I'm not used to being this afraid, not for years.

"You left some lights on. I wasn't going to say anything until you got home, but since you asked." She sighs. "Did you have a nice time with Don?"

There, she's her normal, Don-loving, deluded-mom, compulsive self. I start breathing again.

"Always nice."

It's a stretch to remember a nice time with Don.

"Sweetheart, are you tense? You sound tense."

I'm so tense, I can hear my neck crack when I turn my head.

"No worries, Ma. I'm not."

What I am is pissed that I let Don pull my strings. He's no doubt sitting on his bunk in there, gloating that he made me so frightened that he owns me, counting my false steps down the slippery slope of doing his bidding.

He doesn't own me. Mom is fine. Don is Don: when his jaws are opening and closing, either he's eating or he's lying. And given that there were no snacks, likelier than not, his whole thing was a fairy tale, a campfire horror story to get me to avenge Connie while he's trapped in there; or to get me to ditch my life and do a random hit that he gets paid for; or to prove he's the macho king of brotherhood, upping the ante until I said yes.

"Well, drive safely!" my mom says, as if I had to be reminded not to speed through speed traps.

"Thanks, Mom."

"You're welcome." There's another pause. "And, Jack, I know it's hard to see him locked in there, but Donny's still your loving brother. Remember."

No thanks, Mom.

9

Cat

So maybe the universe did provide.

Slightly.

In the form of a HELP WANTED sign in the window of the Bluebonnet Motor Court Motel. A robin's-egg blue, sagging-roofed building in the middle of a long block anchored by the Five Star on one corner and a bright green Jiffy Taco on the other.

Not that I take this sign as a *sign*. But figuring it for as close to divine signage as I'll ever get, I make myself walk over there. I have to talk myself through it, like when you're learning the fox-trot in seventh-grade gym.

Right foot. Left foot.

Face frozen in a pick-me smile even though (when learning

to fox-trot) Connor was going to knock over the other boys to get to me first.

But this is now. Texas. Bluebonnet. *Go!*

A buzzer is triggered when the door to the lobby opens.

I'm just this side of jumping out of my skin, scooping it up, and racing back to the dump. I pretend that I'm about to face the panel of judges at a pageant. (I only did one, but it stays with you.)

Pick me.

The lady behind the counter is fiddling with a necklace that says *Luna* in gold cursive letters, watching *Animal Planet* in front of an electric fan upwind of me. A good thing, because even if the paper towel scrub removed the stink, the pink liquid soap left me smelling like a gummy bear. Who hires a gummy bear?

The part I'm not expecting is that when she asks, "What happened to you?" my impulse is to tell her.

Which is bad.

Why does every impulse I ever get have to be bad? I've gone so far as to write DON'T on my palm just in case I had the sudden impulse to give it up to Connor at spring formal. This was *after* he plowed through half the dance team and I dumped him.

Luna pours iced tea out of a plastic pitcher into a paper cup and slides it across the counter.

"Was it your boyfriend?"

"No!" I say it so loud, it's like a puppy that scares itself by sneezing and falls over. Only I tip backward into the lobby's one chair.

"Oh, honey," she says. She has a nice Texas twang and a sweet round face. It's the first second I've felt slightly relaxed since it happened. This is also bad. I need to be vigilant, not relaxed.

"The job. Is it still open?"

"Don't you want to know what it is first?" Then she smiles.

I want to trust her so much, it's ridiculous. If I had my phone, I'd be typing in memos to self. *Stop trusting people* would top the list. Just after *Hide*.

"If it's legal, I don't care what it is."

And the legal part is probably negotiable.

"Maid," she says. "You work for tips. Still want it?" I'd nod if bending my head didn't hurt. "We're maybe a third full." Which, given the lack of cars in the lot, might be an exaggeration. "But it's better on weekends, parents visiting over at the college and such. And there's a room—not much of a room, but it's got TV."

"Yes!" There are times when cleaning out toilets in Texas is right up there with a guided tour of heaven.

"I didn't say you're hired. You ever done any heavy cleaning?"

"Tons."

She gives me a look.

I try again. "I really need this. Things didn't work out with my boyfriend. As you can see. Please." My voice catches from hearing myself say this out loud. "If I don't get work, I'll have to go back."

"What did he do, break a chair over your head?"

I don't even blink. "Biker."

Any idea that I'm still a trying-to-be-honest, parties-yet-adheres-to-the-Ten-Commandments kind of girl is dead and buried in Ohio.

Luna nods with a look of lie-induced understanding. "You got ID?"

"I got out with what I had on." Props for thinking on my feet if not for moral rectitude. "But I'm *sure* I could get ID—"

"How old?"

Twenty-one? Everyone who wants to drink says twenty-one. But I don't want to seem like a high school kid either. A beat-up kid so young that a responsible motel clerk would call up the police so they could come right over.

"Nineteen?"

"What's your name?"

Why, why, why hadn't I thought of a name?

I'm staring straight out at the Jiffy Taco three-course Mex-Italian dinner advertised on an easel outside their front door. It's a pizza pie made out of cheese and tortilla chips, with rice and beans.

I say, "Bean." *Bean?* "Uh, it's my nickname." *Bean???*

For the rest of the day, Bean sits on the bed in the maid's room at the Bluebonnet. Listening to the decrepit ice machine building up power to drop its jagged cubes into the metal tray, wheezing and rumbling until the ice clatters to rest.

Every time the ice drops, her heart stops.

10

Jack

When I pull into the cul-de-sac, the sun is setting purple, and the flames are out. The air is tinged with smoke, and there's a light rain of ashes. Two fire trucks are blocking the driveway, an ambulance at the ready, lights flashing, in front of the house.

I leave the car in the middle of the street and sprint between the trucks.

My mother is standing in the front yard smiling, ridiculously calm. Her two settings are overly parental and ridiculously calm. Around my dad, the given was that he controlled everything. Once she got out from under his thumb and into the dullness of desert suburbia, her inner control freak was unleashed—largely on me.

She sees me coming and holds up her hand. "It was the clothes dryer. Lots of fuss about nothing."

Three different firefighters and our next-door neighbor Mrs. Lasky say, "It wasn't nothing." The firefighters keep coming out of the side of the house wearing protective gear, carrying blackened objects to the sidewalk.

The image in my head is Don sneering at me. What I thought were empty, stupid words turn out to be this: someone set my house on fire.

As warnings go, it's impressive. I'm warned. I want to grab my mom and hide her somewhere. Then I want to burn Don, and I want him to know it was me. I can tell myself, *This isn't who I am,* a thousand times, but I still want to do it.

"Laundry rooms." The firefighter shakes his head. You'd think that up and down the streets of Summerlin, Nevada, dryers were blowing up.

"Too much lint in the hose," my mom says as if she believes it. "Probably. Did you know that smoke detector batteries can catch fire spontaneously?"

Sure they can. I ask the firefighter, "Can you check this out? Can you find out what the problem was?"

Because there's no way there was too much lint in that hose unless someone doused it with accelerant and stuffed it in there. This was all set up and ready to launch if I turned down Don.

Someone did this.

I try to calculate how hard it was to make this happen. What skills were required to walk past three Rottweilers and the motion sensors undetected and make a dryer ignite like clockwork when I was driving through the desert, halfway between saying no to Don and pulling into my driveway? This has strategy, planning, and execution so far above Don's pay grade, it's mind-blowing.

This demonstrates what I grew up knowing: *you can get to anyone, anywhere, anytime if you know what you're doing.*

"It's not the end of the world, Jack!" my mother says. "You should see your face. If the worst thing that happens to me in my life is I get singed hair, I'm doing fine!"

"You have singed hair!"

Someone set my house on fire when my mother was in it.

I want to stash her in Witness Protection—except we didn't witness anything, and I'd be ratting out my own brother. She'd never let me rat out Don, even to save herself. If I told her, she'd say I was exaggerating or misinterpreting, anything to avoid seeing reality. I'm the good one, but Don's the son she'd go to the mat for.

Also, if we disappeared, a bunch of guys who knew my dad would figure that my mom had ratted *them* out and gone into hiding. They're cool with her being a lawyer who prosecutes industrial polluters. Poisoning rivers isn't their line of work. But if we vanished, they'd think we'd turned, and they would find us: *Anyone. Anywhere. Anytime.*

Witness Protection would be suicide. Calling the police would be suicide. Calling out Karl Yeager would be suicide. Anything but saluting my smug shit of a brother would be a trip to the morgue.

I say to the firefighter, "Aren't you going to check this out?"

"Don't worry, kid. No one's arresting your mom for appliance abuse." He thinks this is funny.

"Isn't there going to be an investigation?"

He sighs. "Is there something you want to tell me, son?"

"No, sir."

New plan: I'm going to find Nicolette Holland.

I'll tell Don. This girl freaking murdered Connie Marino in the bloodiest possible way. She's a homicidal cheerleader who crossed Karl Yeager. I'm not letting my mother burn while I stand around watching from the moral high ground.

I'm not saying what I'm going to do when I find Nicolette Holland, but I'm going to keep stalling for time while I figure it out.

11

Cat

I keep my head down, look people over fast, and turn my head away faster.

I become a fan of the $4.99 Jiffy Taco lunch special. You can divide it in half and save the cheese enchilada for dinner. I leave money with Luna in quarters and one-dollar bills. The delivery guy never sees me.

I'm hoarding money, for obvious reasons.

Because when I'm not scrubbing up messes and pulling strips of paper that say SPARKLING FRESH across the bowls of newly cleaned toilets, I'm watching crime show reruns about how even if the US Marshals relocate you and give you a new identity, bad guys find you. How even if you've been on the lam as a respectable housewife for forty years after blowing up an ROTC building in 1969, the FBI still finds you.

Every TV show I watch bangs into my head what I already know. Short of locating an armed cult and hiding out in their bunker until the End of Days, I'm toast.

Luna keeps saying, "Bean, sugar, can you please send for your birth certificate and get yourself a new ID? Mrs. Bluebonnet"—that's what she calls the motel's owner, who lives in South Carolina and shows up for surprise inspections— "is all, 'Hire Amurrican, y'all,' and I have to show her something."

Where do I get an ID that says my name's Sabina Magyar? (I told Luna "Sabina" because it was the only girl name I could think of with the sound *Bean* in it. Then she said, "Where's that from?" And I said, "Hungary," because why not? *Magyar* means *Hungarian* in Hungarian. I don't even know how I knew that.)

Where do I get *any* ID?

If I don't figure it out fast, I'm a lot closer to doom.

I don't feel that doomed when I'm busy scraping fossilized nachos out of the hallway carpet. But when I need something I can't get in the lost and found, when my supply of left-behind pink plastic razors runs out, or when I need more quick-change hair dye or tampons or cheap sunglasses that hide half my face, I obsess about whether it's better to go out after dark (when they can't see you coming) or in the light (when you can see *them* coming).

I keep finding South Texas emergency numbers taped up in the utility closet. The number for the battered women's shelter is circled in red.

Bean says, "I'm not a battered woman. It was just that once, when I was trying to leave. It's just, if he finds me, I'm dead."

Luna's completely into it. "He shows up at the Bluebonnet, he's gonna hear one or two things from me!"

"Luna, no! Say you don't know me!"

I feel like an idiot for telling her one tiny fragment of the truth.

"I'll do you one better. He shows up, I'll text you the second he turns around."

About getting texts. I'm not sure how you get a cell phone, but I'm pretty sure you need a credit card and money and a lot of other things I don't have.

I tell her, "Unless Apple's handing out free phones—"

"You don't need a fancy phone does tricks," Luna says. "The market down by Mickey D's has burners. And they're cheap, girl."

Cheap burner phones.

If I had it in me to walk three blocks without a phalanx of bodyguards, I could call Olivia on a totally anonymous, pre-paid burner phone.

This is both reassuring and terrifying.

12

Jack

The homeowners' insurance guy gets one whiff of the burnt laundry room and offers to put us up in a hotel until he gets us "sorted out." I want to stay on the Strip because of the security. Vegas is twenty minutes away, but my mom isn't going anywhere. She hands me a can of room freshener—which is like trying to subdue a rhino with a toothpick—and says, "Spray."

The only way to get this sorted out is if I work something with Don. I have to tell him yes, and he has to get the fire-starter to stop. But you can't drop in on a guy in prison when it's not visiting day unless you're his lawyer. Showing up twice on one visiting day was pushing it.

I'm left praying, white-knuckled, that Don doesn't screw up and lose his Thursday phone call privilege. I'm banking that whoever expects me to do this thing is smart enough to let the acrid smell of melted plastic bring me to my knees. I don't need Yeager's minions showing up in Summerlin with flamethrowers before I have the chance to tell Don I capitulate.

All I can think to do in the meantime is cyber-stalk Nicolette.

I wasn't the guy who could hack into INTERPOL during recess in third grade, but in five minutes online, I can tell that Nicolette leaped off the grid the exact moment Don says Connie got stabbed. The next day, Nicolette was gone.

Her friends' posts read like a collective panic attack. There's a week of *Nicky! Where are you?????* followed by a bunch of cheerleaders praying for her speedy recovery. From what, her homicidal tendencies?

Her private messages from her friend Olivia are more promising, as in:

What's going on? Steve says he signed you
into rehab. For one night of jello shots at
Glen's?!?!? Is he insane?

He is insane. He says you can't talk to anyone outside the program or you'll lose your
resolve. WHAT PROGRAM????

Please if you get this I'm begging you tell
me where you are.

I take from this that Nicolette is tight with her fellow cheer-leaders, Mendes says she's in rehab, and she has a best friend who loves her and is amazed about the rehab. Rehab? Well, we know she does Jell-O shots, but that's a long way from round-the-clock slurred speech and blackouts.

This is my one idea about how to find Nicolette Holland: get to Olivia.

At least she's easy to locate. Olivia's mom has been tagging pictures of her and Nicolette since they were in seventh grade.

Nicolette cheers in a group photo with blue-and-gold pom-poms.

Olivia takes a red ribbon at a science fair in Columbus.

Nicolette cheers some more.

All these albums of Nicolette and Olivia and this Disney-princess–looking girl named Jody rocking prom dresses ought to be captioned *Typical Teen Girls*. I get how people always say, "He was a nice neighbor. He liked gardening," about guys who turn out to have dungeons in their cellars. But there's nothing about Nico-lette that screams "heading to death row."

Also, if Esteban Mendes is nothing to her like Don says, some-one should tell Mendes. Because he shows up at a lot of track meets and fund-raiser car washes, where he can be seen draping a towel over Nicolette's body to cover her smaller-than-small bikini. He looks intense—not a shocker for Karl Yeager's accountant.

There's no bimbo mom in sight. You have to figure that, practi-cally speaking, Nicolette is Esteban's daughter. Judging from all the church bake sales he's attended with her (Olivia's dad, Mr. Pastor, *is* a pastor), Don's idea that Mendes would be fine with his kid lying dead on the altar won't fly.

I wonder if anybody else is coming on here like me, pretending to be "Nicky," looking for hints of her location. For all I know, her log-in info is carved into the bathroom wall at Yucca Valley Correctional.

When I can't stand looking at her anymore, I google Connie Marino.

On a video from a Detroit local news station, her mother's voice cracks as she begs anyone who knows where Connie is to bring her back. Seeing her like that—not knowing that Connie is never coming back, and that this crazy, normal-looking Nicolette did it—by the second time through, anticipating the moment when she covers her face with her hands, I'm choked up.

What the fuck, Nicolette, WHY?

13

Cat

Luna keeps knocking on my door, inviting me up to her manager's apartment to watch TV. She keeps calling me "girlfriend." As in, "Want to watch *Game of Thrones* with me, girlfriend?"

Her *girlfriend* with no ID.

I want a girlfriend so bad, I'm afraid I'm going to tell her something. That I'll accept her offer of Long Island Iced Tea—which she calls Longhorn Iced Tea—and then I'll get all buzzed and talkative and self-destructive.

I sit there on Luna's couch, my tongue stuck between my teeth, biting down to remind myself to avoid anything with vodka in it. Reminding myself to shut up and work on getting her to let me do her makeup.

"It's been a month," Luna says. "Does this guy even know you're in Galkey?"

I shake my head, which at this point has red hair. That, plus thick drawn-on eyebrows and big square glasses constitute my entire disguise.

Luna sighs. "Your a-hole sounds more like the kind of guy's gonna look for you at a biker bar. You really think he's going to track you down if you ride over to the college and hang out with kids your own age Saturday night?"

Set me loose at a college on Saturday night?

It's like offering a crack addict her own little pipe.

You know it's bad for you. You know it's the worst thing for you. But scared as you are of life beyond the walls of the Bluebonnet, you kind of don't care.

I know it's this kind of thinking that got me into the backseat of a Chevy Camaro with the worst guy in the world for me.

I know Luna's theory that the bogeyman isn't going to find me if I head out into the warm Texas night is total BS.

But I want to believe her.

She pats me on the arm. A hand on my skin.

I would have kissed Connor, my second-to-last poor-choice ex, right then, even though he's 90 percent slime, just to feel his 10 percent human arms around me. I'm starting to relate to those baby monkeys in honors psychology who shrivel up and die because they only have wire mothers. Meanwhile, the monkeys with fluffy, soft mother dolls snuggle into the fur and eat their mashed bananas.

"Cheer up," Luna says. "I've got something for you."

Three ancient red bicycles are chained up in a utility closet in the alley behind the motel. Apparently, Mrs. Bluebonnet decided people would rent three-speeds. Nobody did, and here they are.

Luna points into the alley. "Hop on, and you could be at Tech having a good old time in ten minutes."

I try not to pant, that's how much I want to jump on one of those red bikes and book it out of here. Even though I can spot an impulse that bad from fifty yards away.

I half-know I'm lying to myself. Telling myself that if I pedal around at twilight, I'll be basically invisible.

That it's not even that big of a risk.

Eight summers of cheerleading camp, and I know a lot of girls who party on three continents. I get it. But half the time, people can't even tell who I am right away at Halloween when I do weird enough makeup. And who's even *heard* of South Texas Tech, Galkey? It's not like I'm going to a party at Ohio State.

I can tell that how much I want five minutes that approximate normal—five minutes when I can pretend I'm leading a whole other kind of life—might be clouding my thinking. But there's an actual plus column.

If I went out, I could forage for all the stuff TV characters who run away on purpose take with them. Granted, they mostly use these provisions during the zombie apocalypse. But if (when) I have to run (soon), it wouldn't hurt to have it.

Plus this could solve the dilemma of Mrs. Bluebonnet's mandatory ID. Colleges have freshmen in need of fake IDs, and people who know where to get them. To save myself, I have to have some fake ID, right?

And a fake ID procurement outfit from Goodwill. Nice enough to get guys to want to help me find fake ID. Not good enough for them to remember the next day.

And an ice pick.

Plus, I buy a daypack, more makeup, a rainbow of hair dye, and nutrition bars to keep me from having to sneak candy out of any more mini-marts if I get stranded.

There's the cutest dress, summery, backless, midnight-blue. And sandals I can't justify spending seven dollars on, except that they're the highest heels in the place. Being a whole different height is good, right?

What does it say about me that even when life hits its most wretched moment of sadness, shopping is still fun?

I feel so bold, grabbing clothes off hangers, sliding shoes onto my feet.

On the way back to the Bluebonnet, I stop at a convenience store with country music blasting out the open door.

I buy a prepaid burner phone.

"For emergencies," I say to the cashier. I don't know why. I feel so sly and furtive. Like a drug dealer or, I guess, me.

Not that I plan to call 9-1-1 anytime soon, but if I see it coming, at least I want to tell a couple of people I love them before permanently hanging up.

That, and where the body's buried.

14

Jack

I'm the guy who can always concentrate at school. I can shut out anything, turn off my mind and any trouble flowing through it like a faucet turns off water. I was in class nine days after they killed my dad, handing in make-up work.

Now I'm sitting in AP English, seeing and hearing nothing, trying to figure this out. I've run through every conceivable scenario a hundred times. Best case, I disappear into Don's alternate universe for a short nightmare. I wake up with a couple of weeks shot to hell, but to my same life and plans, college, and future.

The most striking flaw is that it's also the least realistic scenario—and how do you have a best case that someone else doesn't wake up from?

My teacher, Mr. Berger, looks pissed.

"*'Two roads diverged in a yellow wood'*? What say you, Mr. Manx?" Jesus, this guy is pretentious. And seriously? This poem has a built-in, teacher-approved right answer, which ordinarily I'd be rolling out, if only to one-up Dan Barrons. Not today.

"It's condescending."

Berger is pacing around like a matador waiting for the bull to charge.

All I want to do is charge, gore him, and leave town.

"All the ordinary jerks take the big road with the streetlights. The superior poetic guy we're supposed to admire takes the cool nonconformist road. Come on, did you ever find one student who thought it was cool to take the *more* traveled road?"

Mr. Berger says, "Did you *read* this poem?"

After English, Calvin corners me by my locker. "What's wrong with you?"

I don't blurt things I don't want blurted, even to Calvin, even when we're plowed and running off at the mouth. But I blurt, "I have to run an errand for Don."

"Are you brain-damaged?"

Don's my go-to excuse for acting brain-damaged, even I know this. And according to my former girlfriend—and Dan Barron's current girlfriend—Scarlett, I'm the least insightful guy in Nevada.

"I have to get out of here. Want to say we're camping until college?"

"Riiiiiight." Calvin doesn't camp. Boy Scout camp with Calvin was me doing all his camping shit for him and him paying me off with poker winnings taken off guys from other troops who thought they knew how to play cards. "You want to tell me where you're really going?"

I shake my head.

"Cool," he says. "A mystery errand for a sociopath."

"No choice."

He waves his arms like a distraught stick figure. "Because free will is an illusion?" *Is anyone not pissed at me today?* "Maybe you need to think this over."

"That's helpful. Maybe you need to go screw yourself."

"Maybe you need me to tutor you on Robert Frost and vocab, asshole."

The most ridiculous part of the day is that I like the poem.

Two roads diverged in a wood, and I—
I took the one less traveled by,
And that has made all the difference.

Only some guys don't get to screw around in the woods in Wherever-the-Hell, New Hampshire, bird-watching or whatever Robert Frost was doing. They get stuck on a third path that leads straight out of the woods.

"Have fun telling your mom," Calvin says.

Unfortunately, I'm not doing that well breaking it to my mom that I'm heading out of the endless subdivisions and strip malls of home. She's the kind of mom who, if you have a condom in your wallet, will find it and want to know what it's doing there. You'd think she'd have been happy she had one stand-up kid: she wasn't. It's hard to figure, if she notices something that small, how I'm going to slip out of town.

I love my mom—she went through worse than I did—but I'm going rogue, and there's nothing she likes about rogue on me. I'm thinking I'll tell her over dinner, but she slides a platter of pork chops across the kitchen table and clears her throat, generally a preamble to me being in for it.

"If this is about mouthing off to Mr. Berger, I'm not apologizing for how I interpret a poem."

"Jackson, look at me and tell me you didn't cut class this morning."

"I haven't cut all year! How can you ask me that as if I did it?"

I don't ever catch a break from her. When I cut one day after APs last year, she acted like I was headed straight to lockup. She made me paint the garage two coats of Navajo White. By the second coat, it was ninety-five degrees outside, and the garage looked fine without it.

The way she sat quietly for her whole married life when she had this in her is a testament to my dad's powers of intimidation.

"Is this a random check to see if I'm a repeat offender? Does the house need painting? Thanks, Mom."

"I'm sorry." She doesn't look sorry. "The motion detectors went off this morning, and the dogs were in the yard. If you came home, that would explain it."

All of a sudden, I don't care what she thinks I did. "When did they go off? Is there security footage? Did the patrol come by?"

"Calm down! Security malfunctioned. It happens. The fire probably destroyed some wires. There's nothing to worry about—unless you cut."

"Seriously, Mrs. *Manx*?"

"There hasn't been a peep from your dad's business associates in years. There's no reason it would start now."

The ways she says *business associates* could make plants wither.

"Somebody was in our *house*. What does the security guy say?"

"Jack, enough! It was a hiccup in the wiring."

It wasn't a hiccup in the wiring.

"Try not to get so overwrought!" she says.

"Yes, ma'am." I might hit the *ma'am* too hard—I go to a school where five hundred kids are forced to speak as if we were alive during the Civil War, so it happens.

"Try that again without the smirk."

Yes, ma'am. No, ma'am. It doesn't matter how respectfully or disrespectfully I do this. I have to get to Ohio *now*. By Thursday, by the second Don calls, I need to be ready. The second after he calls, I need to be gone. I need a plan and I want a beer, which means that I have to push a mound of string beans around my plate until I can get to Calvin's.

I'm sprawled in Calvin's desk chair, flanked by his computers and their many monitors, and the equipment that takes up half his room.

He and Monica are cross-legged on the bed, holding controllers and playing Mermaid Ninjas. Monica made Mermaid Ninjas. It's the most boring game ever conceived unless you're *really* into mermaids. I sit there while they nuke angry mermen and evil aquatic elves.

"What happens if you pause the game?"

Calvin doesn't take his eyes off the screen. "I'll lose my trident."

"I'll buy you a new one. Come on. Get me out of Nevada. Some way I don't fail senior year."

"Good luck," Monica says. "People with *two years* to go in this mind-numbing hell don't get why a few more weeks is such a big deal. Don't you want all your Jack Manx end-of-year whoop-dee-do? Don't you want to see your name on *several* fake gold plaques?"

I resent the hell out of the fact that, thanks to Don, I can't stick around and collect my fake gold plaques. But some guy was in my house, tripping the motion detectors, taunting me, and he wins. The only question is whether my future has to be the spoils of war.

"How can two people who despise Pueblo so much not get this?"

"If whatever you do works, can I come?" Monica says, cuddling up to Calvin as if I weren't there.

"This isn't a joke! This is my life!"

Monica and Calvin snap to attention.

"Damn," Calvin says. "Go with that. Suppressed rage. Very black raincoat."

Monica yelps, "That's not funny, Calvin! Just because—"

"That's the point," he says. "That's why it'll work. Scare them. Go all Manx on them."

Monica is too embarrassed to look anywhere but her lap. "In case you don't know, Manx, that's not how anybody thinks of you."

"Ignore her," Calvin says. "That's what everybody thinks."

Tell me something I don't know.

The headmaster always stares at me like I'm slime that snuck into his school when my application got stuck to someone else's admission folder. The last time he had to hand me a trophy, his look could have melted it down.

So here I sit in his office, using my slimy lineage to my advantage.

"Do you think it would be okay if *all* my seniors up and left before graduation?" he asks.

"No, sir. But I can't take the *pressure*. I need to be outside, not around *people*. . . ."

"You can't go camping in a few weeks?" But he looks worried as hell.

I get his point, but this guy's a douche. He treats me like a criminal fuckup: hello, meet the criminal fuckup.

I say, "I feel like I'm going to *explode*."

You can tell this is why he didn't want me at El Pueblo in the first place, because I'd turn out to be the kid who exploded all over study hall and CNN.

"Should we call Dr. Biggs?" He's reaching for his landline, hoping he can foist me off on the counselor before I combust.

"I had counseling when my father died. No more—*I can't take it.*"

Well played: Headmaster Enright looks like something's stuck halfway down his throat.

"If I call up your teachers, they're all going to tell me your final papers are in?"

"One left. I'll have it on your desk tomorrow."

"And you've got this camping trip planned out—we're not going to find you stoned and playing video games somewhere?"

Insult me some more. Six years of honor roll, and you think I've been waiting for the day I could get stoned and play Call of Duty Black Ops II for a month in my room? Yes, sir.

"No, sir. Zion. Then Yosemite. Then Mercer freshman orientation."

I watch him balance the pain of doing me a favor against the pleasure of getting me out of his school. I watch him start to beam as pleasure wins.

15

Cat

Now that I've got the burner, the whole time I'm planning my field trip to South Texas Tech, Galkey, I'm distracted by terror (good) and obsessed with how easy it would be to call Olivia (bad).

Back when the broken pay phone by the Five Star was front and center in my fantasy life, the fact that I couldn't call home was a lot clearer. Half the little silver number buttons and the entire receiver on that phone are gone.

End of story.

Plus, according to *Law & Order*, you can trace pay-phone calls to a shed in a field full of sheep in Romania if you know what you're doing.

But it's a different episode of *Law & Order* that clinches it.

I sit on the saggy king bed I'm supposed to be making, wanting the police not to be able to track the villain's burner so bad, I can hardly bear to watch.

The villain gets away.

I tear out of there in broad daylight, pedal the red bike as far into the ranchland on the edge of town as I can go and still get a couple of bars. I'm clutching the phone so hard, I'm afraid it's going to crumble into black and silver plastic shards right in my hand.

I have to squeeze the words out individually. "Are? You? Alone?"

My heart is blanched white, the blood wrung out of it. Not because of my situation, for once, but at the realization of my complete lack of self-control.

"Nick!"

"Shhhh!"

Her voice drops to a whisper. "Where are you? What's going on?"

Collapsing lungs. Constricting throat. Eyes full of tears that sting worse than at the eye doctor.

"I just want you to know I'm okay. I'm sorry. Then I have to go."

"You can't do that!" Olivia yelps. "*Why* are you in rehab? Steve's acting like you were cheering on crack."

I'm *where*? Steve's acting like *what*? Rehab because *why*? Three hits of marijuana in Ann Arbor last summer and maybe too much party beer? The only thing I did in the backseat of the Camaro that *wouldn't* make Steve go ballistic is I turned down a whole pharmacy.

Before I remember that it doesn't matter what Steve says.

Before I remember that even though Olivia is rattling on as if everything's the same as always, *nothing* is the same.

She's the person I talked to about everything—cheats-before-spring-formal Connor, and Steve's antiquated ideas of how girls should act, and what I was wearing to school the next day. Now she can't know anything.

I never, never, ever should have called her.

"Nick! Come on. 'Hello, I've been kidnapped by aliens, but I can't talk about it, bye.' Where *are* you? Did you run away from rehab?"

I might not have told her one or two things before, but never in my life have I *lied* to Olivia. Not when she got breasts before anyone else and she wanted to know what people said (only she'll never know the worst bits—vow of silence). Not when we both liked Zak Myer, and she held his hand, and I wanted to slap her. Never.

Until now.

"All right. I ran away, but if Steve finds me, he'll drag me back there. They made me sleep on a cement floor when I wasn't cooperative."

This could happen. If someone stuck me in rehab, I wouldn't cooperate.

"Do you need me to send you money? You're not, like, living under a bridge, right?"

Hearing her voice, it's like there's the possibility I could sit next to her in history again, close enough to pass her notes, and hang out with my friends by my locker. I'm not sure if the actual *im*possibility makes it better or worse.

"Can you delete this number?"

She says, "Why can't I call you back?"

"Liv! I can't be found!"

She clucks. "I'll tell Steve on you. I have *so* much on you. You and the creepazoid in that Camaro burning rubber out on Bayside Road."

"Liv!"

"You know I wouldn't! I'll smash my cell at the landfill in Kerwin if you say to. Just don't disappear. *Please*. When are you coming back?"

I let her pretend that we're still girlfriends like before.

I pretend to myself that I'm going along with her because I'm afraid she'll break down and spill to Steve or the police or the Pastors if I don't. When she says she's buying herself a burner, too, I pretend I don't stop her because I'm afraid she'll get upset and tell someone.

But I know that isn't why.

16

Jack

Thursday.

I grab the phone out of my mom's hands before she can say hello.

I carry the phone into the dining room and shut the door. "Fuck you, Don." I have to tell him yes, save him and my mom, get Yeager off my back, and become a monster in a single syllable: Yes. But my mouth tastes like puke, and I can't stop picturing my mother's hair in flames. "We had a fire."

Nothing.

"Did you consider at least giving me a warning about . . . fire prevention?"

Don snorts, as if I'm amusing him. "Do you think I *knew*?" he says. "Am I God? Can I read minds?"

"What's wrong with you? What kind of moron gets in bed with people who'd do this?"

He ignores this.

"I told you everything you needed to know about *fire prevention*," he says. "Just do what I told you and . . . you know, Jack . . . find yourself a girl."

Then he chuckles as if this were a real conversation, big brother encouraging me to get a prom date on Tinder. It's like he thinks if I set the range at four thousand miles and swipe fifty million times, Nicolette Holland will turn up, mine for the taking in her cheerleader skirt. It's amazing how reasonable he sounds if you don't know what he's actually saying.

"Think about the fire," Don says. "Life is short. Anything can happen."

I picture myself pounding the punching bag in the garage, bare-knuckled, running at the bag and kicking, bruising the outer edges of my feet.

"Threatening me isn't going to help me find a girlfriend."

"Are you *listening*? Do this for me. Like we're one guy in two bodies."

"Don't fucking say that to me!"

"Be cool!" Don says. "Find the girl." There are more chuckles, as if he's morphing from a lowlife thug to a drooling psycho with phone skills.

"*I'm doing it!* I get the point. I'm hitting the road. I hope all your friends with an interest in my social life know that. But"—I go for menacing without a hope in hell of success—"you'd better make sure there aren't more fires. Or anything *like* a fire. That would distract me. I can't look for a girlfriend if I'm distracted."

Don goes, "Mmmmmmmm," smooth and ambiguous.

By this point, I'm yelling at him. "What does 'mmmm' mean? Did you hear what I said?"

"Like I said, I'm not God." There's a new tone, raw and even scarier maybe because he sounds scared himself. "*I* don't control natural disasters."

"So *you* didn't have *anything* to do with—"

"Moron! Shut up! You need to get this done. Because someone controls lightning—but it isn't me."

Part 2

17

Jack

I slide the gun into the trunk of Don's shitmobile, between the rucksack and the cooler.

Then I drive nineteen hundred miles east, playing music so loud, it blocks out rational thought. It takes two and a half days. There might be scenery, but all I see is a loop of Nicolette's face, Yucca Valley Correctional, Connie Marino shooting hoops in the driveway of my dad's spread, and my mother's house on fire.

In the middle of this, there are flashes of my dad coming at me, going, *Think, Jack*. But I'm too busy trying to stay awake in a peeling-plastic bucket seat to think.

Anyone, anywhere, anytime. The world ends. I whimper like a little girl. Connie dies. Bang.

At the point when I realize my mind has turned to the kind of mush that steers cars into the center divider, I pull off and sleep in the front seat, parked at a desolate rest stop in Kansas. I don't have any real dreams, just reruns of what I did to my mother right before I left, and the promises I made that I'm not going to keep.

It started off practical. I said I was leaving. She said my car wouldn't make it.

"I could use Don's car." His uglier-than-shit car was mounted on blocks in our garage, waiting for him to finish up his two-to-five. "He has no use for it."

Pain flashes across her face. Very fast, she turns away so I won't see it. I see it, her sorrow and her mother-love for my thug brother.

"Why are you doing this?" she says. "I don't understand."

"I'm eighteen. Guys my age are in the Marines." This is lame and nonresponsive, but at least it's true.

The reaction on her face is bad enough, and then she starts to talk. "Jackson, Marines are *grown-ups*. Grown-ups don't waltz out of town on a whim. Grown-ups are *responsible*."

"*How* can you say I'm not responsible? In this family, isn't it enough that I don't hold up convenience stores? You act like it's a felony that I want to take a road trip. Don *commits* felonies, and you treat him like the Second Coming."

"Don doesn't have your gifts. Jack, sit down. Be *good*. You're a serious person. Now act like one."

I feel like the exploding guy I pretended to be in Enright's office.

"I want to skip graduation, so I'm Public Enemy Number One?"

Even as I sleep by the interstate in Kansas, *be good be good be good* pounds against the inside of my skull like the clapper of a deafening bell.

"No, wait, didn't you *marry* Public Enemy Number One? Maybe you'd like me better if I screwed up *big*. Maybe then you wouldn't be so obvious about worshipping *Don*—"

"I left Don with your father," she says in her unnaturally calm voice. "It was the worst decision of my life. And don't you ever talk to me like this."

Naturally, her worst decision was a Don-decision.

"Don wasn't the one he was trying to *mold*. I was. You sat there for *ten years* and let him do it."

She reaches out to pat my arm, but I'm two feet back before her hand can touch me. "There are no words for how sorry I am," she says.

This would be my opportunity to be decent, forgiving, kind. I could dream a different outcome and wake up without my gut braided like a Boy Scout lanyard. But it's as if I'm turning into the hard guy everybody always thought I was no matter how *good* I was.

"If you're that sorry, maybe you should have found some words."

She sits down on the couch as if I'd pushed her. "Don't try to get back at me by demolishing your own life, all right? I understand you're furious. I understand why. But I'm not about to roll over and say this is all right. This isn't just monumentally stupid—what about memories you'll want later? Grad night, marching with your class at graduation—"

"I want the memory of seeing Las Vegas in the rearview— tonight." I say this with so much conviction, I almost believe it. "I'll use Manx money if I have to."

This would be the money my father left. My mother thinks of it as tainted. I see it as restitution. Before I turned eighteen, it was her choice. Now it's mine.

"Jack, no!"

There, I've brought my mother to the verge of tears. I feel like warmed-over crap. "It's mine, and he owes me."

I've never said things this harsh or true to her before.

She hugs me, but she's shaking. (Even in the dream, I feel her shake.)

I'm not getting back at her, I'm saving her.

She steps away, and her hands find their way to her hips as if she's about to let me have it. "I'll spring for the tent and all the gear. You don't need *his* money. But I want your itinerary, and I want you to answer your phone. Do you hear me?"

I feel nothing but relief with her back in the mom groove and me in the kid groove—but for now, it's all a lie. "Loud and clear. Thanks for the tent." As for the gear, there's no way she's going to know about the gear I'll need for this trip.

She half whispers, "These are the words. I didn't see what I didn't want to see. I was a terrible mother. I'm trying to make up for it."

I'm not a guy who cries. I start to apologize, but she interrupts me. You would think that asleep in Kansas, in the realm of wish-fulfillment, I'd get to finish apologizing and feel like a stand-up son, but I don't.

She says, "I think you wanted to tell me how angry you are."

"I'm not an angry guy!"

She touches the side of my head. "I hope being in nature feeds your soul, Jack. Tell me what you need, and I'll take care of it. Within reason."

Screw my soul, no one is going to touch her. No one is going to get so close, they can switch off the security and take her down in her own laundry room. I won't let it happen.

I'm going to take a road trip and track down this killer bitch Nicolette and, one way or another, I'm going to solve the fucking problem. I don't care if it takes my mother's money and the Manx money—each dollar of which might as well represent a bullet through somebody's head—and every penny I earned, and was forced to save, from three summers of lifeguarding.

I'm going to do this.

I wake up at dawn, hunched over the steering wheel, back aching, filled with nausea and resolve. A couple of goony little kids pound on my window. My first impulse is to slam the car door into them. Instead, I wave and make a funny face.

Between being awakened and yawning, I've imagined knocking little children over with a metal door.

I'm not that guy.

Nevertheless, my mind turns to destruction. Those are my thoughts.

A thousand miles from Nevada, and the beast is off leash.

18

Cat

Frat row at South Texas Tech, Galkey, is two blocks long but intense. Big wooden houses with torn-up lawns in front. Every one of them having a party.

People cutting across the front lawns, hanging off the porches.

I stash the bike and the zombie-apocalypse preparedness kit between a Dumpster and a broken bookshelf the frat boys are throwing out instead of fixing.

Back home, we fix things. Me, Olivia, and Jody, nine years old, in my room in pajamas after we collapsed my bed by jumping on it. Steve trying to figure out how to put it back together. Us telling him how sorry we are. Him telling us if this is the worst thing we ever do, there's nothing to worry about. Only don't do it again.

Must. Stop. Thinking. About. Home.

It's been so much worse since I called up Olivia. I thought it would make it better, but it didn't.

Must. Get. Head. In. Game.

Now.

All right, I'm in love with this Goodwill halter dress. It's the exact kind I like. And these cute fake-leather heels. The whole outfit looks better than it was supposed to, but what was I going to do? Show up in grungy sweats and ask a guy to do me favors? Good luck, Bean.

Everyone looks so far gone, I figure they'll all be blacked out by two a.m. I won't even be a dim memory.

That's what I tell myself to quell the fear.

That I look like the Little Mermaid with this mass of red hair.

That I'm unrecognizable, only as cute as I have to be to get a couple of drunk frat guys to point me to someone who can scare up some nice-looking fake ID.

I pick Theta Chi. They're the loudest. Lots of girls moving to the music inside, so you figure this is the cool party.

What they say about Texas girls with big hair? True. Only these girls look good. They look top-of-wedding-cake good, if brides danced down the aisle dressed in Forever 21.

The first guy to hit on me is dark and cute in an ROTC kind of way. He asks me if I need a beer (or some sentence with *beer* at the end; it's noisy in here). I need to avoid beer, but I say yes just so I'll get to follow him outside to the keg.

I'm not what you could call a party novice.

I take the red cup. "I wish I could get some Jose Cuervo, but I don't have ID."

"You want tequila? Come with me. I'll grant your every wish. And we've got limes."

I need to avoid tequila even more than I need to avoid beer.

He puts his hand on my waist and starts to kind of dance with me. People are making out all over the yard. I press my face against the guy's neck so I seem friendly but with an unavailable mouth.

He says, "You're so pretty."

"You aren't bad, either." This makes him pull me closer, breasts smashed against his chest. Not a romantic feeling if you like to breathe. "What's your name?"

"Clark."

I don't want to lose him, so I take his hand. I pull him toward the back porch, which opens to a room with guys playing pool. It's a hundred degrees and smelly in there, like boy armpits and moldy Doritos.

"You play?"

"Prepare to be impressed." He pushes up his sleeves and goes to work. Every time he drops a ball into a pocket, I act enthusiastic.

When he goes out to get more beer, I trot along next to him. It's quieter in the backyard now. I say, "Hey, Clark, do you know where a person could get an ID?"

"From your big sister?" He's perplexed and completely unhelpful.

"I need one with my name on it. Don't even ask. I was an idiot."

He shakes his head and takes another drink. Looks more perplexed. "I know someone at UT who *might*."

He smiles at me, white teeth, green eyes. And it's not like I'm waiting for a knight with a pool cue to rescue me, because I'm not. But I'd be lying if I said I didn't feel something. Like the tiny filaments of hair on my arms rising in unison. Like I should have DON'T shellacked on my fingernails.

He hands me his cell phone. "Give me your number and maybe he'll call you." Leaning in. "Maybe *I'll* call you."

This is when it wallops me: I have to stop acting like this is a *party* party. If I don't start acting like this is my opportunity to get what I need, I'm dead. Not the wink-giggle-my-daddy-will-kill-me-if-I-climb-into-your-backseat metaphorical kind of dead. The literal kind.

I'm walloped like, Clark can't help you, and it's disappointing, and it feels like there's a boulder on your chest when you think about how doomed you are.

Do something, because nobody is coming to the rescue. Stop flirting and *go*!

Get in.

Get what you need.

Get out.

Xena, Warrior Princess would.

It's after midnight: Any minute it will be too late. The whole night's risk will be a waste.

I ditch Clark. He's gazing at a knot of college girls (so hot they make me look like a redheaded panda bear) and doesn't notice when the Little Mermaid swims off. Upstairs, doors are open, people hanging out smoking (not cigarettes). People are on the beds and slumped on the floor. Girls too out of it to notice where their bags are.

Girls too out of it to notice where their bags are.

Bags with drivers' licenses in them.

All along the dark, smoky corridor, I search for short white girls with brown eyes. (Good luck determining the eye color of passed-out girls.) I have to find a girl who looks enough like me so the photo on the license I slide out of her wallet could *be* me. Then I have to find her bag and snatch it.

I mumble, almost to myself, "Where's my bag?" Then I scoop a tiny rectangular clutch off the floor and take it into the bathroom. It smells like fresh barf in there. It's no wonder there's no line.

The bag belongs to a 5'10" girl named Zoe. I'm too short to pass as her.

By the time I come up with a girl who looks right—lying on her back across a bed more out of it than sleeping—I have to wait while her friend tries to get her up and staggers off in search of a third girl to drag her out of there.

All I can do is pray that when I pry open her eyes, they aren't blue.

Brown! According to the license in the Prada wallet in the Kate Spade bag. And she's 5'4", close enough.

Also, she just went to the ATM.

The first bang on the bathroom door stops my heart. I yell, "Wait up!"

Because talking yourself into something this bad takes a little time.

I tell myself she's rich. There are Mercedes keys in there. There's a Platinum American Express card like Steve has.

I tell myself it doesn't matter how rich she is, I'm going to be punished for this. That God is watching and bookmarking all this for divine reprisal. Then I try to talk myself into the idea that I was sent to this party by the universe to punish *her*, to teach her a lesson about getting passed-out drunk.

Sure I was.

I vow, if I make it out of this alive, I'll track her down and pay her back. How many girls named Catherine Grace Davis from Tulsa, Oklahoma, can there be?

Then I open the door, and it turns out I was right about who's getting punished the first time.

Standing on the other side of the door is Piper Carmichael, Summer Carmichael's older sister that I've known since I was ten years old, no doubt sent by an avenging God to out me.

"Nicolette? What are you doing here?"

I have the little Kate Spade bag under the halter of the backless dress, which is, duh, my signature party attire. Oh God, oh God, oh God, what was I thinking? Idiot.

I try to look confused, as opposed to shocked and white and shivering.

I say, all Texas drawly, my insides turning to ice, "I have that kind of face. Everyone thinks I'm someone else. I'm Kelly Hill." I slur the words as best I can. I might have said Callie Hale or Kaylie Hull or anything but the name Piper Carmichael has called me since I was in fourth grade with Summer. When she showed us how to put on lip gloss but made us give back her mascara.

Piper's hands fly to her lips, ten flashes of the bloodred nail polish she favors.

"You're *who*?"

She knows who I am.

I run.

19

Jack

Cotter's Mill, Ohio, has a main street with a couple of sad-looking mom-and-pop stores intersecting a side street with a strip mall and Cotter's Mill Unified High, where Nicolette attended before she started practicing her knife skills on people.

I cruise past the hamburger joint where Olivia works weekends. I might come off as a stupid prep tourist, but at least I have the sense not to lead my life online. Olivia, on the other hand, records each minute of every day for the general public. I know when she's on early shift and when her boss, Maxine, reschedules her last-minute. More to the point, I know when the chef leaves, the place is deserted, and she's behind the counter reading a library book: now.

Olivia is even better in person—brown-haired, brown-eyed,

perfect skin, and built. I try to lock in to her eyes to avoid distraction. I order a burger, rare, and a Coke for an excuse to be there.

"The cook leaves at two. Sorry. Just ice cream and pie."

"Olivia?" I pretend to look at her name tag for the first time. "You're not Nick Holland's friend Liv are you?"

Nick, that seems like a nice touch.

There's a quick intake of breath before she starts smoothing nonexistent wrinkles out of her white waitress apron. Maybe I didn't play this right.

"Wow," she says. "How do you know *Nick*?"

No question, I didn't play this right. "Yeah," I say, hoping I'm guessing well. "She wasn't too happy when I called her that, either."

This gets the beginning of a cautious smile. "I'm pretty much the only one who gets to call her that."

"Sorry."

"And we don't have Coke. Just Pepsi."

"I'll have root beer."

"I *know*," she says. "No Coke. So moronic."

"Who drinks Pepsi?" I say. "Listen, is Nicolette around? We were in touch for a while, and then she just . . . stopped. But as long as I'm here . . ."

Olivia is making a big show of wiping off the counter. It's already spotless.

"Come on. I'm trapped at my uncle's for the weekend. On the lake."

"Your uncle has a place on the lake?" she says. "Who is he?"

The smallness of this town is evident. I don't have this down. "Frank Burris," I say, pulling a name out of my butt. "He's renting."

"He's renting a summer place in Cotter's Mill?"

"It's closer to Kerwin." This is two towns over, but she probably knows everyone there, too.

"I'll *bet* it is," she says. This girl can make anything sound questionable.

"Is there something you know that I don't know?" *Such as where Nicolette is? Just tell me, and I'll get out of your hair.* "Is Nick pissed off at me?"

"How would *I* know?" She's fiddling with ketchup bottles. "I don't even know what your name is."

"Shit!" This is involuntary. "It's James." I picked a name that starts with *J.* If someone says, "Jack," and I turn around, it won't be that suspicious.

Olivia, back to me, shovels ice into a glass. "I've never heard of you."

"That's disappointing."

She laughs, just a little.

I say, "Maybe her memory was shot. I heard she got hauled to rehab."

Olivia doesn't take this well. *"Where? In rehab where?* And there's *nothing* wrong with her memory!"

She has no idea. I'm in Cotter's Mill giving out information, learning nothing. Even Don would do a better job. He'd show up, put a knife to her throat, and make her spill everything she knows and then some.

I look down because looking someone in the face and hurling bullshit is getting harder, not easier. "Sorry, it's just what I heard. And I feel bad. I might have encouraged her to drink more than she intended. Shots. I didn't realize she was still in high school."

Olivia is holding up a bottle of mustard and glowering at me. "Where did you say you know her from?"

I'm prepared for this. The Internet is a wonderful thing.

"Cheerleader camp. Last summer."

She gives me an even more disapproving look.

I say, "*I* wasn't at camp, *she* was. In Ann Arbor? I was in summer school. The cheerleaders kept showing up at parties at the Fiji house."

Olivia *tsk-tsks*. "You're a frat boy? You sure you're not that douche Alex?"

"Independent. Things get looser in the summer. And I don't know anybody named Alex." I shrug. "Let me think."

"Don't bother. He came, he went."

Then she stands there, staring at me as if I'm supposed to carry on a conversation about Alex the unknown douche from Ann Arbor. I need to get this back on track. "I just wanted to talk to her. . . . I was in rehab myself once, so . . ."

Olivia squints at me. "You don't seem like the type."

I try to imagine myself reaching around her and snapping her neck. I can't. I'm aware of her chest rising and falling as she breathes, and of her tongue licking her chapped lower lip. She and Nicolette had better not have that much in common, because if I ever find her, I don't want to stare at her like this.

I go back to being James, the bitter U of M drunk. "Some people in rehab are the type. Others were rich kids whose parents needed a place to ditch them."

"Which category were you?"

"Not the former."

Unless Olivia likes guys who pity themselves, the lip-licking isn't a come-on. "At least you *have* parents," she says. Definitely not a come-on. "Not that I'm complaining. I've been with the same foster family forever. Like Nick got Steve. We were the girls who ended up with different parents than we started out with."

How did this go from me trying to pump her about Nicolette to her pouring her heart out?

"Don't look so upset," Olivia says. "Mine are pretty great. I'm staying with them after I age out."

How did this solid girl end up with a bloodthirsty BFF like Nicolette?

I say, "Listen, when does your shift end?" Because this interrogation is not going well, and I need another shot.

"Like, ten minutes ago. We close three to five."

"You want to get coffee somewhere that doesn't smell like a grease fire?"

"Watch it, mister. Someday I'm going to grow up and own Cotter's Mill Shake Shack. It's my *dream*."

I look at her.

"Don't even!" she says. "You're so gullible. Nick must have had you twisted around her pinkie like a rubber band. My dream is to be a microbiologist. Someplace warm. Like Florida. Nick can be my accountant."

Nicolette Holland is planning to be an *accountant*?

Olivia finally gives me a full smile. "Wait for me while I lock up in back."

Her book and bag are on the counter right next to me as if I were the kind of trustworthy guy you could leave alone with your things for five long minutes.

I do what has to be done.

There are two phones in Olivia's bag. The good one's in the pocket where I think phones are supposed to go. The burner's in the change compartment of her massive five-pound wallet. There's only one number in this burner. I memorize it, put the phone back in the wallet, the wallet back in the bag, and the bag back on the counter before the door swings back open.

I look at my phone, and I lie. "I'm sorry! I've gotta head out. Family calls. I obey. Next time?"

She looks disappointed. I did good. "Well, nice to meet you." Then she reaches for my phone and writes herself into my contacts. She says, "Call me if you get back here. I'll tell Nick to call you if I get the chance. If she's up for a drunk rich boy."

"Very sober, very rich," I say—both true. "You do that. Give me your e-mail, too."

20

Cat

I cup my hand over the burner. "Liv, I'm on a bus." I lower my voice. "Somebody saw me."

"I *know*. Piper Carmichael *tagged* you. And this boy from Ann Arbor wants to know why you stopped talking to him. You should let me call you!"

Oh God, oh God, oh God.

I don't know if I say, *This is worse than I thought,* or if I think it. "What did he look like?"

"Super prep. Brown hair. Nice eyes. Knows you from Fiji parties."

It's as if everyone I've ever met is fanning out across the lower forty-eight waving sticks in front of themselves like volunteers forming a grid to find lost hikers.

"I told Summer it was probably your doppelganger," Olivia says. "But she didn't know what that was. So then I said your body double, and she said why would you have a body double, and I said—"

She rattles on. I know she's trying to be helpful, but I can't take it in.

"What was Piper Carmichael doing at South Texas Tech? Why would it even occur to her it was me?"

Olivia snorts. "Well, apparently, with red hair, you look *exactly* like yourself with red hair. And were you wearing *aqua* eye shadow?"

I'm pressed up against the window, curled into my best approximation of not existing, eight rows behind anyone else so they can't hear me coming apart.

"I said it wasn't you," Olivia says. "I said, really, would Nick be caught six feet under and *rotting* with aqua eyelids?"

"Lovely image."

"I said even if it was you—which it *wasn't*—she should tell Piper to take it down because you're supposed to be in rehab and Steve will pitch a fit." She sighs. "But you know Summer. If it's not about her, she won't remember."

I'm undone by my signature backless dress, and the fact that I had a terrible disguise, and what Piper told Summer. I feel like throwing up. And not because I'm tearing into a bag of Dunkin' Donuts, Texas toast grilled cheese, and frosted crullers.

"Don't cry!" Olivia says. "Even worst case, it's not that bad. You get hauled back to rehab, it sucks, you cooperate with their BS, and you're out."

"Olivia, this wasn't about rehab! I wasn't in rehab. I lied."

"What?"

"Just listen. Someone's after me."

"Says Miss Bears-False-Witness who *lies* to her best friend. Forget the Nick Holland show for a minute. Rehab is stupid, but what if you go back and gut it out?"

"Listen to me! Men with *guns* are after me, all right? I disappear or I'm dead."

"What?"

"I saw them. I heard them. Please believe me."

Liv says, "Sweet Jesus Christ!" And it's not like she's taking it in vain. It's more like she's trying to invoke divine intervention. "How did this happen? Stop wailing or someone's going to notice you. Focus. If your hair's still red, you need to get off that bus."

But my hair isn't still red, and I've been completely focused ever since Piper Carmichael said, "Come on, Nicky. I'm not that drunk."

Absolute terror will do that for you.

I could hear blood flow past my ears inside my head, could hear myself breathing, could hear the words *left foot, right foot, left, right*, forming in my head. Directing me out through the front door and into the night.

Picked up my daypack and kept going.

Walked straight into the ladies' room at the first bar I came to.

Cut five inches off my hair. Buried it in the trash.

Standing there in my bra, I pulled a box of dye out of my pack. Squirted foam through my hair. Spread Vaseline around my hairline. Kept spraying room deodorizer to cut the smell, which could have made birds fall out of the sky.

All I needed was twenty minutes for the dye to set.

I got fifteen, then some girl started rattling the door. It was my night for hogging bathrooms.

I yelled, "Just a sec, y'all!" As if I thought if I said *y'all* enough, people would believe I was from Georgia. Or wherever I said I was from.

Dunked my head into the sink. Ran a weak stream of water over it.

"You taking a bath in there?"

I wrung out my hair. Wiped out the sink. Put on jeans and gym shoes.

Walked out the back door into the pitch-black alley.

Tossed my wadded-up dress and fake-leather sandals in a trash can.

Walked away.

You get spotted. You evaporate like dew on a leaf. The sun rises, the leaf dries off, and even if someone can tell you were there, you're gone.

Ask me who I hitched a ride to San Antonio with. How I

found the bus station there. How I bought a ticket on the next bus out. How I managed to calculate the exact number of calories in the junk food I kept shoving down my throat.

I don't know.

The new plan was to alter the shape of my body—put on weight, and quick—before I hit Tallahassee. Because obviously, cheap disguises didn't do the trick. It crossed my mind that with all the greasy frosted doughnut residue, the cream filling and oozing cheeseburger fat clogging my arteries, I'd probably keel over dead before anyone got me in his crosshairs anyway.

So I'm sitting in this bus heading east, eating a chalupa. Wide-awake. Jolted into a perfect state of clarity.

Then it gets worse.

Then it's not that *if* I keep messing up, they'll find me.

I'm found.

Then comes my first and only text. Luna says: *Your biker's back with some muscle. Two guys with shoulder holsters. Looking for you. They have pictures. I said I never heard of you. Get outta Dodge. I'll box your stuff. Xo.*

I'm tagged online for two damn days, and guys with holsters are swilling iced tea in the lobby of the Bluebonnet.

How many screw-ups between Galkey and here? I picture two guys in an Escalade following the bus, biding their time, listening to the radio.

Someone opens the latch on the bathroom door in the

back, and I stop breathing until the bus stops at a multiplex of gas stations and fast food and showers you pay for.

The driver is standing outside, smoking, shooting the breeze with a guy in a T-shirt. No holster. A lady with a half-asleep kid wants off the bus to buy some food.

I slide down the aisle. My pulse and breath and heartbeat are so loud. Out the door and fast over to the on-ramp to a highway going north.

Catch a ride on a truck carrying groceries to Topeka.

Get off. Get on. Change direction. Repeat.

Sleep for a couple of hours in the bushes behind a McDonald's near Memphis.

Wake up.

Stick out my thumb.

Go west.

21

Jack

Two and a half more days on the road, and I slink back across the state border into Nevada, hoping no unhappy coincidence puts Enright or my mother next to me at a red light. I've driven thirty-eight hundred miles without coming six inches closer to finding this girl beyond a phone number I have no strategy for calling.

"What are you doing here?"

I'm in Calvin's room via the ground-floor window next to his closet. I've gotten in this way since we were kids. But that's not his usual response.

I say, "Hello. How's it going? Fine. How about you? Also fine."

"Not fine. Monica can't go to prom with a senior unless she's in a group."

"Sorry. Go with Dan Barrons and Scarlett. Scarlett always liked *you*."

Calvin pantomimes heaving. His geekier friends think prom is crap. I was his group, and I'm supposedly rock-climbing in Yosemite.

"I was hoping for technological assistance."

"Tell me what's going on first."

"Don't you trust me?"

He groans. This question comes from Boy Scouts, when I rowed us into rapids he wasn't expecting. I wasn't expecting them either, but I was slow to admit it. When you know someone long enough, all your history turns into jokes.

I say, "I just need to know. If you call up a burner, is there a way to trace the location of the person who picks up?"

"If you're the NSA. Not if you're you." He rubs his palms together. "That was easy."

This gives rise to Plan B.

Calvin runs his hand through his hair. "Six years of El Pueblo, and all you want is to get As, beat Barrons at everything, and leave for Mercer in a blaze of glory. Now you're gone before gradu-ation. You like cars, but you're driving Don's *thing*. Your mother's a *prosecutor*, but you want me to show you how to put illegal spy-ware in a girl's computer? And of course this has nothing to do with the mysterious errand for Don. One more time, why do you want this?"

"Maybe I'm stalking a girl."

Calvin gapes. "Sorry, man. You have to give me more than that."

"Maybe I'm obsessed with her. Maybe I want to read every e-mail she gets and every word she writes back."

"Doable but illegal."

"Like tapping into Courtney Gan's computer?" Courtney is Monica's older sister, who has bigger everything but no appreciation of smart guys. Calvin wanted her first, explaining the four days of cyber-intrusion. It took him two years to figure out that Monica was the self-proclaimed nerd of his dreams. "Show me how you did that."

"That was ninth grade," Calvin says. "Gerhard found out. I've reformed." Gerhard has a long history of busting us.

"And I need to keep the ID."

"You need it? It's about to be summer. I need the ID."

"Who signed your notes?" Calvin is at war with our second-period math teacher. He won't turn in the homework, which he claims is a waste of time. He got a string of before-school detentions with parental sign-off notes—hence the forgery by yours truly.

I might be a solid citizen, but I'm loyal.

"You need it for how long?"

"Give me a break. I'm hitting the road in the Thing. What if I need a beer?"

"Maybe you should call off your plan. I hear they have beer at senior night. You should come."

"I hear your mother thinks you've been handing in homework all year. Are you going to help me or what?"

Calvin draws diagrams and demonstrates how to use spyware to get into Olivia's computer for the next three hours. "You get her to download an attachment," he says. "Make her think it's a coupon or an invitation or something."

Once I infiltrate Olivia's computer, I'll see everything that comes in or out, every stroke of her keyboard. If Nicolette contacts her from another computer, I'll see every word and emoticon and link Nicolette sends.

Getting the IP address of Nicolette's computer is trickier. I have to get her to click on a dummy website, followed by a series of moves I didn't know existed. But if I do this right, I can get the physical location of Nicolette's computer, leading me to the location of the back of Nicolette's murderous, throat-slashing head.

I flip through my notes, most of which were drafted by Calvin when my speed of comprehension was slower than his speed of explanation.

"Could you go through this again, right here?"

Calvin looks at me as if I were a moron.

"Jesus, were you asleep in comp sci?"

But he explains. It's all in there, my step-by-step guide to tracking Nicolette with marginally legal technology.

Calvin takes hold of my upper arm. He has a wrestler's grip. "*Why* are you doing this? The truth."

"I have to find this girl. Before she gets hurt."

"Don?"

"What do you think? I have to get to her before . . . anyone else does."

I watch the light bulb click on in his head. "You have to find her to warn her?"

This is so plausible and benign. Hell, maybe it's what I'm doing. Either way, she disappears right after I find her. "Something like that."

Calvin likes answers. Now that he has one, he's happy again. He says, "May the force be with you." He throws in a Vulcan blessing to cover all bases.

It doesn't work. I haven't even turned the key in the ignition of the shitmobile when a call comes in with an area code that's probably Helsinki.

There's static. Then Don says, "Shut up. This isn't me."

My first instinct is to toss the phone and floor the car.

My mother told Don that if he got a contraband phone—like half the other prisoners in Nevada who don't mind jeopardizing their release dates—it was the end of his cigarettes. But apparently, to torment me, it was worth the risk.

"What do you want?"

"Is that what you say to your brother who's doing you a favor?"

"What favor?"

"You can turn my car around. She's not in Nowhere, Texas, anymore."

I say, "Thanks," trying to sound as if I know what he's talking about, as if I were already halfway to Nowhere, Texas.

"Word is, guys got there inside of five hours, and they scoured the place."

"If other guys are looking for her, why am I looking for her?"

His voice goes dark. "You're doing more than look for her."

Parked on a side street near Calvin's house, I surf through all things Nicolette. I find red hair and a blurry face that could be anyone, posted on Facebook by some girl named Piper who goes to Southern Methodist. While I was driving straight through like a madman, this was sitting there online, and forty-three people were commenting.

It's possible I'm screwing this up big-time.

22

Cat

I stop when I hit the Pacific Ocean.

Union Station in Los Angeles. Cavernous. Beautiful. Crawling with police. I walk out in a parade of ladies·trailing wheelie bags into a noon sun so bright, it glints through sunglasses in shade. Rows of palm trees. Sky so blue, it looks fake.

Two miles to the library. I know the exact specifications for where I want to hide out. Four turns on the computer, and I've found it and the bus route to get to it.

I sleep at a late-night movie in a mall bordering a commuter college *no one* I know will ever attend. There are people hanging out at an all-night Mexican place. Every hour until seven a.m., I buy some cheap new thing to keep my table. By morning, there are thousands of students milling around.

I'm like Waldo on a two-page spread of ten thousand other Waldos.

If you think I'm going to make the same mistake I made in Galkey, guess again. As if there was just one.

I'm hunkering down until no one can tell that Cat Davis is *me*.

Not people who saw me once at camp. Not people who grew up down the street from me. Not me when I pass my own reflection in a plate-glass window.

Plus, I'm constantly scared.

Which is good.

In real life, if you're so scared, you're debilitated, you're supposed to suck it up. Go to your happy place. Talk it over with your stepfather, who encourages you to stop hiding in your room and go back to fourth grade even if the back of your skirt did get caught in your panties so everyone saw your butt.

In the new real life, *scared* is my motto and creed and religion. It makes me nocturnal, cleaning out offices on night shift. I got the job off Craigslist. At sunrise, when I've mopped my last floor, the boss hands me a wad of cash.

In the room I'm subletting (also Craigslist, also cash), I do hundreds of crunches. Deep knee bends like a manic jack-in-the-box. Push-ups and headstands and walking on my hands between the closet and the tiny bathroom.

Then I eat a bag of frosted Winchell's Donuts.

I'm not actually fat. I pass the pinch test for not being

HOW TO DISAPPEAR

morbidly obese. Let's just say I won't be climbing to the top of
a human pyramid anytime soon.

What used to be empty space between my thighs is filled
with slabs of me that rub against each other when I walk. I'm
cushioned in a muscled sheet of safety.

I live half a block from three bus lines, a quarter mile to
the metro. Be fit. Run. Hitch with whoever gets you off the
street fastest.

When the girls who rent the other rooms in the apartment
are gone, I sneak into the living room and watch Ultimate
Fighting on their cable.

23

Jack

I'm in a crap motel outside Laughlin, where I've been sitting since I left Calvin's house. I paid with Manx cash and signed the register with illegible handwriting. From a hundred miles away, Summerlin feels like ancient history.

It took less than a day for Olivia to download my attachment, a fake contest for tickets to see Taylor Swift live. I might as well be standing right behind her every time she logs on, draped in Monica's Mermaid Ninjas' mantle of invisibility. I'm not pleased to be this level of creeper, but at least I'm not turning on her camera remotely and watching her undress—I could, but I wouldn't. But then, the guy in the cheesy horror movie who chants, "Come out, come out, wherever you are," probably doesn't think he's a freak either.

I keep clicking on Olivia's screen, refreshing it, waiting for it to update with what I'm looking for. As soon as Nicolette e-mails or Facebook messages or contacts her in any way from a computer, I can find her.

I watch Olivia buy a skirt online and shoes that don't have much to them except heels. For hours, all she gets is spam and notices from her dad's church. Her youth group has a Facebook page. She's bringing lemon bars to their next meeting. This gets eight likes, a "yum," and a smiley face.

I eat cartons of KFC, Big Macs, and chili cheese fries.

I wait a day, two days, five days.

Don says, "Aren't you supposed to be the smart one? Speed it up."

"Do you think I want to draw this out?"

"Don't make me wish I got somebody else for this."

"Why didn't you? If you had so many people begging to do your bidding."

"Because *Mom* was in play."

I don't know if he's trying to motivate me, scare me, or hit me in the face with the stakes, but he's three for three. I pull two mini-bottles of whiskey out of the mini-fridge and pour them into the glass I've been using for my toothbrush.

Maybe all the drunk, creative guys had it right. Because then I figure out the obvious. Just because I can't get into Nicolette's phone doesn't mean she's not using it. Why would Olivia get e-mail from Nicolette when they both have phones? Ding, ding, ding: I have to get Nicolette to stop using her cell phone to talk to

Olivia. I need her in Olivia's computer. That's when I'll get to take my mantle of invisibility on the road.

If she loses the phone, I've got her.

It feels like I'm playing Clue against Nicolette, except that I already know she did it and where and with what weapon and to whom. I leave the motel for long enough to buy the phone that's going to lead me to her.

Don's right.

I'm going to win the game.

I explain that there's a new strategy, and he blows. It's pointless to try to explain. He doesn't have the concentration to sit through it, and the likelihood that he'd forgive me for not figuring it out sooner is nil.

I say, "Tell me anyone's closer to finding her than I am, and I'll mail you a finger. Let up. I'm on this 24/7."

"I don't want your friggin' finger! I want results. You're supposed to be the smart one. Do something smart. Because something might happen that I can't stop."

Without thinking, I say, "Whatever happens to Mom happens to you."

There it is: my first death threat.

24

Cat

The first message arrives at 1:40 a.m.

The phone pings.

On the dimly lit screen, a text: *I know where you are.*

My heart stops. I'm still breathing, but there's no pulse or sound or heartbeat. The phone drops onto the bed.

No. No no no no no no no.

I was supposed to be untraceable. How could this happen?

I bite into my lower lip until I taste blood.

Every cell in my body is screaming, *Get out! Get out! Get out!*

Or do they want me to run? Hope I'll be spooked and charge into the open, too scared to think or fight? A moving car's door opens, there's a hand, I'm taken.

The ice pick is in my hand like a sixth finger. I keep it under the pillow.

The phone pings again: *I know.*

Cold hands, cold feet, my right knee bouncing a staccato rhythm on the bed. I'm trying to think, but I can't—not over the sound of silent screaming.

Get out!

Get out!

Get out!

This phone felt like a lifeline. Turns out, it was the human version of the locator chip we put in Gertie when she was a puppy.

Luna has my number. What did they have to do to get her to fork it over? And I gave it to Clark, too, to pass on to his UT fake ID friend.

Damn.

What if *Law & Order* was *wrong*? What if this phone has been pinging my location every three inches?

This phone dies now.

There are footsteps in the outside hallway. The upstairs neighbors shouting at each other. Music coming through the walls.

I hold the phone that knows where I am, waiting for it to tell me something else. I grab my pack and slip out to the walkway that rims the building. Black sweats, faded hoodie, shoulders folded inward from fear. A shapeless gray ghost.

At the corner of the building, a party is overflowing. I stay low, under the railing, slide in the other direction toward the trash room. Open the heavy metal door. Stomp my phone under my heel and toss it down the chute.

How easy would it be to light the paper in the stainless-steel recycling bin on fire? Just enough smoke to trip the alarm and empty the building?

For one second, I see myself waving the lighter over my head at night at the arena in Columbus, swaying to the music with Connor. Feel the flames of the homecoming bonfire throwing heat onto my face, see myself tossing a branch into the conflagration, watching it ignite.

Orange plumes shoot up from the recycling can, and I'm back in reality. The reality in which I just started a fire. Which is bad, for the obvious reasons.

How can I still be this impulsive, how?

But it's a sealed cement room with a fire door. A spritz of an extinguisher, and this will be over.

I smash the glass on the fire alarm with the handle of the ice pick to speed things up. The alarm blasts fast and loud.

I close the fire door behind me as licks curl upward toward the smoke detector. The party crowd heads down the open stairways toward the courtyard as sirens wail. I am indistinguishable from all the other girls who live behind identical apartment doors.

I glom on to a beer-scented guy. Shaved head and heavy-lidded eyes.

I can so do this. Walk away from the fire trucks and the fire fused to the side of an anonymous drunk guy.

He pats my back, all sloppy and uncoordinated. And I wouldn't mind being held—not groped, *held*—even by a comatose bear. But more than that, I want to get away.

I scan the crowd, but who am I looking for? Anyone could be the bad guy. Except for this guy. He's too tanked.

"You got a car?" I'm under his arm all the way to a five-speed Honda Civic. He doesn't complain that I'm hijacking him. He's too far-gone to hear me grind the gears.

"Oh, baaaaabe," he says. Large guys can be so trusting and moronic.

A girl who does what he's doing—gone forever. But he's asleep and I'm driving, so I'm not that unfortunate girl. I'm the girl he won't remember when he wakes up in the parking lot facing the beach, keys in the ignition.

I used to get in trouble for TPing trees and making over girls whose mothers make them dress like Pilgrims.

I've moved so far beyond taking candy bars and licenses and money. I've traded what Steve would have called "playing with fire" (if he'd known what I was up to, which he didn't) for real fire. I'm barely recognizable inside. And I'm working on my outside.

If your life was at risk, would you commit arson in an apartment building?

That would be yes.

Would you risk your soul to save your body?

Yes.

This tops the list of things I wish I didn't know about myself.

I walk along the beach until sunrise. The waves hit the shore so much louder than at Green Lake. Then I run as if I could outrun what I know.

As if.

It feels like the end of a marathon. That's how tired of this I am.

What would Xena, Warrior Princess do?

What she had to do, that's what.

I cut back up to the edge of the road as shades start opening in the houses. I hang behind a gas station on the end of a beach strip mall.

Change into a pink tee I'll never wear again.

Part my hair with my fingernail. Plan what color curly mop it will be a couple of hours from now.

Wait.

Two girls with a San Diego State decal and an empty back-seat pull in.

"My ride was supposed to meet me here an *hour* ago. Could I possibly hitch a ride south? I could chip in for gas."

I sleep all the way down the coast. When they let me off, it feels like the morning after I got monumentally trashed at cheer camp and woke up hungover. I pass an electronics store.

This time I find out which phone has GPS and buy the one that doesn't, never did, and couldn't. I don't even steal it. Still, it seems like lots of money for a thirty-second phone call.

"Are you alone?"

"It's Sunday morning—where do you think I am?" Olivia says.

"Drive the phone somewhere and crush it. Get yourself a new e-mail and write to Cinderella, okay?"

Cinderella3472 is from when we made up a college girl named Desiree to play with online. Not that we got past setting up her e-mail account and an unfinished profile on TrueLuvMatch.com. Who's going to be able to find a nonexistent single who never goes to one website where I ever visited, posted, or scrolled past?

Olivia's voice drops. "What happened?"

"Later."

Then I trash the phone.

I have totally freaked out my best friend while she was sitting in *church*, and I don't even feel bad about it.

I finally get how to do this. Lying and stealing didn't feel that great, but this was a fire, and I don't even feel guilty. On the bus back north, winding through farmland, I'm remembering Steve going, "Don't you think that might have been a wee bit reckless, Nicolette?" I'm thinking, *Freaking-A, I'm reckless*.

Also, still alive.

I'm on the bus in different sunglasses and a marching band

shirt, chomping on a bag of mini Kit Kat bars and a half-quart carton of whole milk to get my fat on.

You can circumnavigate the globe on your tabletop, Steve, but no one, not anyone, not whoever texted me, not a platoon of Texas Rangers or the FBI or a band of scary thugs (or you) will ever find me.

By the time you walk past me on the street, I'll be some whole other girl you don't even recognize or know.

Even I will hardly know it's me.

I feel so maniacally in power, I can't even sleep anymore. So I sit back in this half-dazed state, scanning the bus for bogeymen and obsessing about where Catherine Grace Davis can get a gun.

25

Jack

When it happens, I'm alone in the motel room that by now is strewn with bottles, KFC boxes, and dirty clothes. Nicolette is using Gmail—great for security, bad for me—but Calvin's instructions are gold, and the privacy of the computer Nicolette is using is protected by the functional equivalent of a chain lock made of paper clips.

The computer is in the John Muir Branch of the public library in El Molino, California, a hick town in the Central Valley above Fresno.

Yelling "Gotcha!" to myself would be too much like going over the edge. Instead, I start cleaning up and packing with a vengeance. From this point on, it's all about self-discipline: the kind Nicolette doesn't have.

HOW TO DISAPPEAR

To: Cinderella3472@gmail.com
From: 1SnowWhite5150@gmail.com

I accidently dropped my phone down a well. (Not
really. You know what I mean.) Tell me you're ok
NOW!!!!! Luv u 4ever, Snow

To: 1SnowWhite5150@gmail.com
From: Cinderella3472@gmail.com

Somebody got my number, my fault, I gave it out,
don't even. Total terror-fest. Plus I think it had
GPS. So. Spooked. Might get another for emergencies. Now that I get you have to throw them out
all the time or PEOPLE FIND YOU. Do not trust Law
& Order reruns for survival tips. ♥ ♥ ♥

She's e-mailed Olivia, aka 1SnowWhite5150, twice, and if I
don't get to El Molino, California, fast, she gets her new emergency
burner and she's gone.

I drive there in the dark, guzzling Red Bull.

I'm in an innocuous grayish Prius I bought for cash off a used-car
lot just before it closed as soon as I hit California. Don's car is by
the side of the road in the middle of nowhere. I hiked back. I'm not
sneaking up on this girl in a car you can hear coming a mile away.

It's seven a.m., still chilly, and the library doesn't open for hours. I dig a flannel shirt out of the trunk and cruise. There are FOR RENT signs planted in front of half the apartments abandoned by students taking off for summer.

I want a command post with an ergonomic chair and a mattress from this century, not another sleazy motel. I'm not a guy who throws money around, but I throw some rent at a place in a Victorian house I can get week-to-week. The girl who's handling the rental seems so relieved to get the place off her hands, she doesn't care if I'm in town to commit acts of terror.

I sit in the ergonomic chair and stare at my screen while more days of my life go down the tubes.

There's nothing like a good obsession to keep a guy mesmerized. Four days in, I'm still sitting in the desk chair in boxer shorts, waiting for something to happen. I'm beating myself up for not walking El Molino systematically, street by street, looking for her, when my screen offers her up.

She's e-mailing Olivia from the John Muir branch again. The rush is like a free fall, like bungee jumping where you're not supposed to be.

I'm there in five, scouting.

I watch her hands hover over the keyboard, her arms emerging from the sleeves of a giant tee, her face bent toward the screen. The hair that was once straight and blond, now brown and curly, falls over the side of her face as she leans forward. She has glasses now. I see the thin blue vein in the corner of her forehead, watch her push her hair behind her ear. The diamond studs from the photos are gone, her earlobes curved and white.

I watch her breathe.

I don't let myself feel what I've felt since I saw pictures of her that first time, more difficult now that she's more my physical type, curvier and a little older-looking. She's still small and beautiful and a killer.

When she gets up to leave, I follow her carefully through a leafy neighborhood of big, old wooden houses to a park with a playground. There she sits, reading a book, shading her eyes from the afternoon sun. There I sit on a rock not more than twenty yards behind her, pretending to stare into space.

And it's not that I'm too self-disciplined to move in precipitously, it's that I have no idea what I'm going to do next.

26

Cat

An express to El Molino was the first bus out of San Diego. The ticket lady said, "Whole different state up there."

I nodded like a girl that no one would remember.

But even if she did remember, since LA—with my (sallow) skin, my (stringy) hair, my (unnecessary) glasses, my (penciled-on) eyebrows, my (rapidly increasing) weight, my (lumpy) padding, my (non) style of clothes—*nothing* about me is the same.

This time, if Piper Carmichael sat down next to me, she wouldn't even think I looked familiar.

I probably shouldn't be outside reading anyway. But the point of looking this different is that I'm supposed to be able to walk around in public without being terrified.

I look up to see the little girl fall because she's screaming.

Not in terror, in joy, as she leaps from the swing and soars over the playground's sand floor. Until she lands on a bike and a red wagon. The sound of the child hitting the metal, the bicycle crashing against the wagon, isn't that loud. But it's deafening.

I'm up before I even think, running toward her.

When I was supposed to be as noticeable as a bush, or a slat in the bench, or one more nanny.

The little girl is silent, not making another sound.

A guy runs past me from out of nowhere, outruns me, crouches over her.

You can hear him swearing.

I yell, "Don't move her!"

I've seen enough cheerleading pyramid falls to know this. But there's blood. Her pants are torn above the knee. There's a red stain seeping across the yellow cotton like spilled Hawaiian Punch.

The guy takes off his button-down and uses a sleeve for a tourniquet around her thigh, pressing down on the leg.

In tones of iced rage, he says, "Where's the mom?"

"I'm not the mom!"

"Call 9-1-1."

But there are two women behind him already telling 9-1-1 dispatchers the same identical thing in a duet.

The little girl is pale and still, hair almost white, skin

whitening by the second. The guy is cooing to her. "Can you hear me? Can you open your eyes? I'm right here. What's your name?" And then, in a raspier voice, "Stay with me, okay?"

I say, "Don't talk like that! She isn't dying, all right? I swear, I've seen a bunch of kids fall from way higher than this."

"Thanks, doctor." Then he goes back to telling the girl to stay with him, like she's a police detective breathing her last breath after being felled by a bullet on *Law & Order*.

I'm stroking her arm.

There's blood on my hand.

The mother is running toward us from the ladies' bathroom.

I'm shaking so hard, the paramedic puts a blanket over me after he braces the little girl's head.

The guy who gave up his shirt, now in the wife beater he had on underneath, hands me a half-full water bottle. I take it without even thinking. That's how freaked out I am. Not just about the blood.

He gives me a hand up.

I take in the design of the armband tattooed around his right arm.

For the first time, I really look at the guy. Cute and in extremely good shape. *Extremely* cute. Hazel eyes, shaggy hair, tan. Good smile. Nice taste in tats.

He says, "You ought to sit down."

I ought to run.

"You just stood me on my feet."

"On a bench."

I'm actually gripping this guy's tattoo. I feel him tensing. His biceps don't need any work.

"You've seen a *bunch* of little kids fall out of the sky onto wagons?" he says. "Remind me not to have you watch my kid."

"You have a *kid*?"

"No!" He looks truly taken aback. "You want an ice cream?"

There's a food truck at the edge of the park with pictures of snow cones on the side of it.

"That's okay."

"I'm not trying to pick you up. I'm trying to give you some sugar so you don't go into shock."

"I'm *not* going into shock. Plus, sugar wouldn't help. Complete old wives' tale."

That smile. "Girls often require massive shots of sugar when they first behold me."

"*Behold?* Not grandiose or anything."

"Grandiose? Thanks a lot!" He doesn't look offended.

"Honors psychology." God, now I sound like a high school student. "Who knew that *years* later I'd have insulting diagnoses at my fingertips? Sorry."

"How come you won't let me help you out? You're still shaking."

He's so close to me, propelling me toward the bench, I can feel him shift his weight slightly toward me. Feel his bare forearm against mine. Hear him breathing hard.

He says, "Come on, ice cream. We could still call it cel-
ebratory ice cream. We just saved that kid from bleeding to
death."

"All I did was hold her hand." His foot's touching my foot.
"You did the first aid."

"Boy Scout," he says. "Who knew that *years* later the first
aid would come in handy?"

Great. I've found myself a hot Boy Scout. "Don't make fun
of me."

"I'm not. That would violate the Boy Scout creed. In fact, I
think there's a bylaw that says you have to get Popsicles for girls
covered in blood."

I start to get up to rinse my hands, to get the blood off
me, all of it, now, but I have to sit down again. Dizzy and dry
mouthed. Field of vision narrowing. Passing out.

"Are you all right?" He has his arm around me, but I think
it might be to keep me from falling over as opposed to unin-
vited PDA.

Who am I kidding? I like it.

"You don't look like a Boy Scout."

"This?" He holds out the tattooed arm.

"I like it."

I get that Xena, Warrior Princess wouldn't be cuddling up
to this really cute guy in a wife beater in a public park. She'd
be home making arrowheads. I get it.

But I can't catch my breath or blink or move. His heart

is beating like crazy too, after his virtuoso moves with the injured kid.

Maybe all I'm feeling is like how, after you get spun upside down on the Colossus at State Fair for what feels like forever, you're so hyped up, you want to kiss the random guy sitting behind you in your capsule.

Maybe.

Or maybe I actually want what I want, which would mean I'm insane.

He says, "What's your name? Are you hearing me?"

"*Please* don't start telling me to stay with you like that kid. What's *your* name?"

"J-j-Jay . . ." The slight stammer gets me. As if maybe he's got a slightly (less than 1 percent but still endearing) bashful side. "Just the initial."

No way.

Then he reads my face.

He says, "When I was eleven, I thought it was cool. Then it stuck."

"What's your real name?"

"Don't cringe. Jeremiah. I only got called it one day a year, the first day of school, until I wised up and got to the teachers before they called roll."

"You're pretty serious about this."

"I'm pretty serious about everything. I don't answer to Jeremiah. Try me. Call me from across the park. I won't look up."

"Nerves of steel."

"Who's making fun of whom?"

"Whom?"

"English major. I also recite poetry to impress girls."

This guy is so cute and so close.

I have to lose him.

It would help if I could stand up. But every time I start to lean forward, I get the you're-going-down feeling in my ears.

"Not me! Plus, sensitive, emotional types can't even stand me." Seriously, the lit mag guys treat girls in cheer skirts like a form of plant life. Which doesn't make a girl exactly long for one of them to throw a sonnet at her.

"Lucky for you I'm so insensitive," J says.

Not looking at me like I'm any form of plant.

Maybe I do need sugar.

Maybe I could let a nice guy help me out. He's looking at me so expectantly. Plus, he's athletic.

"Give it up, J. Go get me an ice-cream sandwich, vanilla inside, chocolate out, okay?"

"No stranger to having guys wait on us, are we?"

"Usually they bring me ice-cream sandwiches on their knees, but I'm giving you a pass. Only because you saved that kid."

"Only if you tell me your name."

I'm on such an impulse-driven, plan-defying roll, I don't even hesitate. "Catherine. I answer to Cat."

Part 3

Part 3

27

Jack

I'm sweaty from running and from tension. There's blood on both of us. And I want to make out with her.

When I was next to her on the bench, her head of curly fake-brown hair was half an inch from my chest, and I wanted to hold her—not in a choke hold. I wanted her skin to skin, her head under my chin.

I was supposed to look into the eyes of the girl who carved up Connie Marino and want to close them permanently.

Instead, all I've got is the outline of Don's plan (find; kill; go to college) fighting a ruinous instinct that would undo the plan in one syllable. As I hand her the ice cream, I want to yell, *Don't!* into her ear so loud, it blows out eardrums. Stifling the *Don't!* is making me grind my teeth: *Don't run out of the shadows to help the injured girl.*

Don't take ice cream from a Manx. And don't, for God's sake, tell him your name—your fake name. Don't tell him anything. Run.

Instead I say, "Hey, Catherine."

"Cat." Her eyes are darting all around me, as if she's calculating which stand of trees she'll melt into. "Cat's better."

I have a knife in my pocket—not a switchblade, a legal knife, but it could carve up a small animal. One thrust of the blade could reach a human heart. Her hair covers and uncovers a vein in her neck. I know where all the fatal points of contact are just underneath her skin.

She says, "Maybe *you're* the one who should sit down. You look a little white."

She takes my arm and I'm down, in the prelude to the hookup with this girl I'm supposed to dispose of. There must be a moral code ancient as hieroglyphics that says you can't do this, but I stepped off the edge of the moral universe when I turned over the engine in Don's crap car and rolled out of Summerlin.

"Do you want me to get you another water bottle?" she asks. "I mean, it costs three fifty and it comes from *Fiji*. It probably cures cancer." She's pretty cute, actually, planning her escape route while looking out for me.

"Not a fan of designer water?"

But she's already shot off to the food truck, fast, with a spectacular stride.

I down sixteen ounces. "Thanks. Jesus, it's hot." I'm used to a hundred and ten degrees in the shade, but what the hell, it's conversation. "I thought El Molino was supposed to be balmy."

"Do you believe *everything* people tell you? Does this feel *balmy*?" She extends her arms, palms up, as if waiting for wads of balminess to land in her hands. She shakes her head. "You might be too trusting."

I'm drowning in sweat and irony.

28

Cat

Every part of me is perspiring. My hair is perspiring.

My concentration is shredded.

He says, "Do you have a phone number?"

My mouth is dry. My eyes are too dry to blink. It's distracting to look at him.

"My phone got smashed." Breathe. "I lost it." Breathe. "So no."

He tilts his head the way Gertie does when she's trying to figure out where her doggie treat went after she already ate it. "It got smashed and then it got lost? This phone has very bad luck."

Smartass.

"I lost it, like, 'Oh no, my phone is smashed!' I've lost *the use* of my phone. My phone is deceased. No phone. Is that clear enough for you?"

I don't mention that I smashed it under my foot before tossing it down a garbage chute. And then I stomped on the next one. Or that I bought a new one later, but I'm scared to crack it out of its box. Even though the guy who sold it to me swore up and down that it's an opposite-of-smartphone, with no GPS whatsoever.

"Clear," he says.

I have to get out of this guy's force field.

"Thanks for the ice cream." Licking bits of chocolate sandwich off my front teeth with my tongue. Backing away. "I have to go to work."

"Thanks for the water."

My mouth is cold sugar, but the rest of me is burning. My tee is clinging to my skin like a layer of moist shrink-wrap.

He says, "What do you do?"

I have to go. I know it.

But he sacrificed his shirt. He doesn't deserve a hot mess bitch. "Aide for an old lady. Very glam. I cook a lot of soup."

Soup-cooker for a demented person. She doesn't remember who I am when I get back from peeing. The perfect job. I got it from a tiny want ad posted by her son, who lives in New Mexico. Who's not responsible enough to hire a legit aide for her.

"Could I walk you?" he asks. Undeterred by the obvious fact that I'm backing away. Slowly, with a beauty queen hand wave, a slight swivel at the wrist. I'm fast, but it would look weird if I shot out of the park like bears were chasing me.

Left him to eat my dust.

And the whole time I'm speed-walking away, I'm forcing myself not to look back over my shoulder. Sliding into Dunkin' Donuts in the middle of a bunch of girls who don't even know I'm with them. Cursing the alarm on the back door.

Asking myself how I ended up in the park with a guy, 50 percent afraid he'd catch me and 50 percent disappointed he didn't.

Why does every impulse of mine have to be dangerous?

29

Jack

If I'd been paying more attention to the end game—avoiding the Nevada sun rising over a pile of Manx corpses—I wouldn't be running after Nicolette Holland like a bunglng ass in flip-flops. It's like getting a penalty called on the touchdown you thought won you the game you bet your life on.

I blew the details, and I feel the failure. I should have had THINK, JACK tattooed down my arm in block print, not this Maori armband thing. (It was the night I turned eighteen. I was drunk off my ass. I'm lucky I didn't wake up with Donald Duck on my face.) If I'd thought to wear decent shoes, I could have pivoted on a dime. If I'd thought to wear gym shorts, I could have run in her wake and not looked like a guy sprinting away after mugging someone.

When she came out of Dunkin' Donuts, I should have been

closer. When she slunk into the alley, I should have figured out a way to stick to her. There has to be a way to follow someone down an otherwise deserted alley in broad daylight without being spotted. But I gave up. I crossed the street and circled to the place where the alley meets the sidewalk around two corners.

I'm standing in the shade in the Food 4 Less parking lot, back turned to the mouth of the alley, acting like I'm texting. All I had to do is stay on her until I figured it out—it's not climbing Mount Everest—and I'm still standing here.

I'm so pissed off at myself, I answer Don's call. I've screwed up so badly, why not make it worse?

"Have you got her?" This is what he's taken to saying instead of hello.

"I spotted her."

"Where is she? Is it over?"

"This isn't Yucca Valley Correctional. I can't walk up to her in the shower and shank her."

"You were that close?"

"Figure of speech."

"Figure of speech—straight-A student. You lost her, didn't you?"

I toy with the idea that I lost her on purpose, that I unconsciously engineered this because I couldn't decide how much of a virus spore I was. If so, it was poor engineering because when I look up, she's walking out of the alley and right toward me.

"Shit! Gotta go!"

"Oh no you don't!"

For a second, I'm more scared of her than of Don. It's one short, cold blast to the gut. It's dead Connie Marino and the reminder that this girl isn't who she seems to be. But despite knowing who she is and the blast to the gut that reasonable people know not to ignore, I'm grinning at her. I'm happy to see her. I'm still suppressing the big, silenced *Don't!*—the syllable that's struggling to get out and get out *loudly* while I hold my jaw so rigid, it might crack. I'm still freaking turned on.

I shove the phone into my pocket as she crosses the street, step forward to meet her. I say, "Are you following me?" It's playing with fire, but it's all I can think of.

"You wish!" she says. But it isn't nasty, it's kind of sweet. "How do I know it's not *you* stalking *me*?"

"I do wish." Then I patiently explain how stalking works, and how I'm not, and miraculously, she buys it. "Are you sure you don't want me to?"

She twists up her mouth on the left side, like a cartoon character that's deep in thought. "I'm pretty sure."

Even with the baggy clothes and what she's done to herself, this girl is meant to be on the receiving end of following—and not just by twisted stalkers.

"Okay, lucky coincidence. Can I get you a burger?" She looks taken aback. "When you get off work?"

This is a fail, too much too soon. Her eyes are back to scanning the street. She says, "I'm kind of agoraphobic. Do you know what that is?"

"Isn't that when you can't leave your house? You might be cured."

"Read up. Jeez, do you seriously want to debate this? I think I know what I've got."

"Sorry, rude."

"So rude."

I touch her shoulder. "What happens if you get to work late?"

She rolls her eyes. But she doesn't walk away.

30

Cat

He's standing in the shade in the Food 4 Less parking lot. Hunched over his phone like he's afraid it's going to jump out of his hands.

Then he sees me. Springs up. Comes bounding over. Okay, not exactly bounding. Too puppyish for him. Moving very fast and very intentionally.

Toward me.

I tell myself this is okay. It's an *I*-found-*him* thing and, therefore, meant to be. This is an example of the universe providing.

I get that it's providing the exact thing I'm supposed to avoid.

A human guy.

But it's like stumbling over a lucky penny, shiny and heads

up. The universe doesn't rain lucky pennies. When it does, you pick one up.

No! Don't pick him up! Turn! Walk away!

The space between us is closing, like air being squeezed out of a rapidly collapsing lung.

Then he wants to know if *I'm* following *him*.

Way too self-confident.

"You wish!" My head is so buzzing, I'm talking on auto-pilot. "How do I know it's not *you* stalking *me*?"

"I do wish." J frowns. "Why would I stalk you? You're not that friendly. And stalking entails lurking—correct me if I'm wrong—and there's no lurking going on."

"Great. No lurking."

Then he wants to go out for a burger. I try to tell him how I can't. How I'm agoraphobic, which I might have gotten slightly wrong.

But it's obvious I want to.

It's like my muscle memory of a come-on smile is too much to overcome.

Great.

I'm transforming backward. Turning right back into the self I can't be anymore. The self who hops into the back of a guy's car on a quiet country road because she likes him too much.

The self with no judgment and bad taste in boys.

J tilts his head. "If burgers are out of the question, do we want more ice cream?"

"Seriously, why are you here?"

He groans and looks put out. It's not his worst look. "Because this is the only place other than Starbucks on Hill where I get any kind of reception."

"What's wrong with the Starbucks on Hill?"

J shades his eyes with his hand. Makes a big deal of surveying the parking lot. Looks cute. "Is this your personal domain? Cat-landia, is it? Should I have my passport stamped on my way out of the lot?"

"Stay! Jeremiah, I don't want to interrupt you."

"Jeremiah!" He hammers his right fist against his chest. "Shot through the heart. Remind me of my name, and you'll have to make it up to me."

I'm debating whether it would be weirder to walk away or weirder to stay, act somewhat cold, and induce *him* to walk away. Which wouldn't be a problem if I hadn't crossed the street in the first place.

"It's just more ice cream," he says. "You do eat, right?"

J, you have no idea how much I eat. I ate potato chips for breakfast. In the past week, I've baked Mrs. Podolski three pies, two breads, and snickerdoodles.

He says, "You want a sundae? I have Nutella at my place, and cherries."

Oh God, Nutella! My favorite food group. And he wants to feed me *cherries*.

No way. I have Nutella at home. I have cinnamon bread I

baked Mrs. Podolski to spread it on. I can *buy* cherries.

What am I doing?

Walking down the street with him is what.

Yes, but if he's stalking me, why didn't he follow me all the way home? I live alone in a tiny garage behind Mrs. Podolski's house. It has a window you can open by pushing it with your pinkie.

If he were here to finish me, I'd be finished.

J says, "Or do you want to cut to the chase and get some beers?"

"No chase! No drinks!"

"Kidding," he says. "I figured if I couldn't buy you a burger, most likely I couldn't get you drunk."

"Do girls follow you home when you say stuff like this?"

"All the time."

I sock him on the arm. This seems to make him happy. Everything I say or do seems to make him happy. Just glancing at me makes him grin like an idiot.

He says, "Use your words. You're unusually violent for a short person."

I sock him again.

He lives on the ground floor of an old green wooden house, subdivided into apartments. I figure, worst case, I can kick out a window.

31

Jack

I've got her.

The surreality of Nicolette Holland walking around my place simulates the sensation of reading in a moving car. The room looks to be expanding and contracting to the rhythm of her pulse, despite my disdain for people who lay claim to weird sensory experiences—unless they're in the desert with a bag of shrooms.

I know her pulse because she said my ice cream was giving her brain freeze. My index finger is pressed to the indentation under her right temple.

"No, I'm happy to report that you're still a sentient being."

"Because there's blood flow to my brain? Guess again. Blood flow is overrated. The sweet old lady I work for could run a marathon in her walker, but she doesn't know my name or what I'm doing there half the time."

God, this girl is good, whether she's making this up or if it's true; she's even better if it's true.

"What *are* you doing there?"

"Stealing her jewelry." She smiles up at me and nibbles on the cherry I stuck on top of the spray-can whipped cream. Of course she's the girl who'd be stealing jewelry off defenseless old ladies. At least it's a step up from playing with a blade.

She yelps, "Don't look at me like that! That was a *joke*. If she ever had any jewelry, it's buried in her garden anyway. She buries teaspoons. I have to dig them up and put them back when she's asleep. I don't want to embarrass her."

The girl who steals jewelry from old ladies or the girl who has a nighttime protocol for sparing her senile employer's feelings?

I watch her eat the grotesquely oversize sundae I made because I wanted to keep her in my apartment for as long as possible, ladling on caramel and chocolate sauce and scoops of mint chip. I scrolled through years of her photos online to figure out what kind of food would tempt her. As it turns out, anything with sugar does it for her. She had a Twix appetizer.

Let's just say, she's not the kind of girl who eats only reduced-fat lettuce leaves.

She licks green ice cream off her lower lip. In the bedroom, I have a duffel bag full of weapons any one of which could finish her off before the remnants of the sundae turn to slush. I try to visualize using each one on her. I don't get further than picturing myself shooting her from a distance, and then only when I imagine her flattened into two-dimensionality, a laminated paper target with a frozen face and immobile limbs.

She says, "For sure this is my dinner. Thanks. I might not have to cook myself anything to eat for days."

"I don't cook. If not for In-N-Out, I'd have to eat grass and leaves."

"*I* spent yesterday making peach cobbler and five quarts of borsht. Do you know what that is? Beet soup. It's what the lady I work for wanted for breakfast."

"What's the matter? Did you learn to cook in a giant family and forget to divide?"

When I ask her a question I know she'll have to answer by making things up, it feels as if I'm torturing her, playing with her the way a cat bats a gopher back and forth across a patio before devouring it.

"Six kids," she says. She doesn't miss a beat.

"I'd lose track of their names."

"My parents were highly practical. Angie, Bonnie, me Cat, Davey, Edie, and Frank. Which is a lot of alphabet to stuff in a trailer."

"Don't you call them mobile homes?"

"You're such a know-it-all! Has anybody ever mentioned this to you?"

All my friends and a couple of disgruntled teachers might have mentioned it.

"Ours was definitely a trailer," she says. She has it down. "Not as bad as it sounds. But you know what? *Home*schooled. We never got out of there!"

It's a brilliant idea: no Reunion dot com or googling of the graduating class list or having to tie herself to a specific location where any curious person could find out she never was. She is, I realize, driving where this goes, dishonest and hypnotic.

I say, "Is this trailer nearby?"

"No! They disapprove of me. Religious zealots. I had to take off before they shunned me. I can't go home." She frowns, and if I didn't know better, I'd swear it was real. "I don't want to talk about it."

She abandons her sundae to walk around the room, pausing at the wall of bookshelves, touching the spines of the books. "You read a lot of poems."

"This is a sublet. They're not mine."

"You're subletting from a girl, right?"

"And you know this because . . . ?"

"This shelf. Emily Dickinson. Sylvia *Plath*. In school, when we did this poem she wrote, it was like contraception day in homeroom. You know, boys to the right, girls to the left. Yay abstinence, but if you succumb to sin and personal degradation, say hello to this condom."

I touch the pocket of my jeans containing my wallet and silently greet the condom.

"Interesting school."

I watch her remember that she just said she was homeschooled. Her face registers something and then smooths itself out.

150

"Waaaay down south," she says, returning to her sundae, blocking her mouth from view behind a heaping tablespoon of mint chip. "I got sent there for part of a year so I'd have a school experience beyond the inside of a trailer before college."

"Good move." And I don't mean her imaginary parents sending her to an imaginary Southern high school.

"This poem," she says, "it was about how much she hated her father. Which was a lot. The girls were all having fits about how good it was. The guys were all puking."

"What were *you* doing while all this puking was going on?"

"Remember me? Educated in a tin can. I'm borderline illiterate." She looks as thoughtful as a person can when lighting into a quart of ice cream. "If she'd have just gotten herself out of Dodge and hung with people who were nice to her and shoved her dad out of her mind . . . That's what you have to do sometimes . . . Instead of writing *poems* about it . . ."

"You do know she killed herself?"

"That's the stuff I pay attention to, are you kidding me? Did you know she married a guy who, after she killed herself, married another poet who killed *her*self? So the question is, did he constantly marry suicidal women, or did he marry regular women and drive them over the edge?"

"Is this a quiz?"

"Seriously? Who goes to a party looking for suicidal poets?" She grins. "Unless that's *your* type. Ladies who cry a lot?"

Apart from the sick, intrusive flashes of me with my hands

circling her neck just above the collarbone, it's possible that *she's* my type.

Scarlett, for all her put-downs, for all the times she came on to Dan Barrons whenever she was pissed at me, at least didn't kill people. But after spending three hours with this girl, I like her better than Scarlett. I like that she doesn't take her imaginary self that seriously. I want to off-road with her and Calvin and Monica—despite my reservations about introducing my friends to a girl who could be hazardous to their health. I want to steer into hairpin turns with her thrown against me, riding shotgun. I'm betting she likes to go fast over rocky terrain.

While I'm wondering if I'm genetically impaired in a different way than I've thought all along—if the genes I should worry about aren't my father's, but my mother's (the woman who spent two decades with my father, knowing what he was, but loved him anyway)—Nicolette AKA Cat is polishing off the whole mixing bowl of sundae, and smiling at me between bites. It's that lopsided, endearing, unbearably sexy smile.

I want to rip her clothes off.

32

Cat

Cat is so trampy! She goes to his apartment and starts talking about condoms? Makes fun of abstinence. Plus, factoids about dead poets. Really? Like she didn't notice they were dead and it was tragic?

At least I got out of there without unbuttoning anything.

But it was as if one of those tiny red Disney cartoon devils—the ones that hover over your shoulder encouraging you to do the wrong thing—was going, *Kiss him, kiss him, kiss him.* Until it was so loud I had to do it.

Fast, no tongue, antiseptic. Then I'm out the door so fast, it's like the bad-kiss cops are chasing me.

J's the one who's chasing me, going, "Hey!"

I go faster. So does he.

"Hey!" This guy needs to learn one or two things about picking up girls. But not from me.

"Hey! There are rules against kissing and running."

He's caught up, and he's touching my arm for good measure.

"Says who? The sleazy guys' handbook?"

He breaks out laughing. "Right under the section about aftershave."

"I hate aftershave!" Something Cat and I agree on. "Please stop following me."

"You're not supposed to flirt with guys you're trying to ditch," he says. "Didn't one of your many older sisters tell you that?"

I want to slap myself. Then him.

Acting like I act in real life when buzzed, only worse! Real life being my old life. The one where guys following me wasn't cause for alarm. Possibly should have been, but wasn't. (Definitely should have been. But wasn't.)

What am I doing?

It's not that hard to break it down. I could make a diagram of how my heart is divided into empty sections labeled with things I can't have anymore.

The address of the home I can never go back to.

An aerial view of the trail where I run through the woods and along the lakeshore with (what used to be) home right at the end of it.

A schedule of cheer practice.

A road map from Cotter's Mill, Ohio, to Ann Arbor, Michigan.

Then there's the place right in the middle, full of loneliness and longing, where I'm not allowed to put anyone. There are rules of survival for runners like me. Human entanglements aren't exactly encouraged. Desire for a normal friend, for a normal conversation with a normal boy, for a kiss, has to be squashed.

But how normal is it that the scared-out-of-her-mind girl who spends all her time with an elderly demented person would entertain one or two thoughts about the hot, not-demented boy who was thrown into her path by Fate?

And then removed his shirt.

33

Jack

We're standing on the sidewalk, both of us trying to look inconspicuous.

She says, "I'm going *home*. Do *not* follow me. If you follow me, I'll yell for the police."

No, you won't.

I say, "Understood. But you don't have a phone. How will I find you?"

I'll follow you, and this time I won't lose you.

"You're extremely persistent. I'm not the first person to notice this, right?"

The guy I used to be would be persistently figuring out how to get the hell out of shoving this girl in front of a moving car without ending up with a dead family. He wouldn't be wondering how best to position himself to kiss her back, and how soon he could get to the base of her neck, to that little hollow she keeps touching with her fingertips.

He wouldn't be chasing her down the street, uncertain about whether this is moving toward sex or death.

Fuck all.

Meeting her face-to-face in a place I didn't control was an unlucky accident, but was I supposed to leave that little girl bleeding on the ground? Who would have thought Nicolette Holland would be a steps-up-in-emergencies kind of girl? I wasn't prepared for her holding that kid's hand, spilling milk of human kindness all over the ground six inches from me, where I could smell her hair and get turned on while waiting for paramedics.

I was supposed to be repulsed.

Instead, I'm thinking, *Don has to be wrong*. She couldn't have done this. She's too normal to have done this. She's too cute; I like her too much; I could tell.

I look at her standing in front of me. There's no one else on the street.

I run my hand across her forehead, pushing the fake-brown bangs out of her eyes. Then I kiss her back. It starts out tame. It doesn't end that way. I cradle the back of her head in my hands, with only a brief thought of snapping her neck. Her hands are in the small of my back, and her mouth tastes like chocolate. When I come up for air, she reaches up and takes hold of the back of my head and pulls me back in. I kiss her eyelids and her ear, and I swear she shudders, like in a porno, only more believable. Scarlett didn't shudder.

If there were some way to pick her up and haul her back to the apartment without courting arrest, I could add that to my list of depraved aspirations.

"Fine!" She makes the word *fine* sound like swearing. "Tomorrow. Are you happy?"

I'm happy, but Don isn't.

The respite between his phone calls has diminished to the point that I anticipate by sundown, there'll be one long continuous ring. I'd turn off the sound, but I can't stop listening for it, a regular reminder of how messed up this is.

I have no plan to answer. For once in my life, I have no plan— not even the old plan to hold off figuring out what to do until I found her. Because I have found her, and the brainstorm that was supposed to strike when she was within grabbing range is nowhere on the weather map.

What happens next?

Don's phone calls come in all night, pulling me half out of sleep like a recurring nightmare that won't loosen its grip. It used to be, I was jolted out of sleep by flashes of my father's body, making out his shape in the dark garage, realizing why he was crumpled in that shape over and over until my mother forced me into therapy to "figure it all out." No way in hell was I going to let anyone else figure it out. I knew what I did; that was enough.

At four a.m., I wake up with an image of Nicolette lying crumpled up at my feet. I reach over and answer the phone.

Don says, "Don't you *ever* hang up on me."

"Or what?"

Provoking Don is a dangerous hobby, but it's late; I cut myself some slack.

"You don't want to find out. Did you get her back? This is taking too long."

Lying to Don comes so naturally, it doesn't feel like lying. "There are three hundred twenty million people in the US. How long is it supposed to take to find one of them who doesn't want to be found?"

"How long does it take to walk from the laundry room to Mom's bedroom?"

I'm awake, fighting off the kind of unwanted emotion that makes you put your fist through walls if you don't lock your arms against your sides. It would be easier if what could happen in the four seconds it takes to get from the laundry room to that bedroom didn't come to me so easily—if a parent with his throat cut wasn't already in my mental photo album.

"Don't push it. Mom and I could disappear and leave you behind for Yeager to carve up like *that*."

This shuts him up even though we both know she'd never do it. She'd never leave Don. We both know I've been so indoctrinated to take care of him that I took the envelope, and at some point I'm going to have to do *something*.

Don says, "Don't crap your pants, but you don't have much longer."

"Because you're God, and you'll end the world if I don't bow down faster?"

"Because Yeager is God, and you don't want to piss him off." This has the ring of absolute truth.

"Shit. How much time do I have?"

I'm not the only one who knows how to use silence for intimidation.

"How much time, Don?"

He pauses for so long, I'm afraid my cell will cut out before he gets to the point. "Yeager's getting impatient. That's all I know."

The chance I'm falling back to sleep approaches zip.

34

Cat

So great, I told him where I live.

Semi-safe solitary life as wily fugitive versus life of mad kissing.

Score one for kissing.

There's no point in changing out of a bad-looking outfit to promote the kissing, though. All I have are bad-looking outfits.

Reminders of reality.

The reality in which the safety of bad, brown outfits trumps romance. The one in which loneliness trumps good decisions, and bad impulses trump everything.

I could be packed and gone before he got here.

Race out the door.

Slip down the street.

Duck down alleys and through parking lots.

There are clumps of trees and huge flowering bushes that could shelter a motionless person until it was pitch-black outside.

I could be on a bus out of town with bronzed skin and pink-rimmed glasses in an hour. Less if I pushed it. Or if I hitched.

And then he'd look for me.

Great.

How romantic and deadly would that be? If he made noise about the missing girl with the bad wardrobe.

The noise he's making is banging the knocker on my door.

I just about flatline. Press myself against the wall between the bed and the dinky refrigerator. Know this is bad. Do it anyway.

Unchain the chains. Unbolt the bolt. Pull the key out of the deadbolt.

"Are we expecting a crime wave?" He looks so much larger in my doorway than in his. "Hey, I brought you dough-nut holes."

He steps in over the threshold. Holding out a paper bag as if he gave it a great deal of thought and determined that the perfect gift for me is junk food that gives the sack it comes in grease spots.

What kind of normal girl is happy when a guy brings her this stuff?

"Really?" His face. I go, "No, J! I love this stuff." Happy

face. "This isn't a comment on the size of my butt, right?"

"If I'm remembering correctly, I've never seen your butt."

Perfect. I've introduced body parts into the conversation.

Cat's so forward!

It wasn't this awkward at his place. Then again, the bed was in another room at his place, and we weren't sitting on the edge of it.

He picks up a doughnut hole and gazes at it. "Are these gross? Should I try again? I could run to Food 4 Less and get something else."

"Doughnut hole. Now."

He spreads a dishtowel on the bed and pours out the doughnut holes. Powdered sugar billows up around the mound of them. Three minutes later, when we're both in the throes of a sugar rush, he leans across the dwindling doughnut hole mountain and aims for my sugarcoated mouth.

My hands are in his hair. I'm holding his face in my hands, prolonging this kiss. I am so suddenly aware of the several layers of cloth between my breasts and his chest. When he's kissing me, when he's going after every molecule of sweetness on my lips, there's a total eclipse of reason. I want more than I can have.

Then he starts to lift my T-shirt over my head from the bottom like he means it.

"Don't." This might be the most conflicted syllable ever spoken by a girl on a bed.

Score one for impulse control.

I say, "No, because if we do, you know . . ."

All I want is for him to keep kissing me and stop undressing me.

"I know you better than you think."

Which is unnerving. But it's just master-of-the-universe boy crap. It's not like I've never met a boy before.

Steve, explaining why I was supposed to keep my legs crossed, basically said I had something they wanted. If I didn't give it to them, they'd follow me down the street like a pack of hungry dogs. Which proved more or less correct. (Leaving out the part where girls who hand out doggie treats have even bigger packs following them around. Which I guess he hoped I wouldn't notice.)

I can't make out with this guy while I think about Steve trying to get me to behave.

I say, "Leave my clothes on me." It comes out sharper than intended.

J pulls back. Holds up his hands like I'm arresting him.

Then I think, *What kind of college girl keeps her shirt on?* Either way I go, this blows south very fast. I say, "Religious zealots. Remember? In the trailer. Homeschool. Fire and brimstone."

"I wouldn't want you to burn in hell." He might not be taking me that seriously.

"Next time you want to get it on with someone, try not to make fun of her."

He's sitting so he isn't even touching me. "I understand the word *no*. Not that I've heard it before, but I get it."

"You're so full of yourself! Did anybody ever tell you that?"

"So we can assume the zealots beat the sense of humor out of you?"

The only thing in reach is a handful of doughnut holes. Which I throw at him.

He pretends he doesn't like this and returns to kissing. Maybe just to distract me. I feel it in places I don't want to be feeling.

Not now.

Not when I'm hiding.

Not when I have to be on top of my game and not under some guy who doesn't even know my real name.

35

Jack

Doughnut holes might have been the wrong thing to bring. She eats them, but then she wants to know if I go out with a lot of girls, the message clear that guys who go out with lots of girls know enough not to bring doughnuts. I tell her the truth, maybe because no matter how this goes, it's not destined to be a lasting relationship where things you said at the beginning come back to bite you later.

I say, "There was one long thing, not much else."

"When did it end? It *did* end, right?"

"Six weeks ago. Something like that."

She screws up her face. "Was she an evil bitch?"

"No."

She tosses a doughnut hole at my face, presumably aiming for my mouth.

"Don't worry," she says. "I'm not looking for touchy-feely. I'm just not helping you two-time anybody while we have a good time."

"Do people say 'two-time' this century?"

"They *should*."

I have my hands on her shoulders, and all I want to do is kiss her and anything else she'll go along with. I slip my hands under her big shirt, fingers against her skin, which is so soft, softer than you'd expect, softer than Scarlett.

She says, "Uh. Not that good a time."

This is when my phone vibrates again. Don has a seemingly endless supply of cell phone minutes and an unerring ability to call when I least want to hear from him. She's pressed against me, so she feels the phone's vibration.

"Speak of the devil," she says. "Is this her? And if it is, you'd better *lie* because I'll hand you your ass tied up in ribbons."

"You'll hand me my six-foot ass with your hundred-pound-girl hands?"

"Does your girlfriend like it when the six-foot ass tells sexist jokes?" She sighs. "Not that you can't see *tons* of other girls. It's not like we're together or anything. Just not *one* cheated-on one."

"No girlfriend."

I take her hand, and this time she doesn't pull away from me. The phone starts buzzing again, and I tighten my grip. There has to be some other way out of this damn yellow wood, a shortcut I can find before Yeager finds it for me.

Somewhere in this confusion, there's a workable syllogism.

Cat is girl; I like Cat; therefore, I don't dispose of Cat?

Then I think, *Hurray for me; I only get rid of girls I don't like*. What a stand-up guy. I only get rid of girls I *don't* like who cut the throats of people I *do* like. And I only do that when my pathologically dishonest brother says my mom dies if the girl doesn't.

Girl-whose-pants-he's-trying-to-get-into versus mom-he'd-prefer-not-to-see-burned, and the guy stands there lusting after the girl in a converted garage, waffling about whether he's going to answer the phone and deal with his shit brother. What a sick story that makes.

She says, "Did I just do something?"

"You want to finish eating carbs and go for a run?"

"*Those* are my choices? Let you take my shirt off me or run around the block? Very romantic."

"I saw you running in the park. You run."

She grins. "I hope you're not the competitive type because I'm going to run circles around you." She stretches out her legs straight in front of her, points her toes, and bends until she's folded on herself.

"A little overconfident, are we?" I say as she looks up to see if I noticed how limber she is. I noticed. "You want to go right now?"

"Later, okay?"

Of course running should happen later, when it's dark and no one who's looking for her can spot her. "If that's not romantic enough, I can always recite poetry to you. We know how much you love that. *Two rooooooads diverged in a yellow wood . . .*"

"Kill me now," she says.

I can't help flinching.

She's very close to me, still touching my hand, as if she wants me to touch her again—about time—but as I'm reaching for her, she flops back against the pillows. "You're not obsessed with poetry, right?"

"'The Road Not Taken' is the story of my life, but you don't have to like it."

"Don't get upset, but that poet guy was probably tromping through the woods to drop in on his mistress," she says.

"Did Robert Frost rise from the grave to tell you that?"

"Poets! Take Shakespeare. And that poem is for his coy mistress."

"Not Shakespeare, Andrew Marvell. I thought the coy mistress was his wife."

"You don't think he was cheating with some coy girl?" she demands. Obviously, she does. "It's all about getting girls on their backs," she says. "Geez, *Had we but world enough, and time*, but we don't, so lie down? Give me a break."

"You *memorize* poetry? Hand over the borderline illiterate card." I hold out my hand and she slaps it, palm to palm, as if we were playing the game where you extend your hands to see who has faster reflexes, and she wins.

"I'm not *completely* ignorant," she says.

Then she throws back her head, laughing, her mouth lining up with mine. How am I supposed to resist this? I pull her back onto my lap, and she melts into me like warm wax, perfect fit, soft lips, her hands in my hair—for thirty seconds.

Then she says, "I've gotta go to work. Right now. Go write yourself a sad poem."

36

Cat

I'm sitting on the bed (alone) finishing off the doughnut holes with a chaser bag of Funyuns. I'm staring down at my thighs as if I could see them expand before my very eyes. I'm moaning into the burner.

This is because I made him go away before I was ready. I told him I had to work. Right then. That minute.

Total lie.

Then I got stuck waiting for a computer at the library so I could talk to Olivia. And when I finally got a computer, after this tiny girl finished playing a video game with Barbies and twinkly sea horses, no Olivia.

She checks her phone constantly. Where is she? Probably eating dinner with her folks. I can see her on her screened porch, eating Mrs. Pastor's famous (kind of bad) tuna noodle casserole.

I can see the look on Steve's face when Mrs. Pastor offered to show Rosalba how to make it. Me, later, begging Rosalba to make it. Rosalba batting at me with a wooden spoon that had tomato sauce all over it because she was using it to make something that actually tasted good.

The kid who's signed up to use the computer after me taps me on the shoulder. I gasp so loud, he jumps back.

I've let an eight-year-old creep up on me.

He could have been someone else. He could have slid a switchblade from between the pages of *Grimms' Fairy Tales*, cut my heart out, and fed it to a flock of magic pigeons. While I'm thinking this gruesome thought, he's staring at me.

And so's his mother.

I bolt.

What am I doing?

Seriously, if J had said, *Hey, babe, let's run away to Bora Bora for forever*, I would have started packing.

Nothing like total deprivation of pretty much everything to make a person crazy.

He makes me feel safe. I lay my head against his chest, and it's like I've got a bulletproof wall between me and everything. Or maybe it's that he distracts me so much, I don't think about being *un*safe.

I think about how much I like him.

And contraception.

How stupid it is to be with someone I like so much, I'd even be thinking about that?

The library's out of the question, I'm out of my mind, and the burner is out of its container and in use.

Olivia says, "I don't care if he's God's other son, you can't have a boyfriend. Aren't you supposed to be living in a cave until you look unrecognizable? You *said*."

All true.

"But I like him so much! Liv, he's so nice! And no matter what I do, there's no way I'm going to start looking like a frumpy twenty-five-year-old until I'm twenty-five."

"That's a long way from looking like yourself with bad red hair."

I swear, if there were no burner phones in the world, I would curl up and die.

If I had to spend years without anyone looking at me or touching me or caring about me.

If I had to be completely alone until I grew out of being at all like my current self.

If there were no J.

Olivia says, "Well?"

"I was wearing *mom jeans*, all right? But I still didn't have to encourage him."

"Do. Not. Encourage. Him!"

"I'm *joking*. We're only slightly past first base."

"What's wrong with you?" she shout-whispers. "Do you want to end up with a baby? Do you?"

"I'm not getting pregnant."

"Said fifty thousand other girls just before they had to hit Planned Parenthood. And that's not the only reason he's not safe!"

"I'm getting off the phone. I really like him. And if he was going to do something to me, why didn't he just put a pillow on my face the first time he came over?"

"He knows where you live? Are you crazy?"

"Yeah, well, next time it's at his house."

37

Jack

One minute it feels like I'm a normal guy moving in on a normal girl. I want to hang out with her, make her like me, protect her. The next minute, the fact that I'm the person she needs to be protected from is making me choke on the dessert she's feeding me right now.

I knew all the roads were dead ends when I started this.

If I don't do it, Yeager comes after my family.

If I do it, I'm a murderer, and Nicolette is dead.

If I don't do it, everybody still ends up dead.

Even the variation that has me hiding out in a dark corner of the world with Nicolette and the Manx money leaves my mother dangling in the wind.

Anyone. Anywhere. Anytime.

When I was a kid, I was always searching for remote places my family could set up camp. Becoming the Swiss Family Robinson seemed like a better alternative than what we had going.

But here I am in El Molino with no idea how to extricate myself or anybody else, no exotic island backup plan, nothing. And Don keeps calling to remind me I'm fucked.

I say, "Just a minute," leave Nicolette in my living room eating lemon meringue pie, and hit the front porch. It's as if Don has a sixth sense for throwing people off, and I've reached the time limit for how long I can ignore him today.

"I thought I told you to pick up!" He's pissed, resentful, frustrated—a brew of classic Don emotions that spew all over anyone in range.

"I'm in the library. Better databases." Because what does he know about libraries? Nothing.

"I'm calling time, Jack." He sounds harder than usual. "It happens right now. Find her and end it."

Ignoring the Weedwacker to the gut, I say, "Get off my back. It takes how long it takes."

"Don't get high and mighty! You know what you have to do. Now do it."

I think about our relative heights and might. Maybe I've descended into the gutter, but he's in prison, which has to be lower. "You think you can do better? If you weren't somebody's slave boy, you could buy me more time."

I know his anxious, angry breathing from the years of being

smaller than he was, when I had to know when to get out of his way or risk drowning in six inches of water in the bathroom sink, groping to break the headlock. I have three inches on Don now, I'm armed, and I have martial arts training he dropped out of at age twelve. But when I hear that breathing, I feel it in the pit of my stomach, and all even a black belt would be good for is wrapping around his neck and pulling.

Everyone has the power of life and death over everyone else. Anybody walking down the street can jab anybody else between the ribs with something sharp. Man's march out of the ooze toward civilization—a march that passed the Manx family by—is all that saves mankind from a continuous bloodbath.

Through the window, I see how nice Nicolette looks perched on the arm of the couch. She breathes at my discretion.

What happens next?

I can live with moral ambiguity. Grow up with a dad who executes people and a mom who sits there while he pounds on you—grow up loving your mom and your dad and your shit brother who'd sell you out for a carton of cigarettes—and you *get* moral ambiguity.

I'm eighteen. I'm legally qualified to judge guilt and innocence. If there were a DA stupid enough to put someone named Manx on a jury, I could determine someone else's fate.

Would I be the lone juror voting to acquit the guy who killed somebody crazy-bad to save his mother, his shithead brother, and maybe himself? Maybe.

Would I acquit the guy if he slept with the crazy-bad girl first, fully consensual, everyone smiling, nobody drunk, victim and victimizer with protection and clean sheets? That guy should burn in hell.

Don says, "Pay attention. If you need reinforcements to do it for you . . ." He trails off. I keep him waiting. "Two more days, and I'm sending in helpers."

Helpers? This is all I need. The only upside is he doesn't know where to send these helpers. I don't have much leverage, but if he knew where to find me, I'd have none.

"Here it comes: threatening Mom."

"I'm not threatening. For now, we're in this together. The day you quit, that's the day you start triple locking your door."

"I'm not together in *anything* with you! I'm doing this because you're ten-feet deep in shit, and you're dragging Mom down with you! If your guys do *anything* to Mom, this is over. I drive straight to a police station."

"Big blowhard Jacky! These wouldn't be my guys. These would be Yeager's guys. I don't control what they do or where they do it. And the police—that's what you've got?" He belly laughs like Santa's evil twin. "Death certificate. Didn't Dad teach you *anything*?"

I visualize Don facing the wall of his cell, his hands cupped over his phone. I take some pleasure in the fact that I can tell he wants to scream but can't. I'm not proud of it, but there it is.

"If you don't have what it takes to do this," he says, "tell me where the girl is, and I'll get it taken care of."

"I don't know where she is!"

"Come on, Jacky. We both know how good you are at fingering people."

"Shut up!"

Don says, "Open your e-mail."

My in-box pings with an attachment from an unknown sender with a long string of seemingly random letters and numbers for a name.

```
Hey bro,


Hope you're still looking for love on the
road. Cuties all over and you only need
to find one. There's some bad news. They
found Connie Marino's body. It's a sad day.
What kind of person would hurt Connie?
```

I can't read any farther. I start clicking on links, one after the other:

Citizens of sleepy Cotter's Mill, Ohio, were shocked earlier this week when a body was found in a shallow grave on a public access trail to Green Lake. Today, police announced that the body has been identified as twenty-two-year-old Constance Marino, missing from the Detroit suburb of Birmingham.

And another:

The Ohio Bureau of Criminal Investigation is looking into the murder of Constance (Connie) Marino, a Detroit-area nursing student, found buried four hundred feet from Northern Ohio's Green Lake on Tuesday.

Shit, Nicolette.

Right when I've made every excuse I can think of for you—ignoring the obvious, staring down reality and calling it bogus, ignoring the facts—my screen opens on the words "Cotter's Mill, Ohio," in the same sentence as Connie Marino's body.

How can I still be this turned on when your house is 324 yards from where a hiker's curious Newfie found the corpse?

38

Cat

We're sitting in J's living room, eating lemon meringue pie.

All right, I'm sitting on J's lap on his green scratchy sofa, and I'm feeding him pie. He's extremely appreciative.

This is what zero to sixty without taking off your clothes looks like. After nobody touches you or gets anywhere near you for what feels like forever.

"Could you at least *try* not to get it on my nose?" he says.

"Sit still and open your mouth." I do the babysitter-feeding-the-kid thing, chugging as the fork circles his mouth.

"If the next step is I'm supposed to talk baby talk, it's not happening," he says.

"Says you. If I took off my blouse, you'd talk any way I wanted." (Cat's a lot more direct than the actual me.)

This is when he gets another phone call. I'm pretty sure from his ex. Every time that phone buzzes, he tenses up.

He takes the phone out onto the porch. Through the front window, I watch him making angry faces as he talks.

He scrolls, and then he shoves the phone back into his pocket. Wipes his hand on his jeans, hard, like he's trying to scrape off poison ivy.

From the doorway, he says, "Where were we?" He reaches under the tank top that's beneath my blouse and runs his fingers up and down my spine. I tense every time he gets close to the clasp of my bra, but he ignores it and keeps going.

He's *nice*.

I like this so much.

I'm like a camel binge-eating affection and physical touch at the oasis. So it can do without when it treks through the desert for months.

Enjoy the heat, binge-feel the feels, and take off for parts unknown with enough stored-up satisfaction to last until I'm someone else. In theory, if I store this up, I won't miss it.

In theory, I won't miss *him*.

In theory.

J is massaging my shoulders, one after the other, one hand under my shirt and one over.

I say, "You want some of this? I'm not completely greedy. Take off your shirt."

Because (holy crap, Cat!) when you don't want to get

attached to someone, make him take off his shirt.

"No way. I'm not taking off my shirt until you take off your shirt." He crosses his arms across his chest. Wads up the cotton of his T-shirt in his fists. "You'll lose all your respect for me."

I swat him. "Don't tease me!"

I shove a forkful of meringue against his lips when his mouth is closed, and he pushes it in with his fingers.

"Who's teasing whom? Besides, I have to keep you in line, or who knows what you'll do? We know how violent you are when you don't get your way."

I'm pushing him down. "How violent? How violent? How violent am I? You want to find out?"

J pushes back, he's bent over me, and I'm pinned. "I won't be finding that out," he says. "Don't try."

It feels, just for a second, like he isn't playing. His voice is lower, and he's not letting me up.

"This isn't funny."

He says, "It's not meant to be funny. Don't smear pie on my face. Don't push me with a fork in your hand, got it?"

I'm not actually scared, but my body is acting scared. Highly adaptive sweating so I could slither away like a greased piglet. "I got pie on your mouth, so you're holding me down? Asshat! Let me up, because do you see where my foot is?"

I don't kick him. But his face looks like I did. Like I kicked him just after I caught him pulling the wings off a fly.

"Oh shit! I'm sorry! I apologize."

At least he's got his normal voice back.

He pulls away, lets go of my wrists in what looks like a spasm. "Sorry!"

Great, I'm getting my camel fix of romance with a scary lunatic.

"You can't do that kind of stuff! Are you stupid?"

He says, "Don't call me stupid!"

I swear to God, I'm going for the ice pick if he gets off the couch. Except he'd twist my hand and grab it. It would take a much better strategy than that to bring him down.

Strategy is my strong suit.

39

Jack

What the hell thing was that?

I hold down a girl I outweigh by 100 percent, whom I could lift by the collar of her blouse using my thumb and index finger, because she comes at me with a dessert fork? It's not even the heavy, silver-plated kind of fork she could use to poke holes in me. It's cheap stainless steel, the weight of a plastic picnic fork.

I knew what she was when I started this. Now I'm pissed Don rubbed it in my face?

I hold out my hands, and they look like someone else's— someone I despise, I'm ashamed to be, and I wasn't supposed to turn into. Someone who just took a call about how soon he has to smoke the girl he's making out with.

She's backing toward the door.

Is this Nicolette, America's mouthy sweetheart, who's afraid of a guy who just demonstrated what an all-powerful creep he is? Or is this Nicolette, the throat-slasher who has to be stopped?

It doesn't freaking matter. She's not the crazy bad one in this scene. I am.

I start apologizing again, and I don't stop.

Her hand is on the doorknob.

"Stop. Please accept my apology. I know how bad that was." She looks enraged but also undecided. "I'll make you a Nutella sandwich."

"Making fun of me doesn't help!"

"I'm sorry, also for bringing up the sandwich."

It's not my natural inclination to start telling her the truth, but I don't see any other way to go in for the save.

The first try, I can't do it. I say, "I got a shit phone call."

She gives me a look. "Well, that explains it. I feel so much better now." Acid is dripping off her tongue.

I say, "How about this? I lose it when people come at me with things that look like they could hurt me." I feel like a dog rolling over and showing his throat in submission.

"It was a *fork*."

"Do you think I'd embarrass myself like this if it weren't true?"

Her eyes are angry slits. "Are you sure it's not, some girl pushes you over and you have to prove what a big strong jerk you are?"

"I swear. Push me again, and nothing will happen. Kick me, and I'll stand there."

"Fine." She drops her pack onto the floor and storms over, stands facing me, a head shorter. There are blond roots growing out on the top of her head. Then she lands a kick on the middle of my shin, swift and well-placed.

I force my hands flat, my fingers extended, no fists, and I don't respond.

"Fine." She does it again.

She seems to be winding up for another assault. My eyes are tearing, and however bad holding her down was, I can't let her go for it.

I put my hand on her shoulder. At least she doesn't flinch at my touch. I say, "Twice was enough."

"Are you *ordering* me?"

"I'm telling you."

She's rubbing her wrists together. I left marks on her wrists. There's a wave of nausea so powerful, I have to sit, buckled over, forcing down the glop that chokes my mouth.

"Maybe you should go."

She straddles a kitchen chair, facing me over the back. "Don't have to. I made my point. *And* I got to watch you control yourself. Which was *quite* the spectacle. I want my Nutella sandwich."

It's starting to feel as if all my buttons are lined up on the coffee table, screaming *Push me*, and she's obliging. I'm close to pitching over the edge for the second time in ten minutes.

"*Now* can we get something to drink?" I say.

There's no excuse for this. I've lost control and I'm on the verge of losing more control, I have no plan, and I decide it would be good to drink a shitload of alcohol? *Think, Jack.*

But I don't want to think.

I have never in my life wanted to be drunk this much. Drunk, stoned, or punched in the face—any one of those would do it.

40

Cat

On the bright side, if anyone comes at me when I'm next to him, he'll probably break them in half.

On the dark side, what happens if you pat his cheek too fast? He shatters your wrist?

I squirt a bunch of his chocolate sauce into my mouth right out of the squeeze bottle. This makes him seriously annoyed, but he tries not to let on. Ha. I drip it onto my tongue and stare straight at him.

I say, "If you ever do that again, I'll cut important parts off you. You get that, right?"

"Got it. On a not-joke note, I'm sorry. I'm not saying it to look good."

"That wasn't a joke. And it doesn't make you look good."

There. I've made him turn white.

He says, "Jesus." He might be praying I don't cut him up.

"Plus, I'm leaving. Go play with a two-hundred-pound guy who likes to wrestle."

"Feel free to take the fudge sauce."

"I'll have more fun sitting at home imagining you trying to sterilize the nozzle without getting soap in the chocolate."

He sits down on his sofa, laughing.

I want to sit down next to him, but having some tiny shred of impulse control, I don't.

He says, "Let me get you a beer. Think how much easier it will be for you to cut me after I knock back a few."

It's going to sound like I'm a stupid pushover girl. The kind who lets guys smack her around if they cry and give her candy and say sorry. But I'm not. I'm more like a girl taking pity on a guy who feels like a prize moron for losing it over an incoming dessert fork.

It's going to sound like I've completely given up on personal safety and all of the rules of survival. Yet again.

This would be correct.

41

Jack

I'm driving a dirt-encrusted Prius with eighty-five thousand miles on it, and it looks it. I bought it unwashed, and I haven't remedied the situation. I can't say what I'll find under the dirt, apart from knowing that whatever shade of charcoal gray it turns out to be, it'll be less conspicuous than Don's red shitmobile.

Nicolette walks all the way around it. "Are you sure this is your car? If you didn't just do that, I'd be totally nice. I wouldn't mention the existence of *soap*."

"If I weren't such a spectacle of self-control, I'd tell you to zip it. If you want to go somewhere that's not teeming with frat boys, you'd better get in."

"How do you know I don't love and adore frat boys?"

I open her door, realizing that the passenger side handle is sticky.

"I was flattering you. I was assuming that if you wanted to be with a frat guy, you'd be with a frat guy."

She climbs into the front seat, stows her pack in the backseat, and wriggles. "Do uncomfortable seats save energy, or do tree huggers just like to suffer?"

"We like to make our *passengers* suffer. And where I come from, they have more cacti than trees." This is a slip but not a grievous one. I say, "Arizona," and hope she hasn't been there.

"I'd say something mean about hugging and cactus and what you deserve, but it's almost cheating to slug that slow a pitch."

"You're not a very forgiving girl, are you?"

"Excuse me!" she says. I'm getting used to her punches on the arm. "I'm totally forgiving. But people have to pay. *Then* I'm forgiving."

She shuts her own door and lets me lock the car from the driver's seat, not even checking to see if she can get herself out. I'm still thinking, *Don't. Don't get into cars with strangers. Don't take Nutella sandwiches from strange men. Don't go to bars with Manxes.* Which is some heavy-duty sexist shit but applicable under the circumstances.

She puts the bottoms of her sandals up against the glove compartment.

She says, "Just so I don't feel like Miss Bad Judgment out drinking with a guy who loses it over tiny forks, you want to tell me why?" There's a long pause, when she touches my arm very lightly, just where the sleeve of my T-shirt ends, her favorite spot to sock. "Just tell me. If that had been a three-pronged serving fork, would I be dead?"

Yes. No. Maybe. I'm not in a good frame of mind. I can hear Don coaching: *End her.*

She says, "Tell me what's wrong." These are maybe my least favorite words from a girl's mouth, any girl, under ordinary circumstances. This is worse.

"I wish I hadn't explained." I more mutter this than say it. "Clearly the wrong path in the yellow wood."

"Not *poetry*! First you impersonate King Kong, and then you give me *poetry*?"

"Sorry."

She closes her eyes. I want to tell her to keep them wide open. "You don't get to hold girls down *and* quote poems. Worst of both worlds. Brute butthead who tries to intimidate girls *or* deeply sensitive butthead who likes poems. You have to pick one or the other."

"Thanks. I'll remember that next time."

"You're welcome." She looks up through her bangs. "And don't even *think* next time. No next time."

"Sorry." She certainly provides ample opportunities to apologize. I'm rubbing my shin under the dashboard. I'm driving along waiting to be forgiven by the girl who cut Connie Marino.

42

Cat

When you drive inland from El Molino off the interstate, you hit Crothers. Beyond that, Los Arroyos. Meaning creeks. Except there aren't any. We drive over a gully on a wooden bridge, but there's no water in there.

We pass a 7-Eleven, a gas station, and a feed store.

I say, "Not to complain about the field trip, but aren't we getting kind of far from civilization?"

J drives exactly at speed limit. When it says to go twenty-five around curves, we go twenty-five. When a sign shows a family of cows in the road, he slows down in case there's a parade of heifers just around the bend.

He says, "There's a bar down the road where they're not picky about ID."

This bar would be a shack if it was made of wood, but it's concrete. The only light is a flashing red-and-blue neon sign. Fifty motorcycles parked in front. Guys with club jackets hanging outside the door. Women far more trampy than Cat will ever be glued to them.

I mean, get a room.

I'm sitting in the front seat, facing karmic justice. The Circle of Life. What goes around comes around. I *knew* I shouldn't tell Luna my biker boyfriend beat me up. Also, it occurs to me that while I'm a killer beer-pong player, I've never been in a bar. Not a real bar.

Not the scary kind of bar with bikers swarming it.

J opens my door, very old school. He says, "You don't like it? We could go somewhere else."

"Like the feed store?"

He wants old school, fine. I take his arm.

If this happened in a movie, you'd be chomping on your popcorn and moaning, *Oh, HELL no.*

43

Jack

I know this place from when I wanted a beer, and the checker at Ralph's in El Molino looked from Gerhard's license to my face and said no. I wanted the beer. The candidate most likely to ignore drinking age was a biker bar. This worked a couple of times in Nevada. Twenty miles out of El Molino, you can take your pick.

But last time it was morning and easy to drive up to the emptiest one.

In the almost darkness of the gravel parking lot, the idea of approaching the cinder block building with Nicolette on my arm seems like less of a plan.

When I lean down to open her door, there's a chill along my spine, fighting the hot night air. I'm not sure if this is the kind of cue reasonable people know not to ignore or me turning into a wuss who buys shots for his prey.

She swings her pack over her shoulder.

There are guys standing outside the door, lighting up, girls sticking to them, the acrid smell of weed in the air. There's a blast of music and shouting every time the door to the bar opens and people fall in or out.

I say, "This might not be the right place."

She leans against the car, arching her back. "Without a Harley, you mean? Or without biker mama arm candy?" She unbuttons her massive shirt, and I'm staring down a tank top. She says, "It's hot out. Do you mind?"

I force my eyes up to her face, her chin tilted back, her hair curling around the edges of her forehead.

She puts her hand on my arm, grasping it. I'm acutely aware of where we are, where I've brought her, and how stupid this is.

I say, "Let's get out of here."

She wriggles all the way out of the shirt until she's all bra straps and tank top and skin.

"Just trying to fit in," she says.

I can't tell if she's making the best of a shit date or teasing.

"You come here a lot?" she asks, not waiting for an answer. "Not that a lot of bikers in zero-cylinder electric cars don't come here."

"Get back in the car! And it's a hybrid, not electric."

She resists, and after what happened in my apartment, I'm not about to exert any physical pressure, not even to hold her hand tightly.

She nods toward the side of the bar, where it's pitch-black shadow, the back of the place verging on dark bleak empty farmland and the creek bed that winds through the town. "*Or* we could go over there and get high on fumes."

"No, we're leaving."

She yanks on my arm. "That was a *joke*! Don't be so master-of-the-universe!"

"You stop undressing at a biker bar! Get in the car!"

A sloppy drunk guy heading to a pickup says, "This little shit bothering you, miss?"

We say no simultaneously.

He seems to be turning back toward his truck, but he's just swiveling wide toward us, straight on.

I hold out my arm like a crossing guard.

She says, "I'm *fine*. We were just going."

"This boy pressuring you? You said no and he don't get it?"

I say, "She's fine! Back off."

He keeps coming. You could light his breath on fire.

She says, "Oooookay, look, I'm getting in the car. Everything's fine. Don't turn this into a B-movie, all right?" I'm not sure if she's saying this to him or to me.

He says, "*You're* fine. You're a little movie star." Still coming.

One chop to the neck right now, and he won't be bothering girls again for a while. But he just seems like a drunk asshole, not a threat.

She says, "Oh crap," and pulls on the door handle. Things turn instantly. All of a sudden we've got the Prius behind us and this guy advancing on us.

He reaches out for her, and without any thought, I land a punch on the side of his face, swivel his head. It should be enough to knock over a drunk guy, but it's not.

I assessed my target, but I assessed wrong.

He's grabbing for her, tearing at my shirt to reach her, pushing me down to get to her. I land an uppercut to his chin, then I go for his eyes. But he's fast, and I'm paying too much attention to where she is. He's got hold of my belt; he kicks the outside of my knee. I'm in the gravel, and he's pounding my face. I'm in that state of combat where nothing hurts too much for you to keep going, or even distracts you.

I tell her to run, but she's frozen against the Prius, rifling through her pack, which, unless she's got a bazooka in there, isn't going to do us much good.

"Will you *run*?"

I dig an elbow into the gravel and push the drunk guy with my other shoulder, unbalance him, roll on top, go for a knockout punch. Blood pours out of his nose, and then there's a knife: his knife. The blade is curved and moving fast.

I remember mine, lying useless in the trunk. This is a bloodbath of poor calculation. I go for the hand with the knife, throw my weight into getting it down and keeping it down. Because this guy can't get up. He's not getting to her. If he stabs me and I die, he takes her—not on my watch. His arm is bent, the blade's six inches from my face. My left hand versus his right arm, and every molecule of energy in every cell of every muscle in my body is pushing him down, pushing a lead oar through a river of molten lead. I'm not dying in a parking lot, not adding myself to the Manx legacy's body count.

My endorphins open up, or maybe it's rage, but I've got his hand down, still clutching his knife. I'm going for the game-changing punch when whatever she's got in her fist sails past me, a slight fast glint, and through his arm.

He howls as she withdraws the spike, and his hand opens. I chop his face where I can break the most things—cartilage, nose, bones, skin—all to the rhythm of a blast of music from the bar.

"What the fuck?"

"Ice pick. Come on."

44

Cat

I stabbed a drunk guy in a parking lot.

The ice pick slid through his forearm like a skewer spearing shish kebab.

Most of the blood came from his nose.

J was pounding him into the gravel. Smashing his face with pinpoint accuracy. J's mouth is torn up. Two black eyes forming.

Would you, could you, can you, did you?

Yes to all of the above.

Try leading the life of a fugitive sometime. Those Sunday School questions just keep coming. Would you stab a drunk guy through the heart to save your boyfriend in a bar fight? And he's not even my boyfriend. And we weren't even *in* the bar.

But yes. Obviously. I would. If it had been just me, alone in the dark with a guy with a hunting knife, one of us would be dead.

Probably not me.

That guy's lucky he jerked to the right when my arm was coming down. Because I wasn't aiming for his arm. He's lucky J grabbed my wrist when the ice pick was coming down the second time.

So no regrets beyond the fact that I need to barricade myself in Mrs. P's house and marathon-watch the Home Shopping Network with her until I figure this out. Until there's zero possibility that what we did will blow up in our faces.

J says, "How're you doing?"

I'm crying, and there's an ice pick in my lap.

I say, "How are you doing?"

J isn't crying, he's bleeding. I blot his face with my shirt, but he keeps looking at the road. Like a robot packed with life-like spurting blood.

He pulls out of the lot as if nothing happened. Windows open, but I don't hear anyone sounding alarms. Then there's shouting.

At least there's no dead guy. Probably.

I think he's still breathing when we peel out. The J version of peeling out. Perfect driving until he thinks someone is after us. Then it's NASCAR.

Before that, he was pounding that guy like he's used to pounding guys. Only he's not acting that way now.

He pulls off at an exit just east of El Molino, idles behind a gas station that's closed for the night. Kills the lights.

I say, "Sorry."

"She apologizes. Jesus weeps."

"Don't get sarcastic about Jesus! I'm just saying, I should have gotten back in the car. Duh. All right? And that was self-defense."

"Do you want to tell that to the police, or should I?"

"You get really sarcastic when you're upset. Did anybody ever tell you that?"

He takes several deep breaths. "You have to get rid of that ice pick."

"I'll clean it off and stick it in the kitchen drawer."

"Blood doesn't clean off."

"I watch *CSI*, all right? First I'll dip it in bleach, *then* I'll use it to pry open a couple of cans and stick it in the kitchen drawer." This feels completely unreal. Except it is real. "He wasn't dead, right?"

J shakes his head.

I say, "Stop looking at me like that! This isn't my fault or your fault. It's that guy's fault. I *hope* he's dead."

J gives me a worse look.

I say, "Give it up. I'm not saying, 'Hey, cool, dead guy.' But what do you think he was going to do with that knife? I'm not getting raped by a drunk in a pickup."

"That was the general idea. That's what I was stopping! That isn't what I do for fun."

"I know. I'm not an idiot. You totally saved me."

"What are you doing with an ice pick?" He sounds like the vice principal of a reform school. My reform school.

"Ladies' self-defense. I'm not getting dragged off and praying for my life. I'm poking a hole in his eye."

"Poke! That was a *poke*? I had him close to unconscious."

"Like you're upset I helped you clobber him?"

"You don't *clobber* people with ice picks."

"Fine! *Gouge. Eviscerate. Dismember.* And if you have to know, I think you did great, but he was a giant crackhead. I was going for his heart."

"You can't do that!"

"If it was him or you? Why not? You deserve to live, and he deserved to die—what's wrong with that?"

"I already had him on the ground."

"You saved me and then I helped save you. Can we please figure out what to do next?"

He's quiet. It looks like he fell asleep with his eyes open. "I take you home and you change how you look while I get rid of the car."

"I know the drill." He has no idea how well I know the drill. If we broke into this Chevron's padlocked restroom, I could come out looking different in no time flat. "What about you? You're going to have black eyes and, wait a minute—"

I reach over and push on the bridge of his nose.

"Stop!" He's all but yelling at me.

"Noses have a *very* small window to get pushed back into shape. Do you want to hit an ER, or do you want to let me touch it?"

"You know this how?"

"Brawling boyfriend and YouTube."

He sighs.

I say, "You'll look kind of normal in maybe a week." This is highly optimistic, but I don't want him any more freaked out. If cops are out looking for a bruised white guy, he'd better call in sick. "I could do makeup for you."

J looks miserable. I've come up with a Boy Scout who doesn't like to brawl. Even though he's good at it. Even though he saved me.

I say, "He was coming at me. Not that I think going to the police would be the best idea. But if they believed the truth, they'd hang a medal on you."

He puts his arm around my shoulders and kisses my head with his split lip. Romantic. No, really. His arm feels heavy and warm. The fact that it just beat the crap out of some armed guy who was going to hurt me isn't lost on me.

I hug him back. "Lucky for you, I was loaded for bear."

"Lucky for us, you missed his heart."

"Lucky for *him*."

Before he drops me off, he leans across and kisses me again. It's a there's-no-tomorrow, soldier-off-to-fight-intergalactic-war, train-leaving-the-station-in-the-rain-and-everybody's-crying kiss.

He says, "I'll be back. Don't go anywhere."

"You won't recognize me."

"I'll recognize you fine. And I'm sorry. This was my fault."

"I told you, it was *his* fault."

"It was *stupid*. I shouldn't have let you get out of the car."

"You're not in charge of me! You don't let me do things and not let me do things and push me around! Who do you think you are?"

"The ass who took you to the scene of the crime and *committed* the crime."

"So we shouldn't have gone there. I get it. You shouldn't have picked it, and I should have said, 'What the hell?' and we shouldn't have opened our doors. But after that, it was totally *him*. He got what he deserved. That makes it self-defense. That makes it *fine*."

45

Jack

I had him down, and she stabbed him through the arm. There wasn't a qualm, not a shred of hesitation. I had him on the ground, I had his knife arm secured. For all practical purposes, she was saved. It was over. Then she stabbed him.

Maybe she couldn't tell it was done.

He was big and more than drunk. He could have been dusted. Don likes to sample any mind-altering thing anyone hands him. I've seen him try to walk through walls when someone gave him PCP.

I'm the one who beat the drunk guy to a bloody pulp, not her, all but sitting on the guy, whaling on him without brakes.

Maybe she's right, and he was going to drag her off and rape her. Maybe he would have carved me up, and I wouldn't have been alive to hear that her body turned up half naked in a field in Crothers.

Either way, I did the job. And then she stabbed him. Damn. She's who I should have known she was all along, but I wasn't expecting to see her in action.

I wait to blend into the morning's highway traffic and ditch the car in San Jose. I pull off the license plates, wipe it down, and leave the keys under the seat. Then I buy an old Chevy with a FOR SALE sign in the window and a price that says it's scrap. I look under the hood—Gerhard built a car from a kit while Calvin and I, age thirteen and in awe, stood there and handed him the parts—and it's better than expected. I claim I'm going to the bank, walk around for twenty minutes, come back and slap some Manx cash into the owner's hand.

My beard is neatly trimmed. My hair has some crap in it that old guys use to cover graying temples, turning it the color of rotted-out rust. My face is plastered with the stuff Nicolette ran back out to the car and gave me, for people with nasty scars. I don't see how girls can stand makeup. It feels like I've rubbed my face with scented crankcase oil.

I try to convince myself that this is the classic all-American boy's tale: boy meets bear; boy vanquishes bear; boy saves a princess in a tank top. I liked winning, even with the complicating factor of the princess stabbing the bear.

I've spent my life not beating guys who were begging for it, all the while being trained to go for it. But I just kept punching. If she hadn't stabbed him, I might have kept going until he stopped breathing.

After driving around for a couple of hours, trying to calm down, my cell phone vibrating continuously, I pull over to talk to Don.

He's pissed, as usual, but I don't have the patience for it.

I say, "I hit a glitch. I had to deal with it."

"A *glitch*? Isn't that when ladies are late because they couldn't pick what dress to wear? You have trouble picking your dress?"

"Fuck off. I had trouble ditching a car."

"What did you do with my car?" I enjoy him knowing that, in some ways, locked up in there, he's helpless. I focus on that and not on worrying what he'll say when he finds out his car's been abandoned in the desert for a while.

"You want me to do this? I can't drive a red shitmobile with no muffler."

"You decide to do something, you get my permission!"

"Will you listen? I got in a fight. I had to lose a car." I'm thinking this is something Don could relate to, but I'm thinking wrong.

"*You* got in a fight? What, the checker at Rite Aid overcharged you for gum so you bitch-slapped the bitch?"

"It was a drunk guy in a parking lot."

"Shit. Were you drunk?"

"No."

"Figures. Anyone see you?"

"Besides the guy? Maybe. I don't think so."

"Straight-A moron, aren't you? Did I tell you to get in a fight or did I tell you to get your hands on her?"

Maybe I am a straight-A moron, but I'm not letting him do this.

"Answer me!"

I don't. But the playground rule that if you ignore the bully, eventually he'll forget what he was taunting you about and go away doesn't apply to Don.

"Do you have her or don't you? And the answer better be yes."

There's no answer from me for maybe a second too long.

"Jesus," he says. "You found her and you took her drinking, didn't you? You found her, and you're playing with her."

"No!"

"What's wrong with you? Fuck her after you off her—just finish this thing!"

"What kind of perverted shit is that? What's wrong with *you*?"

"You don't have the balls for this, do you? You're gonna take her to the movies and ask her to prom."

"No!"

"Where are you keeping her?"

"I told you, I don't have her!" Even to myself, I sound like a liar. "Nobody wants this over more than I do."

There are a couple of minutes of listening to Don's uneven breathing and static. Finally he says, "You need to get your butt back up here."

"No."

"Jackass," Don says. "This is real. Bad things are going to happen. Get in my car and get back up here and convince me to believe you."

"I told you, the shitmobile is history."

In a voice I remember from childhood, from when he was

cornered with no way out, short of scratching a hole under his feet with his toenails, he says, "You need to be here. Right now. If these guys don't think I have you under control, Mom's the carrot and the stick. You're disposable, and so am I. *Get back here.*"

I want it not to be true. I want this to be Don offering up the same self-serving lies he tells regularly without blinking. I want this to be his effort to manipulate me like the little bitch he says I am. But I believe him, or close to enough to tell Nicolette a fairy tale to keep her at Mrs. Podolski's while I drive to Nevada.

I believe him, and I need him to know that so he won't do some angry, stupid thing to show me how serious he is, and get us all killed.

I say, "Yes, sirrrr," in the exaggerated slur we used to use when we were sassing our dad behind his back.

Don says, "Don't you sass me, boy," imitating the voice I haven't heard for four years but that still gets me going—along with the guilt that I closed it down.

46

Cat

I'm hunkered down with Mrs. P. Curtains drawn. Getting groceries delivered to the welcome mat. Watching TV and baking.

I'm not waiting for him.

I'm hiding out.

Not feeling a tenth of the way safe.

The Home Shopping Network doesn't have news. Every
time Mrs. P nods off, I grab the remote and hit up the local
news on channel nine.

Nothing.

No armed assaults. No barroom brawls. No murders.

I mean, somebody thought she saw a bear cub in a tree.
That was news. They interviewed her for five minutes.

If we killed the guy, it would have to be news.

Where is J ditching the car anyway? Peru?

I think he's coming back.

Maybe.

I grill Mrs. Podolski lamp chops (into the yard for mint leaves, back in under ten seconds, world record) and return to the Home Shopping Network for an ongoing sale of loose gems. Mrs. P's birthstone is the opal. Cat's is aquamarine. My real one ought to be rubies.

I keep coming back to bloodred.

The brightest thing I wear now is beige, but bloodred is my signature color.

Mrs. Podolski says, "The price of a good woman is above rubies. That's a proverb for you, Cathy."

This might explain one or two things.

By Thursday, Mrs. P is so sick of pastries, I have to stop rolling dough. When she grabs my hand with her little, liver-spotted fingers, I can't believe her grip.

"I'm going to read your palm, Ruby," she says.

For a second, I'm terrified she's going to figure out who I am and why I'm in her living room by tracing the lines of my hand. Until I remember that nobody can do that. There are no real fortune-tellers or real witches or real bogeymen.

Maybe bogeymen.

I let her massage my palm with the tips of her fingers.

Meet a dark stranger. Check.

Go on a long journey. Check.

She gets distracted by a mound of cubic zirconia on TV before she gets to long life.

After a while, she's so sick of me folding her afghan over her knees and waving my palm at her for the word on long life, she's ready to throw me out of the house.

She thinks I poisoned her coffee. When J finally shows up, tapping on the kitchen window, she thinks he's come to arrest me.

I want to hug him until my arms are too tired to keep hugging. But he swoops in and hugs me first. I'm enveloped in it. Also trapped. But all I feel is relieved.

When he steps back, he looks me over like the vice principal checking for bra straps and too-short skirts and random inappropriateness.

He says, "Good job! You look great."

I have black hair parted down the middle, black eyebrows, and red bow lips. I turned one of Mrs. P's old thermal tops into a white waffle-weave shirt. Over a black skirt.

Blah.

But a different style of blah.

"Like I looked terrible before?"

"You were supposed to look different, that's all I meant."

"Joking." I reach up to touch where his cheekbone is swollen, but he pulls back. "You still look pretty beat-up."

I'm so glad to see him, it's borderline pathetic. I tell myself I'd be happy to see a friendly dachshund. Facing the fact that I don't like being alone. But it's not the same thing. The dachshund wouldn't have its paws under the waistband of my awful skirt.

He says, "Can I get into the garage?"

I start to hand him my key ring, but why? There isn't any reason Mrs. P can't see him. It's not like she'll remember. And what if she did? What if she told her totally indifferent son, Walter? I could go, *No, Walter, it wasn't my boyfriend, it was a praying mantis.*

The worst part is, it would be plausible.

No, the worst part is seeing J with her. How sweet he is.

I wish I could keep him. Bag him and drag him back to Cotter's Mill. Go, *Hey J, I'm not who you think—fooled ya! Wanna be my boyfriend?*

Pretend he never saw me stab that guy. Another episode of things that look like the fun kind of bad spinning out of control. Him spinning with me.

He walks through the kitchen door like nothing happened. Like he's my playmate with a half-assed disguise. Not my partner in what might have been a crime.

I have to keep reminding myself that him-and-me isn't real.

That even if I don't ever go back home (reality), if I accept that and go, *Yay, new life with permanent bad hair and giant thighs* (reality), he'd still be with a made-up girl.

If I'm with anyone ever from now on, that person will be with a made-up girl.

Mrs. Podolski yells, "Officer!"

J says, "Can I get you more tomato soup?"

He looks over at me, smiling at me, and I try to think about something other than the fact that at some point I'm going to have to shed Catherine G. Davis and never see him again.

Such as, how weird is it that a lady who buries her silverware can still tell if her soup comes from a can or from a fresh tomato?

And how hot J looks in oven mitts.

I settle Mrs. P in front of the TV with soup and Sprite on her favorite tray (violets painted on a white metal background) and her favorite nighttime show (QVC selling handbags).

Back in the kitchen, J is staring down my stash of Toaster Strudel and Oreos. The cupboard door is hanging open. If my life didn't revolve around avoiding death every minute when he isn't underfoot distracting me, I'd die of shame.

"You don't feed her this crap, do you?"

"Constantly. If I stuff her veins with enough cholesterol, who knows, I could inherit that couch."

I swear he's trying to figure out how many bags of Famous Amos chocolate chip cookies it took to pad my behind. Calculating how big I'll be once I've emptied that cupboard down my throat.

"Do you ever worry about malnutrition?"

"Do you ever worry girls will smack you?"

"I feel relatively safe as long as I outweigh you."

"Not for long." I pull a box of Hostess Sno Balls from the cupboard, take out a Sno Ball, and bite into it.

"Are we going to share?"

"Nope." But I hand him one, a pink one. I don't even know why I eat this garbage when the kitchen's full of things I baked.

He says, almost casually but in a tight, tight voice, "I'm supposed to be in my cousin's wedding. This is probably what they'll serve. I was going to cancel, but maybe I should keep everything looking normal. You think?"

This is it. The kiss-off. He leaves, and I'm out of here. I'll call Walter from the bus, tell him to get another aide for Mrs. P. Fast.

I say, "Classy. Where is it?"

"South Dakota. The drive is going to take longer than the whole event."

"Come on. No bachelor party and rehearsal dinner and binge drinking with the bridesmaids?" (Camel chitchats while exiting oasis.)

"Maybe the binge drinking."

"When?"

"Tomorrow. I should be back by Monday. Tuesday if I'm passed out in a drunken stupor with a couple of bridesmaids."

Tomorrow?

I feel something I'm not supposed to feel. Big-time. I make myself smile. My face is the kind of mask that doesn't have tear ducts. "Help yourself. You want a drunk bridesmaid, go to. It's not like I'm your girlfriend."

He looks relieved.

I feel miserable. Resent that this wedding is cutting into my temporary true romance because I can't do this again anytime soon. Gainesville, Florida next. Or maybe Pullman, Washington.

I hate this. I hate that he can't know Actual Me. Hate that I can't go sneaking out with him in Cotter's Mill. Take him to a party on the lake where Liv and Jody get to look him over, and Summer embarrasses herself with shameless flirting.

I hate how not-normal and approaching expiration this and everything else is. I hate that I can't keep him. I hate everything about this.

Then he hands me a box.

"What's in here?"

"No big deal—it's a phone."

"You can't go getting me phones!"

"What if I'm up in South Dakota and the only thing to talk to for miles is a cow?"

"You got me this because talking to me is better than talking to livestock?"

"Don't forget phone sex."

"What?"

"That was a joke."

It's a cute green burner. Expensive for a prepaid.

I want to hurl myself around his neck.

He kind of grabs me, followed by neck-wrapping.

Sweet.

Sweet sweet sweet sweet sweet.

I really like this guy.

Damn.

47

Jack

This is a bad idea.

I don't look like the prep guy who shows up at Yucca Valley Correctional with clockwork regularity because his mother makes him anymore. I look like Jeremiah from El Molino, unshaven and scraggly haired, a cross between a hipster and someone who's been camping for too long.

Don says, "Nice hair, Jacqueline."

"Nice jumpsuit. You have something to tell me you couldn't say on the phone?"

Don's eyes narrow. "You're here to dance like Pinocchio. Some people need to see me pull your strings." His head bobs as if he's inviting me to stand up. "So dance."

I don't move. "You're the one in the cage, not me."

"Don't be such a smug bitch! You think you disappear in the middle of this, ditch my car, and *nothing happens*?" His voice is rising. He glances across the prison yard. "Try to look like a guy getting a message. Is that too hard for you? You don't want to be sorry."

A *you'll be sorry* from Don is his most reliable promise. He saves it for special occasions.

"Fine!" I sound just like Nicolette with the defiant little *fine* of the defeated person: not as much fun when you're the one who's defeated. "Everybody knows you made me come. Take a bow. Can I go now?"

Don says, "Are you stupid?"

I look around the yard, wanting to figure out who he's trying to impress.

"Words need to start coming out of your mouth, Jack-off," Don leans in. "And when you get around to doing this thing, make sure it's an accident."

This thing I've been pushing further and further into the realm of the theoretical, parsing out directions I could go as if they were equidistant points on a compass. But here's the reality: I'm taking concrete instructions from a man I visualize with slime dribbling out of the corners of his mouth when he speaks.

"That's why you wanted me to take your gun? So I could stage an accidental shooting? Clever plan, Don."

"Just finish her."

For a second, I hope she's on a bus out of El Molino right now, heading for somewhere I'll never find her. Then the thought of never seeing her again makes me feel something close to panic.

Followed immediately by the image of my mother's house burned to the ground.

"Jesus! I'll just make her disappear. She'll go on a hike and whoops—something like that. Does that float your boat?"

"It's not my boat you have to worry about." Don looks around as if he's still trying to spot someone. "It's Yeager's boat. And you'd better float it good."

I'm making every muscle in my face stand down, a skill well honed when kids wanted to meet up after school to see who was the badder ass. I knew I could break them in half but declined, seemingly impassive, afraid of what I'd do to them if I said yes.

If Don sees me panic, he's right, I'm his bitch. I try to sound as much like him as I can manage. "How much longer does this puppet show have to take?"

With an intensity that spews up through his rage, he says, "I flap my lips, you nod like a good little boy."

I start nodding.

"Not that much!"

"Fine." I stop and sit there glaring at him while he tells me the plot of a science-fiction movie he got to see for good behavior. I nod at appropriate intervals until the buzzer goes off and visitors are ushered out.

Just before he stands up, he says so quickly that it's almost as if it didn't happen, "The thing with Mom. I don't know how long I can hold them off. They're not nice guys. You've got to get this done."

"Don!"

221

He's on his way out before I can even get a read on his face. "Have a good one," he calls to me casually, as if he didn't just tell me his friends are going to execute my mother.

This whole thing is a play I don't want to be in.

"Whatever you say." I try to sound cowed pretty loudly on the chance he's sneaking glances all around because we've got an audience that has to think I'm going to do what I'm supposed to do. I try to sound like I'm afraid of him.

It's not much of a stretch.

The sprint to the car, the fumbling with the phone, the attempt to sound something other than scared shitless is getting old.

Fortunately, my mother is so annoyed, she doesn't notice.

"Where are you, Jack? And where's your phone? And why did you turn off the tracker? You're supposed to be camping, not hiding."

I've called my mom on the burner. That's how thrown off I am.

"I might have left it somewhere. Sorry. I bought this cheap one." There's a long silence while she waits for me to elaborate. It's like playing chicken with someone who doesn't even have eyelids and couldn't blink if she wanted to.

"*What* did I say about being responsible?"

How do I answer that?

"Jack! Where's your itinerary? Or are you just wandering through the countryside losing things?"

"Just the phone. And a sweatshirt I could care less about." I throw in the sweatshirt to give her something trivial to call me out on, and to distract her—a tactic developed over years of trial and error. It doesn't work.

"This isn't safe! You were supposed to be sending me your *detailed* itinerary. And answering my calls!"

"Come on." I play the military card again. "Guys my age are fighting in Afghanistan."

"Don't equate driving around aimlessly and letting your sweatshirt walk away with *fighting for your country*—"

"The fact you don't know where I eat lunch doesn't make it dangerous for me to have a sandwich! It'd probably be *more* dangerous if you knew because then I'd be the wuss who has to ask his mommy whether he can have a beer."

"You *can't* have a beer! You're not traveling with Don's old ID, are you?"

And the save: "I just visited Don. With my own ID."

"You did?" Her tone softens as she imagines the loving-brother reconciliation that's never going to happen.

"He says hello." He didn't. The sentence tastes like rotten fish on my tongue, but the words have the desired effect. The thought of Don saying hi makes her sigh as if she just saw a cute bunny.

"Here's the thing, kiddo," she says. "Why I've been calling you *all day*. There might be something hinky with one of my cases." Her voice is very strained, like she's choosing every word and laying it down gently in a careful sentence.

"Hinky how?" She doesn't say *hinky*. She doesn't say *kiddo*, and she doesn't talk about her cases.

"I'd rather discuss this in person."

I don't say anything.

She says, "Exactly where are you? Are you still in Nevada?"

Given that I'm not telling her where I'm headed, or why, or anything like why, all that's left is irrational shouting. "Isn't the point for me to be wherever I want? Isn't the point for me to be free for a while?"

"You're in a state of unreality! Drifting around with plenty of money and no responsibilities to prove you *can* isn't being free! It's being a child with a car!"

"The deal was you were going to go along with this. That's what you said."

"Jack!" she says, as if repeating my name would bring me to my senses. "It's probably nothing, but get back here. Park Don's car and hop on a bus."

This is when I start to feel sicker. "Did something happen?"

"*Come back here.* How long will it take?"

"Did something happen to you?"

"Don't raise your voice to me!"

"I'm expressing *concern*, not coming back at you!"

My mother sighs. "It was probably nothing. It's not as if industrial polluters run around jimmying lawyers' cars."

"Did somebody fuck with your car?" I can't keep the panic out of my voice.

"Language!" Then, deep breath, restrained tone. "Maybe someone made a mistake when I had it serviced. Maybe someone nicked the brake line accidently." It's as if she's trying to convince herself. "I just think you'd be safer here."

You can't miss the irony, how she thinks I'd be safer playing momma's boy at home, when the only way she's safe and I'm off Yeager's shit list is when I seal the deal with Nicolette.

Only I have to do it faster. This thing with the fire was the warning. Turning a car into a deathtrap is pure intimidation.

Oh Jesus, Don, how could you let it get this far? This is Mom, not some live lizard you roast on a spit over a campfire. You made me watch that, too.

I know what I have to do.

I play my part. "You think I'd be safer with the lady some industrial polluter wants to ice than on my own?" I'm the road-tripping kid who has inexplicably lost all respect and reason. That's what she believes, anyway. I think, *Believe what you want. I'm saving your life*.

"*Ice,* Jack? This isn't a joke! There was something with the steering column, too. Are you listening to me?"

Who messes with a prosecutor's car, not even bothering to make it look accidental?

"Do you have security? Good security, not the old guys in the golf carts."

"The police are treating me like the crown jewels. Sweetheart, there's nothing to worry about. But you have to get back here."

There's plenty to worry about. But she's got police watching out for her. This buys me some time.

She's saying, "Jack, be careful!" as I hang up on her.

Part 4

48

Jack

I don't drive straight back to El Molino.

There are things I have to take care of, steps to take. This requires planning and precision, a time and a place. I drive along the crest of the mountains and onto a service road that barely exists, carved into the precipice. Courtesy of Google satellite images, I'm here.

The pavement of what used to be a parking lot is rutted, the trash cans upended. The NO OVERNIGHT PARKING signs are aerated where they were used for target practice a long time ago. There are no signs of human life, no telltale beer bottles, not a wrapper or a plastic ring that holds six-packs together anywhere.

This is the place.

Ravines and rocks, cliffs, and enough vegetation for cover: it's harsh, rugged terrain. If you tried to run here, the likeliest thing is you'd go down without any help from me—it's that rocky and uneven, unstable underfoot.

I map where I've been with merit-badge accuracy until I find my spot. Then I stop charting and start memorizing.

I have equipment to take down anything that comes at me. If it has a blade, I've got one: ax; bowie knife; camping gadget with corkscrew, box cutter, nail file, and useless little scissors; and a big, dull thing that looks like a machete that hacks through underbrush.

Also, I've got what's in the holster.

The gadget is from my mom, from when I was a Scout. The bowie knife is from my dad. Compare: a gift that would be good for opening a bottle of white wine at a campsite ringed with Winnebagos versus a gift that could decapitate a bear.

I get them both two weeks after my dad hears I'm not coming to his house on his weekend because my Scout troop is hitting the wilderness. He says, "Shit, Bella. My kid's going into the desert with grown men in *shorts*?" I can hear him from ten feet away through the receiver my mom holds away from her ear.

My mom says, "It's Boy Scouts. It's harmless."

My dad makes the sound that says he's glowering.

But my mom knows how to play him when he's not too far gone. "It's for survival skills. What's the harm?"

Two weekends later, when I'm at his house, my dad starts quizzing me on what plant roots to eat if you run out of food, and how to purify water. All I know is what kind of plant not to eat and a couple of birdcalls. He tosses me a survivalist hand-book with sidebars about keeping your gunpowder dry and rebuilding a constitutional democracy from the ruins of the US after Armageddon.

He says, "I bought you this. You get stuck out there with those assholes, I don't want you to die."

I read the book.

Don reads the book because I got it first.

At night, Don and I trek onto the ten acres of manicured back-yard. We pretend we're Special Forces soldiers stranded between rows of ornamental shrubs, camped out by an Olympic-size swim-ming pool outside Kabul.

I follow the diagrammed instructions to make Molotov cock-tails, which we hurl across the diving board. A chair catches fire. Three guys who work for my dad come running outside, ready to take down an invading army.

In the morning, my dad is there, eating bacon and eggs.

He says, "What was wrong with that?"

For once, Don doesn't point at me. He's figured out that I could blow him up. But my dad isn't asking Don.

I say, "It was in the book."

He keeps eating.

I say, "I didn't know it would start a fire."

Then I say, "It was stupid?"

"It was *loud.* Do we want the police at this house? Do we want to attract attention to this house?"

I'm not just afraid he's going to hit me—that's a given. I'm afraid I've caused something terrible to happen.

The guy standing guard by the back door says, "Come on, Art, at least he didn't put shrapnel in it."

My dad laughs so hard, the guy comes over and pounds him between the shoulders so he won't choke on the bacon.

He doesn't say anything when he slaps down the knife between us on the console in the front seat of his car. The blade says, *Life is gruesome, be prepared, go camping with assholes in shorts if your mother insists. But get ready, be armed to draw and quarter anything that comes at you because the insurance agent troop leader dads sure as hell won't.*

I wrap myself in the space blanket, but I can't get warm. I fall asleep thinking about Scouts and toasted marshmallows, playing with Don, hiding in the bushes and throwing incendiary bottles at deck chairs.

I imagine Don in an open coffin, eyelids folded down over dead eyes. Even for my father, in his closed, black coffin, my mother's face collapsed and never plumped back up, not ever. And this happened after he'd divorced her and she hated him. Don's a shit, but he's not dying the kind of prison death it makes my mother sick to think about.

My mother isn't burying her kid or going up in flames when her dryer accidently on purpose blows up again, this time singeing her hair down to the roots, blackening her bones.

Her car isn't accidently on purpose losing its brakes on the interstate.

No one is going to touch any of us.

I have to do this.

I have to make Nicolette Holland disappear.

That's why I'm here.

49

Cat

"Did you miss me?"

He's standing in my doorway.

He's tanner than before. It suits him.

He's back! I hope looking shocked suits me.

My getaway can wait. Underneath my new and different exterior, in this rapidly transforming vessel of moral decay, I'm still *me*. It's got to be okay to like guys. Why can't I have whatever extremely low level of fun is possible under the circumstances?

I pull him inside, bolt the door, and kiss him.

Kiss him some more.

He says, "You're depraved. I should beat on drunks and leave town more often."

He hesitates for a second, looking at me. Hands me a bottle of rum. Then he kisses me back. And then some.

"You smell like a campfire."

J crosses his arms behind my back, pulls me in closer. "It was South Dakota. You're lucky I don't smell like a cow patty. I was going to shower when I got back to my apartment, but there was this cop car outside when I was unpacking. So I ducked out the kitchen window."

"A cop car?" Does he even get how bad this is?

"Calm down. They drive up and down my street every ten minutes looking for jaywalkers. What else is there for them to do around here?"

"Look for us?" Then I might make too big a show of sniffing the air. His face. I say, "No, you're fine. Really. Was it nice?"

"Was what nice?"

"Uh, the wedding. Groomsman. Bachelor party."

He sits down on the edge of the bed, looking embarrassed. Does the thing where he grabs on to the back of his neck and massages it. It must have been one amazing bachelor party. "It was home on the range. No strippers—just a lot of cows."

"Did you meet any cowgirls?"

"You're depraved and jealous."

Now he's massaging *my* neck. Much better.

"I'm *so* not jealous. We'd have to be together for me to be jealous and we're *so* not together."

"Not us." He stretches out on the bed, closes his eyes.

I nudge him slightly. Nothing.

"Did you drive all night?"

He doesn't answer. He's asleep.

I roll the desk chair next to the bed and sit there reading, my feet draped over him on the bed. His hand closes on my ankle.

After dark, I wedge myself between him and the wall.

Fully clothed, on top of the blanket.

Not totally depraved yet, but slipping fast.

50

Jack

I wake up in her bed.

The only time I've ever woken up with a female in a bed was on the class trip to DC with Scarlett after we figured out our chaperone was useless. I made Calvin go bunk with the guys across the hall.

But that was intentional. This isn't. Her chin is tucked over my shoulder. I can't move without damaging her jaw. She's lying there, the tail of my shirt in her sleeping fist, all but volunteering for anything I want to do to her.

She shakes her head loose and props herself up on her elbow.

She wakes up looking good. She even smells good in her day-old clothes.

She wakes up looking scared.

Then it strikes me that being this close to her messes with my head. The only problem here is that *I* made myself vulnerable to *her*. I passed out in her bed, my wallet in one pocket, my cell phone in the other. Who knows what she found out while I was unconscious, sprawled there with my throat unguarded?

"How long have I been here?"

"Weeks," she says, smiling a little. "That wedding took a lot out of you."

"Driving for twenty-four hours took a lot out of me."

"Didn't your mother ever tell you about roadside motels?"

I reach back into my pockets to make sure everything's still there. It is. Then I start wondering what's in her pockets. A scalpel? Piano wire? Every weapon I think of for her to have stuffed into her bra—which might as well be welded to her skin—I think, *I should have that*. Then I think, *No, I shouldn't have that*.

I'm running my fingers over her eyelids and those stained-dark brows. "I thought girls got warned against roadside motels."

"Everyone gets warned against driving for thirty-six hours. You're just being a macho blowhard, right? You didn't actually—"

"I pulled over and slept. Not enough, obviously."

"Do you want coffee?"

She starts to climb over me, but I take hold of her arm. I want out of this errand for Don so bad, every muscle in my body is tensed up and ready to spring. Only I want to take her with me: her, me, my money, Costa Rica or Belize or Trinidad or any number of places I researched as a well-prepared little kid, aware that at some point my family might have to leave town. I could take her to an obscure island off Indonesia. Someplace nobody I ever met would take a vacation was the old rule. I could buy a coffee plantation or a rubber plantation or whatever kind of plantation they've got.

I say, "Do you ever think about going 'screw it' and getting away?"

She says, "Like a week at Disney World or life in Argentina?"

"Argentina."

Her hand covers my hand. "Was this the plan? Pass out for ten hours, then strike with your lame romantic fantasy?"

"Ten hours?"

"That might be an exaggeration," she says. "Just slightly." Then she starts unbuttoning her shirt.

Once it's off and she's still kissing me, I reach around her and unhook her bra.

She says, "Nuh-uh," batting my hands away.

I say, "I'll do it." But I've never hooked a bra back up, and they're not as stretchy as you'd think. I'm trying to get her bra closed again without breaking the mood, hoping she'll say it's okay to leave it open. She doesn't, and I feel like a clown. Finally, she does it herself, behind her back, not even seeing where the miniscule hooks are.

Then she touches my hand, still behind her, pulling it onto her skin.

I say, "That was close. Thanks for preserving my virtue."

"Sarcasm," she says. "So unromantic."

Then she takes the hem of my T-shirt and she starts to lift it up over my torso. Reflexively, I pull it back down.

She says, "What? You want to stash me in Paraguay, but you won't let me kiss your naked shoulders?"

"Gotta keep you in line."

"Take off your shirt."

It's not like everyone who's ever been to a pool party with me, and dozens of crew teams, haven't seen me without a shirt. I know the drill. I've got my story down if anybody asks. That doesn't mean I want to be here now, showing her.

"What?" she says, touching my hair. "Do you have a tattoo that says, *I love my wife* or *I love Mommy* or *I love boys*? Do you have a giant birthmark in the shape of a weasel? Do you have a terrifying scar?"

She stops right there.

She says, "I'm sorry." She sits there, waiting for me to say something. "I swear, I thought it was like you thought I'd hate chest hair or something. I was joking about the scar."

How transparent am I? One day I'm calculating in minute detail the staging of a murder in the mountains, and now I've lowered my guard like a drawbridge for her to cross.

She says, "I really was joking. Sorry, okay? Don't be mad."

There's more silence from me. It's not that I'm fuming; it's that I don't know what to say.

"It's just kind of weird getting this naked with someone who's not equally naked," she says. "That's all. I keep the bra, you keep the shirt, okay?"

240

I raise my arms.

She says, "You don't have to do this." Then she eases my T-shirt up past my pits and over my head.

I wish I could see her face, but she's behind me now on the bed, her legs pressing against me on either side. I think, *Perfect, this is the A-number-one position to get garroted, one thin stretch of wire to my neck, quick, followed by instant death.*

I'm in the A-number-one position for a stupid guy who trusts a girl, shirtless, without anything between me and the truth, between me and her. I'm acting exactly like a person who trusts people, specifically her, the girl I just invited to a South American country, whom anyone in his right mind would know not to trust.

I feel her eyes on my back, fixed on the expanse of skin where my biography is etched.

I feel her finger tracing the scar that runs across my back, first the faint lines and then the one where it's hard for me to feel anything but a vague pressure, where I can't feel the location of her finger on my body unless she pushes down hard, because the sensation is gone: the ugly one. The scar twists across my back in uneven knots of hard white skin, like a deformed centipede.

She says, "Who did this to you?"

The story is that Don did it. It goes, we were playing with fencing swords, one of them with the dull tip broken off, leaving a jagged metal point. The story is that we were too young to understand the danger, that we both thought we were Zorro until I started to bleed through my cut-to-ribbons Sunday School shirt.

I don't know why I put the Sunday School shirt in there, nice detail though.

The story is a lie.

"'*Two paths diverge in a yellow wood,*'" she misquotes. "Are you going to tell me or not?"

The idea that a month ago I was sitting in AP English and cared what Robert Frost had to say is remarkable. It's amazing how false it feels for that to be my memory, as if high school and AP English and raising my hand and being called on could never happen to the thug I am now.

But the AP English in me speaks. "Roads. It was roads that diverged."

"Show-off. Are you going to take the path where you tell me what happened to you?"

I try to get myself to feel better about this so I can keep some semblance of control here. I say to myself, *I might as well tell her, she already suspects.* She'd probably admire someone who could cut up a kid, her being such a master of cutting up humans.

But it feels as if the girl who's a slasher and the girl on the bed this close to me are two different people. I don't want to hurt either one of them.

I want her to know, God knows why.

I try to convince myself that coming out with it would have a strategic advantage. If I go with the truth about this thing, it will make me look honest as hell. I could be the trustworthy guy who gets to unhook the bra.

Okay, there's that. I'm trying to have sex with her, which, under the circumstances, makes me a monster—a respectful monster, but a monster.

I say, "I tell people my brother and I were playing with a broken saber."

"But that's not true?" I'm not sure if this is a question or a statement.

Suddenly, I'm not turned on. She's put my T-shirt on herself, snuggling now at my side. The shirt hangs like a charcoal gray tepee, which on her could still be arousing. It's not arousing now.

"My dad had an anger-management problem." The words come out slowly. They feel stuck in my mouth.

"That's one way of putting it," she says, her fingers still wandering the surface of my back, between the shoulder blades and down my spine as she curls around me. "You don't have to tell me if you don't want to."

She can say that, but she's waiting for something.

"My dad beat on me." It doesn't even sound like my voice. "Not often. Jesus." She's moved to where she's next to me, holding me, touching my face. My face is in her now-black hair where it gets fluffy around the neck, soft as a cat.

Her arms wrap around me. She says, "I'd never have kids if I thought I'd do that *once*."

"You don't think anyone can lose it if they're angry enough? If everything lines up, perfect storm?"

She's hanging on to me from the side, straddling me, clinging the way those stuffed animal toys with hinged arms and legs cling to the ends of pencils. "You seriously think *anyone* could beat on a kid with a meat cleaver?"

I have to stop myself from saying *You should know* or *Got hypocrisy?* or *What the fuck were you doing with a knife and Connie Marino's jugular vein?*

But I don't say any of it. I say, "Belt buckle."

I've told the other story so often that the truth feels like a lie. Having Don shred my back sounds a lot more plausible than my dad losing it. Of course, my dad losing it isn't what happened either. My dad always did what he intended to do. He didn't lose it.

It's hard to breathe because my throat is closing. I force words out across my tongue and through my lips, which are freaking quivering—*quivering*! I don't get like this. I will not.

I say, "It wasn't his anger-management problem. He didn't real-ize how much it would show. It was a big PR disaster."

Maybe I can't breathe because she's holding me so tight. She's pressed against me so hard everywhere, I couldn't get any closer unless I were literally inside her. But I'm the opposite of turned on.

Her hands are kneading my shoulders. She has a lot of hand strength for a small girl: surprise, surprise. I lean forward, away from her. The places we were skin to skin peel apart with a little stripping sound.

I'm making satisfied noises against my will.

She says, "Do you want to keep having this conversation?"

"No! I don't ever want to discuss this again."

"Don't yell at me."

"Sorry."

"When I was joking about wounded, sensitive guys? The part where I said they can't stand me and they make me sick. I'm sorry."

"I'm *not* wounded. And I'm *not* sensitive. Give me back my shirt."

She pulls it right off, slides it fast over my head and down my shoulders. Once my eyes are uncovered, there's the pink polka-dotted bra. It's a don't-touch-me, purest-girl-on-the-cheerleading-squad, don't-think-about-going-all-the-way bra.

I wish beyond wishing that the truth wasn't true. I wish Connie Marino were alive and well and acing nursing school in Michigan. I wish this girl with the unfettered evil streak didn't make me feel this way—this crazy protective want-to-be-with-her-all-the-time way.

51

Cat

Pull on the snag, and the sweater unravels.

Everyone knows that.

I know that.

I didn't mean to unravel him. I would knit him back up if I could. But all I get to do is hold him, sensitive and wounded, leaning back against me on the bed.

I want to say, *Be all right. Don't let me mess you up. I can knit. Let me fix this.*

I know there's no way to fix this.

If I could face down the man who did this to him, the so-called father with the belt, I would—with my own hands, with the rush mothers get that lets them lift boulders off their half-crushed babies—give him what he deserves.

I hum and stroke J's head, the babysitting move that puts the kid to sleep.

He relaxes into me.

I want to be a real girl holding a real boy. Not a fake person from a fake trailer full of fake religious zealots pretending to care about someone she's going to ditch ASAP because her whole life is all me me me, staying alive.

The plan is to slide from place to place. Score a birth certificate. Get a real job. Save up. Go to college online. Get plastic surgery. Do everything intentionally missing people on TV shows do, and come out as a living person who's not me.

The problem is, I hate this plan.

Tell me how it's being alive if you can't stop for one freaking second and care about someone? And not just because he's distracting you with charm and hotness. When he's not one-upping you with his macho boy thing. When you just accidently pushed him into his own personal dark cellar full of spooks and things that snag and snag and snag.

Please, please get out of the cellar.

Said the fake girl to the real boy crashing into her. Through his T-shirt, I feel the raggedy line of the strand I yanked on. I feel it in the scar across his back and in the tension in his shoulder blades.

I say, "Please. I'm so sorry I did that about your shirt. I'm an idiot."

He says, "No harm done." Touches his neck. He's so lying. Harm done.

"Tell me how to make you feel better. Anything." Then I wish I could take back the *anything* because it sounds like I'm offering up sex like it was Krazy Glue to stick broken guys back together.

"Anything?" I can tell it's a tease.

"Not *that* anything. Some other anything. Where I'm not an idiot and I bake you a pie."

"I'm not getting psychoanalyzed for a metaphorical pie."

"Actual pie. I don't do metaphorical anything, duh. I'm not literary, I'm practical. Do you want it or not?"

He swings his legs over the side of the bed. His face looks semi-normal.

I say, "Don't even answer. All straight guys want pie and bra removal. It's a fact of life."

He shakes his head. "Is this chiseled on stone tablets? Because I wouldn't want to mess with the eleventh commandment."

"On bedrock. Do you mind store-bought crust?"

You can tell he's so glad he's not fending off a conversation about his back, his father, or anything that makes him seem, look, or feel weak, he'd eat crust made of crushed gravel. This guy likes weakness even less than all other guys like weakness.

It seems like I actually see him, weirdly so, since we're busy burying his actual feelings in pastry. Even from this place of total fakeness, I get him. I do. Not Cat. *Me.*

"Store-bought?" He shakes his head. "I might have to dump you."

"Ha! I'd have to be your girlfriend for you to dump me, and I'm so not."

Only maybe I am.

Or maybe Cat is, and how's that supposed to work?

I run across the backyard to Mrs. Podolski's kitchen. I grab a crust. I bake him a blueberry pie in the garage's miniature oven.

We make out while waiting for it to cool.

Do I know how idiotic this is?

Do I know we should be dealing with what happens now? (About blowing town. About the guy he pounded and I punctured. About disappearing.)

Do I know I have to go, and going with him would be mind-blowingly stupid?

Yes to all of the above.

52

Jack

Walking back to my apartment from her place, I'm whistling. Then I'm not whistling so much.

I know to check if things are as I left them. I've known that since I was five, and not just because Don took my stuff and put it back broken.

Trip wires, threads, twigs, tiny wads of lint—you wouldn't think a person so conversant with the fine art of self-preservation would be facing down two guys in his living room.

Correction: I'm facing one guy. I walked in, and there he was, sitting in the dark. The second guy was pressed against the book-case, a yard from the door. But I missed him, and now he has a hard metallic thing just behind my head. I force air up and down my nostrils, smell the dust in the apartment, and the humans.

Nobody says anything.

Every breath seems to take thirty seconds: time to plan. First you assess your target, then you plan. You hit them hard enough to get away, and then you get away.

If they falter, I'll duck, jab backward, kick, and try to take out a knee in a bastardized Krav Maga move. I wish I were wearing hiking boots and not sneakers. I'm so pumped with adrenaline, I could probably bench press a Hummer. Dislocating a kneecap with a Converse sneaker should be nothing compared to that.

I wonder if they've found Don's gun in its hiding place. If they're that good, I'm fucked whether they've found it or not.

The guy in front of me is built like a bouncer. He's bulging out of his suit, his pants riding up over the top of zip-up ankle boots. His weapon isn't pointed at me. It isn't even out. Why should it be, given what's behind my head?

He settles in the green easy chair, his bulk spilling over the armrests. I make myself stop thinking about Nicolette in my lap in that chair, the rough mohair on skin, her skin against my skin.

I can't let myself get distracted. These guys figuring out who was in that chair would make things worse—much worse. Because they're not here for me, they're here for her.

The guy behind me doesn't move. I don't think he's big, and either he doesn't use deodorant or he's scared shitless. The worst kind of guy to have pointing something at the back of your head would be a scared little guy.

It runs through my head that the wedge sitting in my chair will collapse it, the guy behind me will freak, and I'll only make it if the thing in his hand is a knife.

"You should get a better lock," the big guy says. "Word to the wise." He sounds as if he's auditioning for a part in an episode of the kind of old black-and-white crime show my dad liked—or maybe a parody of that kind of show.

He's not getting the part.

I say, "Make yourself comfortable."

"Cool customer." Crap, this part of the nightmare has a terrible script.

"You're in my apartment. Your boy has something aimed at me. Do you know who I am?"

I'm trying to sound like a prodigy crime lord, Son of Crime Lord, any heavy-duty thing I can think of.

He laughs at me.

There's nothing to lose. Something bad is going to happen here. The guy behind me is leaning against the bookshelves (I can hear them creaking), lazy.

I swivel toward him, take the knee without too much trouble, my hand on his wrist, the only challenge how sweat-slick it is. The knife falls against my calf. I kick it to the side, out of reach, the payoff for ten years of martial arts.

The hulk in the chair barks, "Manx! Chill!"

The little sweaty guy is lying on the ground, swearing at me. All I've got going for me here is my lineage and a lot of sparring with an Israeli Krav Maga instructor who took me down every single time. I'd rather have metal in my hand.

The guy in the chair raises his eyebrows. "We don't want trouble from you."

"You ambush me in my apartment? Seems like trouble." I'm doing the best possible imitation of my dad, or maybe the Godfather. I hope it's good enough.

The guy in the chair takes his gun out from under the jacket and lays it across his lap. "Just tell me where she is, and we'll leave."

"Where who is?"

This was stupid because, in his line of work, he's got a temper, and there's a Beretta in his lap. He puts his hand on the gun and gives me a significant look, exactly like bad TV except for the real possibility of sudden death.

I say, "Okay, sorry. But if I knew where she was, do you think I'd still be here? I'd be at the beach."

He's looking me over, trying to decide if he believes me. "You find her, we take her," he says. "Easy."

If I say *easy*, maybe he'll go away.

He'll also know I'm blowing smoke.

I shake my head. "That's not what I heard."

He half-rises from the chair, his hand suddenly cradling the gun, the barrel and the silencer pointing straight outward. He shakes his head. "I know who you are, kid. Do you know who I am?"

"Karl Yeager's cousin Bob? Cops who've been undercover too long?"

"Watch yourself!" his friend growls from the floor, the terror effect he's going for undermined by the fact that he's flat on his ass.

Beretta Man says, "You find her, we get her. Understood?"

I realize they have no idea where Nicolette is.

And, shit, they're here because I led them here. How else? That was the point of Don's making me visit him—not him showing off how much power he wielded over me, but Yeager's guys being able to follow me out of the prison parking lot. And if they found me, they can find her. I've led them straight to her.

Now is when I have to do it, *now* before they find her, *now* before somebody other than me gets to her, and she and my whole family end up dead. But where? If they followed me back, they had days to do recon at the campsite. I was the hotshot, hiking around memorizing the terrain, and I didn't notice these two? Or what if it was someone else? What if they tag team? How many people are looking for this girl?

Nicolette, why did you have to do it?

I say, "I can do this myself," with more bravado than confidence.

"Sure you can," the guy in the chair sneers as the guy on the floor edges toward his knife. I kick it into the kitchen.

Then there's the choke hold. It's not even the big guy, it's the little guy I put on the floor—the one I thought was harmless. He comes up at me so fast, I'm just standing there, looking stupid. I can't move, can't breathe, his arm is pressed around my neck. My field of vision narrows to a speck. If I struggle against it, my windpipe is crushed and I'm dead sooner, and Nicolette is dead too. I hear them. "Arrogant little pissant." And I'm thinking my last thought: *Pissant, are you kidding me? Who says that?*

Then my head implodes.

53

Cat

Abandon nice old lady in a house of food she won't remember to eat, and disappear into the night.

Not exactly.

I tell Mrs. Podolski's son, Walter, I have a family emergency.

He doesn't even care.

He says, "She'll be okay till you get back."

I can't tell if he's stoned. Or a bad person. Or a moron.

I say, "No, she won't! Seriously? You have to hire somebody else. Do you want her to eat safety pins?"

"She hated those other girls. When do you get back?"

"You have to hire someone *right now!*"

I clear any number of Sunday School hurdles.

I don't take Mrs. P's stash of emergency twenties.

Plus, I feel bad about walking (running) away from J right after I made him all mushy and soft. Which he hates.

Oh God, I like him so much.

Normally, this isn't when I leave guys. It's when I peel off my judgment like a pair of used gym socks. Reducing myself to a bundle of impulses, dangerous attraction, and bare feet.

Not suited to running.

But I can't be anywhere within a thousand miles of police looking for a girl with an ice pick. I can't.

Wait while he ditches the car. Check.

Wait while he goes to a freaking wedding in South Dakota. Check.

Wait for him to go, *I'm back, now let's get out of here.* Nothing.

And I'm not about to twist his arm. Or wait.

Come with me to Argentina, babe.

Yeah, right.

I wish, I wish, I wish. But seriously? Yeah, right.

I'm keeping my socks on, and I'm gone.

Plus, I can look him up later. Years from today. When I've bought a new face and a passport that says I come from Paraguay.

I can go, *Hola, Jeremiah.*

How many Jeremiah Jenkins can there be?

54

Jack

I'm on the floor where they dropped me, ears ringing, head pounding, mouth full of sewage that belongs in my stomach. Something stinks. They emptied the kitchen garbage on me—nice touch. The place is trashed. It's dark, and I can't raise my head to take in the full extent of it, but I can tell it's time to go.

How many words do Eskimos have for stupid? Not as many as I deserve, or they'd all have been eaten by polar bears.

I pull myself off the floor, not sure if I'm supposed to be alive. It's not easy to breathe with a neck that's been pressed closed, or to deal with the humiliation. The little one got me? *Jack Manx, arrogant pissant*: words to live by.

I dial her number. Very quietly, I ask her, "Are you alone?"

"I'm with my other boyfriend. What do you think?"

I say, "I can't sleep. Let's go somewhere."

There's a long silence. "It's three in the morning. You know that, right?"

"Let's get out of town and see some stars."

"Like stars over Crothers or stars in Argentina?"

"God, you're picky. You say you like romantic, and I give you stars." She says, "I've created a monster."

"I was already a monster." She has no idea. "Are you coming or not?" I know she's coming.

"Dress warm—I'll be there in thirty. Make sandwiches, okay?" My throat feels like someone buffed it with sandpaper, but I'm hungry.

I spend five minutes throwing everything into my duffel, shovel the trash back into a black plastic bag, put the drawers back in the dresser and the cushions back on the couch. Cleaning up isn't on my top ten list for the night, but neither is having the girl who rented me the place show up to what looks like a crime scene.

I go out the kitchen window for the second time in two days. That cop car that scared me into avoiding the front door and instead climbing over my sink and out the back window to get to Nicolette's place is what kept these two guys from following me straight to her yesterday. Hats off to community policing. It's the first cop car that ever did me any good.

I look around the side of the apartment. I'm pretty sure which car the two guys who threatened me are in, meaning they didn't intend to kill me, just to leave the taste of death in my mouth so I'd know what I was up against: people who are better at this than I am.

I drop down behind the bushes that surround the building, then sprint to the side of the house next door. I don't hear a car start or see one following when I shoot around the corner.

I cut through alleys and behind buildings to get to my junker. It's parked far enough from my apartment that they can't see it from where they're sitting—but only just barely. Starting it up, it feels as if I'm pushing the button on a detonator. I drive without headlights, park between a couple of bigger cars in a lot a few blocks from her place. The only person who could have followed me would be an invisible guy with night-vision goggles and a jetpack. I close the car door so quietly, it's hard to differentiate the sound from the ambient night noises—crickets, branches, muted traffic.

I approach carefully, making sure there's nothing strange, no one watching the street or watching me. She's good to go in sweats, toting a grocery bag full of food and the ubiquitous daypack. She leans up to kiss me.

"We could just stay here and have a picnic, say, on the table," she says.

I look around the garage she lives in. I can come back sometime after and wash it down, but what's the point? You can't get rid of all traces. If anyone figures out what happened, I'll be too busy exporting whatever you export from Madagascar, holed up in a tropical paradise fighting off poisonous insects, to care.

I tap her on the butt. "Let's go."

She finds this extremely annoying. She says, "Could you *please* not go all master-of-the-universe on me?" She does half an eye roll. "That's what my friend says you are, too."

"It was an accident. Sorry." And then, damn, "You just talked to your friend about me?"

"Oh no!" This is her at her most tender. "Not about what happened to you. I would *never* tell anyone. Please trust me."

Frankly, how bad it was with her running her fingertip along the scars, how naked I was, how much I wanted her to shut up, how important it seemed, how sorry she was—now it's like it was nothing.

"I'm not the most trusting guy."

Her face falls. I know I have to fix this fast, but all I have room for in my brain is getting her out of here and processing that she's been talking about me, that when she goes even more missing than she is right now, somebody out there will know God knows what about me. At some point, someone—Olivia most likely—is going to put two and two together and get four, and this won't be good for me.

I just want to get her out of here and into my car before we have company.

We're leaving now, and we're leaving fast.

55

Cat

It's stars. And it's the middle of the night. And it's romantic.

The affection-binging camel is a glutton for this stuff.

Plus, how bad could one more night be?

The gym socks slither down my ankles.

J says, "Wait here. I'll get the car."

"I think I can manage to walk two blocks without breaking."

He grins the hot grin. "Said the agoraphobic wreck."

Really? He tells me his secrets. He comes apart. I stick him back together, plus pie and a lot of making out. But now it's three thirty in the morning, and he isn't being very nice.

"I never said I was a *wreck*."

"You came very close."

"Not that close."

He seems nervous, looking around my room, pulling the curtains over the bed closed tighter. Switching off lights.

"If you're looking for evidence of all my other boyfriends, I had a half hour to hide everything." Exactly one half hour. J is punctual.

"Can we go?"

"*You* invited *me*. Aren't you supposed to be all happy I'm coming?"

He puts his arm around me. It's so rigid that stretched out, it could be a battering ram. Which makes me feel kind of secure. I might need a battering ram.

But he was so smiley before. After we changed the subject. After we buried the whole conversation about his horrible dad in three boxes' worth of baked blueberries and lightly whipped cream. He ate seconds. He had a purple tongue from all the berries.

God, I don't want to leave him. Have to. Don't want to.

"Can we *please* go?" he says. He takes the grocery bag and drags me out the door.

All the way to the car, he's bent over me like a live raincoat with a hood. My head is under his chin for part of the walk, and then he's moving from one side of me to the other on the sidewalk, like he can't make up his mind.

I say, "You're acting kind of strange."

He says, "Hurry up."

We drive through student housing, south of the college, and then pull onto the freeway. Then off. Then on again.

I say, "Do you even know where we're going?"

"It's a surprise."

Then it occurs to me that maybe this is the big seduction scene.

A car that smells like peanut butter sandwiches so isn't what I had in mind.

He reaches behind my head and weaves his fingers through my hair. "We could be in the mountains in two hours. It'll be awesome."

Except he's changed directions twice.

I say, "Are you all right? Listen, if you'd rather go to a motel instead of the mountains, I might be open to it."

One last slight fling.

Why not?

I know why not, but I halfway don't care.

"You *might* be?" he says. "I have to keep outwitting you to hang on to my virtue."

"Stop teasing me."

"I'm sorry." He sounds kind of shocked, actually. "You want to go to a motel with me?"

Shock is not what I was after. "That might not mean what you think it means. You know, fool around a little. Not conceive your first-born child. Sack out. Beats going into a ditch when the driver falls asleep."

"So fooling around with me . . . or whatever . . . would be a step up from being in a car wreck?"

"Possibly two steps. Even three." I have no idea what I'm doing to freak him out, but he's driving like a crazy person. Perfect speed limit, checking his rearview constantly. First we were pointed south, then west, and now we're pointed toward the mountains.

I say, "We could park and eat sandwiches. We could wait a while. Maybe you'll feel better."

"Wait for what?" He's shouting at me.

"Don't yell at me! It's not like I'm questioning your manhood. Do you want me to drive?"

He shouts, "I'm fine!" Looking straight ahead, he says, "I need to talk to you. Let's get out of here."

We need to talk??? This is *so* not what I had in mind.

"Just so you know, you can't break up with people after you drive them two hours from home. It's bad form. If that's what this is." I'm rethinking my stealth breakup by disappearance. If this is what breaking up with him feels like.

"How can we break up if we were never together?"

This feels like a blow to the head until I remember I'm the one who said we weren't together in the first, second, and third place.

"Are you teasing me?" I say. "Because I *thought* all was forgiven. Only *then* you call me at three in the morning because you're pissed off and you want a sandwich."

"Are you angry? You sound angry."

I snap, "I'm not angry!"

"Because if you're angry that I didn't spill my guts about how it felt to have a guy three times my size come at me with a belt buckle, get used to being angry."

"*You're* the one who's angry. And I wasn't pressuring you to spill anything. When you said you couldn't talk about it, I respected that."

J accelerates around a curve so fast, I'm afraid we're going to spin out.

I try again. I touch his arm. "I hate what happened to you. And"—giant leap—"I understand. I do. I get what it's like to have somebody you lean on turn on you. I get not being able to talk about it."

He tightens his grip on my hair. "Why, did somebody turn on you?"

"I can't talk about it."

He pulls his hand out of my hair. "That's not funny." Scary voice I do not want to hear again. Ever.

"You so don't get me! I wasn't mocking you! Stop growling at me!"

How could he think I'd tease him over something like that? I was being *honest*. We're miles from civilization. We've turned off the main road and we're heading into the national forest. Soon we'll be fighting on hairpin turns. In mountains. Narrow roads, sheer drops. Fighting.

I'm from Northeast Ohio. It's flat from crushing sheets of glacial ice. Taking the Greyhound bus across the Rockies was a nightmare. Being scared that you're about to crash through a guardrail because the driver is yelling at you isn't romantic.

"I want to go home."

He doesn't say anything, just presses down on the accelerator.

"Turn the car around! I want to go home!"

He puts his hand on my hand. I don't want it there. He says, "I'm sorry. Let's go make up somewhere, okay? This is stupid. If I floor it, we'll be there for sunrise."

"Don't floor it! Are you insane? And where will we be, exactly?"

"I planned this. This will be special."

"Not that special! The first time we do it—*if* we ever do it—it won't be make-up sex. Don't even bother."

"We have to talk. Not about that."

"Talk to me *now*."

"Wait until we get there."

"Don't order me around!"

"Don't start!"

It's like this all the way up into the mountains until we're at the ridge of wherever we are—just us and the coyotes and whatever else they have around here that bites.

56

Jack

After three hours of acting like an asshole because, apparently, it's my nature, I'm driving along with no idea of where I should take her. I had it planned out. I knew the terrain. Now all I know is I can't go back there because I already led the lowlifes who followed me west from Yucca Valley Correctional to what was supposed to be the crime scene.

Where we go now is anyone's guess, or, if I'm lucky, nobody's guess.

Normally, I'm good under pressure. But this is life-and-death and, right now, I wish I had a sliver of my father's lethal grace.

I pull off onto a gravel fire trail until the car is out of sight of the main road.

She looks so upset, I start to stroke her hair, but she pulls away. She says, "You've been yelling at me all the way here. You have to say sorry like you mean it before you start making out with me."

"I was patting your head!"

"I'm not your cocker spaniel!"

"Do you have a compulsion to turn things to crap?"

"No wonder your ex is your ex!"

She storms out of the car and runs into the unfamiliar woods, kicking the door shut behind her. It's first light, and she's running toward the rising sun. I squint, but I can barely see her.

I'm so pissed at her. I shout, "Wait up!"

She shouts back at me, "How could I be with such a jerk?"

I go running after her. This isn't the way this was supposed to go down. I reach out—I'm about to grab her arm—but I wasn't supposed to be overpowering her. There wasn't supposed to be physical force and certainly not me yanking her arm out of its socket.

I take her hand instead, my fingers clamped like the jaws of a wrench.

"Don't make me chase you down! Crap, Nicolette, I get that you—"

Nicolette?

What have I done?

Her hand twists out of my hand. I go for her wrist as she breaks away from me. A sharp kick to my ankle, and she catapults off me. There's a yell like the cry before you break a board in half in karate, that *kiai*, and she's gone. She's racing deeper into the woods, and I'm running after her.

Every time my ankle comes down anything but straight on, where the terrain is uneven—every stride—I get a thrusting blade of pain. I want to kick her back. Then I have this feeling-like-shit moment because what kind of person wants to kick a girl who's a foot shorter than he is?

And then the deeper thrust of realization: what I was supposed to be doing to her went far beyond kicking her. And the fact that I'm chasing her through this desiccated landscape with a gun in my hand doesn't look good for me. But it doesn't seem as if she's going to stop long enough for me to tell her that the gun was in case the guys who decked me followed us. She's not going to slow down long enough for me to say it's in my hand because I can't even walk fast with it stuck in the back of my jeans, and I couldn't exactly drop in on her wearing a holster for her to discover while making out.

The girl can run. It's the damned Cotter's Mill Unified High School track team. Who knew she could sprint like this? When I catch sight of her, she's bouncing off things like she grew up getting chased through the wilderness. She makes it over rocks and outcroppings of thistly bushes like Bambi—not Bambi in the headlights but surefooted Bambi.

She's running toward the precipice, toward the cliffside of the narrow stretch of woods between the road and oblivion. When she realizes, she dodges back into the woods.

I'm waving this gun in front of me like a fool, like I was planning to shoot someone with it. This is something I'm not going to do.

I start to tuck it back into my waistband, not paying enough attention. I go down, the thing in my outstretched hand, slamming a rock as I fall, and the thing fires. I fire it, and then my hand closes on nothing. I fire a gun, and I'm so startled, I don't even hang on to it, don't even brace my fall. I hear the thwack of my head against a tree trunk before I even feel it. My hands go to my head, without thinking, which you can't do when there's a gun involved. You can't stop thinking ever (*think, Jack*) but especially not then.

I hear my head cracking open against the tree, and the gunshot, and myself saying, "Shit!" all at once, although they couldn't have happened at once.

My forehead is wet, I'm bleeding from the temple, wet fingers, and Nicolette has the gun.

She's crouched in a good position, a two-handed stance, the gun in her right hand, right arm braced with the left, not crying, not shaking, not in any way weak or hesitant or anything you'd want a girl with a gun on you to be.

"Did you shoot me?"

"Are you serious?" Her voice is vibrating with indignation. "You bumped your head when you ran into a bush. It's a boo-boo. When I shoot you, you'll need more than a Band-Aid."

Then she lowers herself onto a rock, not losing her aim for a second.

"It's not what you think. Cat, it's not. Put down the gun."

"Nicolette," she says. "My name is Nicolette Holland. But you already knew that."

She doesn't put the gun down.

57

Nicolette

His name isn't J.

And he isn't my boyfriend or my semi-boyfriend or my friend.

He's the angel of death. Maybe not death in general. Just *my* death. The opposite of my guardian angel.

The opposite of what I thought.

I'm staring at his face across his gun. I have to get this right the first time, because the kickback is going to throw me off. Also, the sight of him, his head coming apart in pieces like a clay pigeon, could be bad. I know it won't happen like that, but I imagine his face breaking apart like a porcelain plate you drop on a tile floor.

This doesn't upset me as much as it should.

Maybe answering the Sunday School question of whether, if it was either you or this other person you were deeply into until five minutes ago, you'd kill the other person.

It isn't down to him or me yet, but I'll shoot before it gets there.

So, yes.

I don't want him looking at me like this.

Scared out of his mind but planning something.

I don't want him to see my face.

I mean, I want him to see how much I want to kill him, but I don't want him to think I'm weak because I haven't pulled the trigger yet. I want him in the dark.

My whole life is turning into a can-you-top-this fest of getting as angry as I thought I could possibly be. And then topping it.

This angry.

No, *this angry*.

No, *THIS ANGRY*.

I got therapy for this a long time ago, where the point was to figure out I wasn't actually angry. No, Nicolette, you're actually *sad*. Unbearably sad. Your mom is gone, and you're left with this sweet Cuban stepfather you hardly even know.

But face it, as unbearably *sad* as I am now that my freaking boyfriend wanted to take me to see a romantic sunrise where he was going to freaking shoot me, the main thing is anger. Righteous anger.

Even if I deserved everything he planned to do to me, it wasn't supposed to be *him*.

I'm this angry, and I'm not going down.

He is. Whoever he is.

I order him to close his eyes.

He just keeps watching me.

"Close your eyes!"

He says, "I can explain."

I say, *"Shut the fuck up!"*

58

Jack

I shut the fuck up because when the person with the gun tells you to do that, you do. We sit there as the sun gets hotter and starts to fry me, long enough for me to sweat through my flannel shirt, just this side of forever. The gun is trained on me. She doesn't look away from me for a second, the whole time glaring at me.

And I'm not my father's son as much as I was afraid I was because it's taking a lot of effort not to piss myself.

I need to be thinking about ways out of here as I tense and untense my muscles, preparing to flee or lunge. I ought to be calculating what to do tonight—if I last that long—when it's so dark, she can't see me unless she comes so close that I can overpower her. But I'm just staring at her staring at me.

I can't tell if she's talking herself into shooting me or out of it—or if I'm already dead. I wonder if the gun got messed up bouncing across the rock, and if she knows how to shoot it. But I look at her stance, the way she's crouched, the way she's got the gun braced, and I know she knows what she's doing.

She says, "Eyes closed!" She sounds ferocious.

"What?"

"You heard me. Close them!"

I do, but not completely—I can still see a sliver of light and underbrush.

She says, "Keep your hands on your head!"

I sit there, frozen, not wanting to spook her. I keep trying to look at her through the slit between my eyelids, remembering the part of the equation I'd rather not remember—Connie Marino with her throat cut.

I make an inventory of the parts of my body that don't hurt, in case I need them later: my left leg, my hands, my right arm up to the elbow.

She says, "How were you planning to do it?"

"Do what?"

"Shoot me? Push me over the edge? Shoot me and then push me over the edge?"

"I wasn't."

"Were you going to rape me first?"

"You think I'd *rape* you?" I rub my left shoulder, which is starting to throb.

"Keep your hands on your head! Just if you value them."

"You're going to shoot up my hands?" I can't stop marveling at the strangeness of this conversation, how fast everything tanked.

"I grew up in Cotter's Mill, Ohio, asshat. I know the dates of hunting season. I can shoot a Canada goose out of the sky and gut it."

"Really?" I don't know why I'm even asking. Skills with a knife is one talent I've always known she had. I just didn't know how she acquired it.

She does one of her little sighs. "How hard could it be to gut a goose? I've watched enough times." She's using that tone she gets when she's admitting to something. How cute I thought it was—not so cute now. "Here's the thing, J, or whatever your name is. I can shoot up any part of you I feel like shooting up. I have a pretty good idea of where I'll start."

I don't like where I think she's looking. "Cat—"

"Nicolette. And I could blow the slider off your zipper at twenty-five yards."

The fact that she says twenty-five yards, not some other number, but exactly twenty-five, makes her a target shooter. Shit. I've been disarmed by a cute, cheerleading target shooter. Shit, shit, shit.

"I didn't mean to insult you. Sorry. I didn't realize you were— I'm sorry."

"Do you think I care how sorry you are?" she shouts, rising, approaching. I'm so fucked. "Do you think I believe *anything* you say? All I care about is how to get you tied up in the car without taking this gun off you so I can turn you in."

"Please don't do that."

"Why not?" she shouts. "Do the police already know about you? Am I just one in a string of girls you hooked up with and threw off cliffs?"

My head hurts, my shoulder hurts, and I think I'm a lot closer to getting shot than I was five minutes ago.

She screams, "Answer me!"

"No! Cat. And I swear on my father's grave, there was a change of plan. I was trying to save you."

"I don't believe you! And *don't* call me Cat."

"Okay. I don't see why you *should* believe me. But the hitch with turning me in is you'll have to turn yourself in." There's silence from the armed girl. "Think about it. Even if you get off in the end, do you want to spend the next decade on death row in Ohio?"

In a gritty voice, she says, "Open your eyes."

She's just a couple of yards away now, still aiming at me, and even if her reflexes were below average, if I took a run at her, I'd have a hole in my gut.

"What do you think you know?" she says.

Two roads diverged in a yellow wood. I tell her the truth, which is short and pretty simple, or I draw it out all day until it's dark and I can take her: maybe.

I say, "Connie Marino." She's stone-faced. "I know what you did to her, how you stabbed her." I sound like a bad guy on TV, like the bozos in my apartment, like the guy who pulls you out of the story because he needs acting lessons. I try again, "She shouldn't be dead."

"Somebody told you I *stabbed* someone?"

"Shit. Do you even know who Connie Marino is?"

Her face is screaming before anything comes out of her mouth. "I don't know who *you* are!" She aims down at me. "And I didn't stab anybody! So I won't be on death row anytime soon." She sighs. "Unless I shoot you."

Her arms look so muscular from this angle, and so at ease with that gun. She probably could take down a duck in flight. Or bag a guy.

My gut is a rock, rolling into my throat, defying gravity and my will.

She doesn't have a clue. I've brought the wrong girl to ground.

Or maybe the point was for me to take out an innocent, know-nothing girl, hiding for reasons I might never know if she takes me out before I ask her.

"I'm going to throw up. Don't shoot me." I barely finish because I'm puking into a bush, gagging and wiping my mouth, heaving some more. I'm going to be a vomit-crusted carcass, devoured by cougars and maggots in the Sierras.

"You must think I'm an idiot," she says. "You find me, you con me, and I just *leap* into your car. *Oh, J, I've never felt this way before. Oh, J, do you want to kill me now or later?*"

"It wasn't like that. I swear."

"On the imaginary grave of your undead dad?"

"I'm going to toss you my phone, all right? Google him."

"You think I'm going to let you pitch your phone at my head? I'm going to take my eyes off you to play Candy Crush? You must think I'm so stupid. *Oh, J, why don't I take off my bra so you can strangle me with it?*"

"Please, baby, don't—"

"I'm *not* your baby! Put your hands back on your head. What kind of moron gets turned on by a guy who's there to kill her? I don't exactly trust my instincts right now. I have such bad impulse control." She sighs. "Which is *not* great for you."

Here we have a girl who would tear my heart out with her bare hands if she could do it without giving up her weapon.

"I'm sorry."

She just glares. "So what should I call you?"

"Asshat works."

"I mean it! What's your name? And when I look in your wallet, that better be your name."

"Jack. It's in the pocket of my rucksack. My license. The one that's in my wallet says I'm twenty-one, and it says 'Gerhard Rheingold.'"

"*Ger*hard *Rheingold*?"

"My friend's older brother is Gerhard, all right? My name is Jack."

She's resting her hands on a rock, aiming low. "J wasn't very imaginative."

"I'm not that good at this." This isn't what I'd intended to say, but once it's out there, it sounds true. "I started to say 'Jack,' and I was stuck with the *J* sound. Remember in the park?"

She hisses, "I remember Every. Single. Second. I thought you were the one good thing in what you were *trying* to turn into my very short life."

There's a silence, and then in a flat voice she says, "How much was he paying you, anyway? What was I worth dead?"

"It wasn't for money. I have a shit ton of money from the not-undead dad."

"*What did he pay you?* Or is this your hobby? Hunting girls for fun because you're so rich and macho?"

"My name is Jack Manx. My dad was Art Manx. Is this ringing any bells?"

"I don't care who your dad is. I *hate* you!"

"Will you let me explain? I have a brother in prison in Nevada, okay? He's been locked up off and on since he was fourteen. He's a bad guy."

"You're the *good* guy?"

We've come a long way from her running her finger along the scar and getting me—me telling her things I've never told anybody else—to this. It occurs to me that I don't want her to hate me, and not just because she has the gun. "My brother, he said..." How do I even say this to her? "He told me you cut somebody's throat. And you knew some things this thug Karl Yeager didn't want you walking around knowing."

Her face keeps vacillating between skepticism and pure horror. "So you're *attracted* to girls who kill people and know things about thugs? I'm so not buying this."

"But you didn't do it."

"You didn't know that! Maybe I'm a really good actress and a total liar. Maybe I . . . you know . . . *cut her throat*, and now I'm going to cut *your* throat. Ha!"

Damn fucking Don.

"I don't know what's wrong with me. My brother said you did, and some bad things were going to happen if I didn't find you first." Finally, her hand is shaking. "But I wasn't going to do it! I was starting to tell you so we could fake it. People would think you were dead. You could get away."

"There are no *people*." She's screaming and holding the gun out with rigid arms, waving it at me. "The only person I have to worry about is *you*."

"*Nicolette, listen to me.* Two guys came to my apartment last night. Do you see the side of my neck? I'm going to pull down on my shirt, don't freak—"

"Don't patronize me!"

"That's why it had to be tonight."

"Save your story with your imaginary bad guys! How much am I worth to Steve dead?"

"Who's Steve?"

"Steve! The guy who hired you. The guy I thought was my *dad*." Her voice cracks on this final syllable.

I figure if I try to put my arm around her, she'll misinterpret, and I'll end up dead. I say, "Steve is Esteban Mendes?"

She nods, miserable and ferocious.

"You think Esteban Mendes wants you dead? That makes no sense."

This is when she hits me on the head.

59

Nicolette

The second I hit him, I know I shouldn't have.

I mean, I'm armed, and he's already on the ground. A gash in his forehead. Blood on his face. I'm so freaking angry at him, I want to kill him.

So I bash him on the head?

Not hard enough to put him out of his misery, either.

Just enough force to pause the conversation.

Not that it was a totally irrational act, even if it had *terrible impulse control* written all over it. Every second he was woozy was a second I didn't have to worry about him jumping up and tackling me.

He was a lot more manageable woozy.

I got him to fork over the car keys and walked him,

half-staggering, to the car. I told him to climb, semiconscious, into the trunk. I left it all the way open. So if anyone says I wanted him dead, I didn't. Or I would have let him asphyxiate in there like those poor pet dogs whose owners leave them in cars in shopping mall parking lots in the summer. Whose owners I actually *do* want dead.

I sit down under a tree so dried out that it barely provides shade, and I wait for him to come to.

I drink a can of warmed-over Coca-Cola I packed with the peanut butter sandwiches. I come close to pouring in the rum I brought that J or Gerhard or Jack or whoever he is carried back from South Dakota or wherever he really went.

But I don't.

I'm in the stay-alert, don't-get-drunk, don't-lose-control, don't-die track.

I'm on the numb, not-feeling-much-of-anything side. A good thing, because I'm in an isolated part of a forest I don't know how to find my way out of. Although aiming the car downhill would probably work.

I'm with the guy who was supposed to throw me off a cliff.

60

Jack

I'm in the driver's seat, the gun at the base of my skull. My head feels as if a grenade just burst between my ears.

"The only reason you're not closed in the trunk is I'm afraid you'd figure out how to trip the latch. But I could change my mind," she says.

I hope she realizes that, on a road like this, if I die driving, she dies.

I start the car and shift into gear.

She pounds on the back of my seat. "That's too jerky!"

"Sorry, there's a gun pointed at my head."

"Whose idea was it to bring a freaking .45 on our big romantic getaway?" Christ, she knows the caliber of it. She probably knows how to disassemble it blindfolded. "If you hadn't been such a jerk all the way up here, I would have thought this was your big romantic move. Ha!"

I say, "My big romantic move was going to be to save your life."

A minivan comes barreling around a curve, straddling the center line. I swerve onto the narrow shoulder between the road and the sheer drop and hear Nicolette bump against the inside of the rear door. She yells, "Don't do that!"

"Did you want a head-on?"

"Do you want to live?"

I'm trying to control my breathing, the thin line between hyperventilation and uncontrollable shaking. "I was going to fake your death—that was the plan. I was going to tell my slime brother it was done and take him a trophy, and you were going to do a better job of hiding. Or maybe"—the embarrassing component of all this, but what the hell—"if you wanted, I was going to go with you."

Nicolette's ability to remain withering under stress is stellar. "Tell me why I believe this again?"

"Because if I wanted to kill you, why aren't you killed?"

She doesn't even pause to think. "Because you're incompetent? Have you ever even shot a moving target? And you didn't want to get caught."

"Right. I spend all this time hanging out with you, shed cells all over your apartment, and make a bunch of phone calls from California. I wrote the textbook on how not to get caught."

More silence.

I say, "Why are you running?"

"I thought you already knew why. Because I stuck a knife in someone."

"That someone was buried a quarter of a mile from your house. Her name was Connie."

This is when she starts to cry again. She's crying so hard, I want to pull over and hold her. But more than that, I want her finger off the trigger of Don's gun.

61

Nicolette

I tell him how it was sunset, and then it was dark.

Voices and then nothing.

I tell him how I was supposed to stay in my room, but Gertie wasn't there.

I whistle for her, but she doesn't come.

The screen door is banging in the wind.

Downstairs, the lights are out, Steve's office dark.

I call Steve's name. Nothing.

We live in a house on the edge of the woods, the yard running down to Green Lake on one side, merging with forest on the other. Coyotes could eat Gertie if she got outside by herself. An owl could.

I whistle for her again, but there's still nothing. Just wind and the slap of branches against the roof, creaking under their own weight, shedding pine needles like raindrops.

It's already the worst day ever. I'm stuck in my room. I'm not losing my dog.

I tell him how I headed down toward the lake, toward the shed where Gertie likes to go poking around, but she's not there.

Behind the shed, I see a beam of light by the trail that winds past the edge of our property to the lake. I trot toward it along the lakeshore and between the trees. Like a moth so stupid that her whole species is about to be wiped out by survival of the fittest.

The moth that spreads her white wings against the porch light and fries.

The girl who follows a beam of light into the woods.

There is a body in the woods, wrapped in a yellow blanket. The arm, the hand, the chipped blue nail polish. Two men dragging her along, Steve illuminating their way with a flashlight.

Disbelief.

All the eight-by-twelve glossies of father-daughter dances, the years of posing with the fireplace stockings for Christmas cards, the scrapbooks that jump from holiday to holiday, are sucked through a shredder.

The shovel is raised higher when they see me. Steve's shouting. I'm frozen. The blow to the head. My fingers pressed around the handle of the knife they toss into the grave.

My fingerprints buried with the dead blue fingernails.

Darkness. The wind. The sound of water lapping at the edge of Green Lake.

"We have to get rid of her."

Steve says, "Not to worry. It's done."

I'm on my back in the shed. Smelling fertilizer. My head resting against the metal prongs of a rake, hips and shoulders hurting as if I'd been dropped from a height in this exact position. Pain behind my eyes that's almost worse than seeing what I saw.

Almost.

"You're going to handle this?"

Steve says, "We've been doing business for a long time. I'll do what has to be done. It's taken care of. Go!"

"You're sure? It's your kid."

Steve says, "It's not my kid. It never was my kid. Go! Maybe she was cute when she was eight, but she turned herself into a useless whore. Some mornings, I can't stand to look at her. Believe me, it's nothing."

I'm the it.

The it that's not his kid.

The it that's done, the useless whore, the it that's taken care of.

The it that has to be killed.

"She's out cold. I'll walk you to your car."

The voices fade into the wind.

I tell him I know what Steve does for a living. I do.

I file things for him in the home office.

I'm not an idiot. I know he does taxes for people named Yeager. People who do a whole lot of business in Colombia. People who, when you google them, you figure out they didn't actually make that much money importing extra virgin olive oil and exporting scrap metal because *there isn't that much olive oil or scrap metal on earth.*

But I thought he loved me.

I thought I was his little girl. Like his daughter. His kid.

I thought he'd do anything for me.

Not to me.

I say how I rolled onto my side in the shed, crouched, stood, squeezed out under the board loosened by years of hide-and-seek, and took off along the shore.

Hid in a tree house.

Climbed onto a truck.

62

Jack

I thought things were bad, but they're worse than I thought. I was supposed to kill a *witness*—not a killer, but the witness to the killing. She knows squat about Karl Yeager's business.

Does Don know? *"She might know things,"* he said. Yes, he knew, and yes, I'm stupid. Don winds me up, gets to me with some story about Karl Yeager—whose name is enough to make people shit their pants—and once he's got me good and scared, he sends me off to kill an innocent as ordered by Esteban Mendes, a stepfather who eats his young. And being Don, he throws our mom into the mix for good measure. Or Mendes does.

For Nicolette, it's even worse. Her *dad* is gunning for her? Her dad is the top of a pyramid, and Don's in the ooze at the bottom,

calling the shots for his dupe brother: me. I am the murder technician for Esteban Mendes.

"Why didn't you walk into a police station?"

She says, "Why didn't *you*?"

"The truth—because if Karl Yeager says your family is dead if
you don't do him a favor . . . Come on, you looked him up. . . ."

The truth is, I rejected the possibility of telling the FBI, the
Nevada police, and the fire department that didn't investigate
obvious arson at the outset. Telling didn't figure into the equation when Don was handing me my marching orders, or when I
was driving home, or when my house had smoke pouring out of it,
my mother regaling me with the fairy tale about the spontaneous
combustion of smoke detector batteries.

Telling anyone was too risky, too messy, too counterproduc-
tive, a death sentence . . . for *me*, not for Nicolette.

No, I went off to solve the fucking problem, to find Nicolette.
And if the whole point was to warn her, why didn't I?

Because I'm Jack Manx.

The truth is tearing at me like a detonated land mine. I'm the
guy who didn't consider the normal possibilities because the normal course of action wasn't even a road in my twisted yellow wood.
And this, Mr. Berger, proves that taking the *much* less traveled road
can be a bad thing.

I say, "They would have believed you."

She kicks the back of my seat. "Blame *me*, why don't you?"

Turns out, there are five police officers in Cotter's Mill, Ohio, and four of them shoot geese with Mendes—geese, and maybe sitting ducks.

My dad avoided police, crossed the street, drove in the other direction. But Cotter's Mill is a backwater town in Ohio, and if she believes Mendes owns the police department, what do I know? You could fill Lake Tahoe with the nothing I know. They might not hurt a kid outright, but how normal would it be for police to return a runaway girl to her dear old dad? Ignore her wild stories? Scoop her into the squad car and drop her off at home?

"Is that good enough?" she spits at me from the backseat. "Because maybe it was binge watching *In Plain Sight* on TV, where every single protected witness gets shot at. Maybe telling the police my fingerprints were on the knife because someone else put them there seemed like a bad idea."

"Baby—"

"I'm not your baby, J. Jack. Whoever."

"Do you want to come in the front seat?"

"Why? So you can grab the gun?"

I take a deep breath and blow the air out through my mouth. "The only reason I want the gun is so you don't shoot me with it."

We drive in silence until we're almost all the way out of the foothills, driving west toward the coast, back to civilization.

I switch on the radio.

"Turn it off."

Then she says, "You swear you thought it was Yeager sending you out after me? *Swear* no one said one word to you about Steve."

"That's how it happened. Don said Mendes had nothing to do with it. He said it was Yeager. He knew hearing 'Yeager' would scare me. And it made sense it was him."

What doesn't make sense is that I went along with it.

I hear her fingernails drumming on something hard—the seat belt buckle, I hope. Then she says, "God, you believe anything."

I wish I could see her face. She's probably sorry I ever came to.

I say, "You're lucky it's not Yeager. Once he starts, he won't stop until he's dead—or you are. He's relentless. His brother's wife divorces his brother, she marries a dentist, his brother remarries, everybody's happy. Three years later, she disappears. She's gone. She's never heard from again."

She says, "Stop! I get you thought it was Yeager."

"That whole Yeager clan is a bunch of rabid pit bulls."

"I get it! All Yeagers suck. Fine."

And then there's absolute silence. This goes on for miles as we swing through what would be farm country if there were water. The headache she gave me when she clobbered me could be classified as blinding if I didn't have to see well enough to drive.

I whisper, "Are you asleep?"

"You wish."

After a long time, Nicolette says, "You're in deep shit, aren't you?"

"Yeah." When I think about the deep shit I'm in—beyond Don, beyond my mother, beyond the guys in my apartment and whoever set our laundry room at home on fire—I can't believe I let this happen.

I'm Art Manx's kid. Law enforcement has preconceived notions about me. They find reason to search my trunk when I drive, stone sober, through a sobriety checkpoint off the Strip. And now Nicolette can tell them how I chased her with a loaded gun. No one will believe that I was planning to convince her to come with me to Guyana or some other unspecified location I never revealed to her before she had a gun on me.

I say, "More like quicksand. Unless you want to run away with me."

Nicolette laughs, but not her fun laugh. "Sure. That's definitely on. Argentina. As if that was a thing."

"It would save us both a lot of grief. There's cash in the trunk."

"You're *so* full of yourself! I already tried disappearing—you think you'd be so much better at it? I'm tired of disappearing. I'm done."

I say, "What's your alternative? You hand me over to the police and go back to being a target? I was never going to hurt you."

"Liar! You *know* you had a plan!"

"My plan was to stage it. We'd get to the crest, and I'd explain to you."

"At gunpoint?"

"The plan was for you to believe me. Give me a bloody shoe for Don. And then we could take off."

"What if I didn't want to take off with you?"

Admittedly, I didn't have that part of the equation mapped out. "I'd give you cash? You could hide better with cash, admit it."

"So I was going to leave with your money. What were you

going to do? Like, if somebody checked to see if you actually killed me."

"I don't know!" This is the frustrating, embarrassing truth. "Rat out Don? Kill my mom?"

"*Kill* your—"

"It's a figure of speech. When I rat out Don, it's going to break her heart."

"Your brother said it was her or me?"

"And me. There was an element of self-interest."

"If you think you can charm me by being slightly honest, you can't."

I want to charm her, but I don't know how.

I really am fucked.

63

Nicolette

Everything's different from what I thought. I was hiding from the wrong thing. I had the wrong plan.

This is where I make a better plan.

The plan where I stop paying for things I mostly didn't even do, and everybody else who did terrible things starts paying up.

Big time.

Jack is lucky.

All he has to do is help me out, and maybe I'll let him out of this. Maybe? Who am I kidding? I will. All I can think about is whether I gave him a concussion, and how bad that is, and if I should make him drive us to an urgent care center somewhere in this burned-out brown landscape so a doctor can check him out.

I wish he'd say something. Such as apologizing more. But

he's just driving along like a law-abiding maniac at thirty-five miles per hour.

I just want to hurry up and get out of here.

At least Ohio is green. This place looks like it just had a forest fire. Jack says people consider this golden. I consider it a wasteland that I'm leaving.

I hate the West.

I like Ohio. I liked my life. I want it back.

I'm done with rolling with the punches.

Finished.

Despite all the credit that you get for rolling.

How resilient you are.

How you land on your feet.

How you're slightly screwed up and require counseling and have no judgment whatsoever, but you're rolling with those punches. Good girl. Steal nail polish and roll, roll, roll.

I'm tired of going along with every damn thing with slight, girly rebellion that doesn't actually change anything. Just reminds you that you're a private with no say in Fate's army.

So, Nicky, we're moving to Ohio where I'm marrying this man you've never even met named Steeeeve, and we're going to be soooo happy. Fine.

So, Nicky, she's gone, she's looking down on you from heaven, and here's this tooootally nice guy you've known for six months, Steve, and he's going to be your dad. Don't look back. Look forward. Fine.

So, Nicky, smile or nobody will like you. Be fun, only not so fun you're reckless, not so reckless you worry your nice dad, and if he's going to be that worried, sneak out. Fine.

So, Nicky, you need a 3.3 or Steve will be pissed and you won't get into college with Olivia and everyone will think you're an idiot and you won't get a smart boyfriend. Fine.

Only don't get too upset when your smart boyfriend, Connor, that you love and adore, is sleeping with every other cute girl with a 3.3 in Cotter's Mill because, hey, you're only kids.

Don't be so upset you decide to get even with him with the next guy.

Only the next random guy you think is your new boy-friend is so not your boyfriend. Big U of M college guy and his stupid muscle car and his stupid SOG SEAL knife he shows off all the time. You think the sun rises over his left shoulder, but he's only standing there to eclipse the light. You're the idiot who doesn't get that hooking up with the devil is bad news. Until it's too late.

So, Nicky, the people you love and adore want to kill you. Didn't see that one coming, did you?

You should have, but you didn't.

You'd better hit the road and turn into someone who won't even need that 3.3 to go to college on the Internet because she has to hide for the rest of her life. Fine.

So, Nicky, you can't go back to looking like yourself or

being yourself, and you can't get your life back. Ever. Fine.

So, Nicky, this J, who acts like he loves and adores you even though you're not petite and cute and the purest, funnest girl on the cheerleading squad anymore, well, he's actually planning to kill you.

Not freaking fine.

I am so tired of rolling.

I am so *punching.*

I liked you, Jack. I really liked you, and I get what happened to you. Plus, it's slightly a relief that even Boy Scouts with excellent judgment can screw up this royally. I kind of believe you weren't going to off me because even a total incompetent already would have.

So I mostly forgive you.

But really?

None of this is fine. I'm Nicolette Holland, not Bean, not Cat Davis, Kelly Hill, Kaylie Mills, Cathy, Cath, Catherine— I'm *Nick.*

I'm punching and not rolling.

And as for anyone who's coming after me?

Watch out.

64

Jack

I keep driving.

I want to talk to her more than I've ever wanted to talk to anyone, but she's got Don's Glock. It would be stupid to get her riled.

Whatever she does to me, I have it coming.

It's good the car's a five-speed, and I have to pay enough attention to shift.

I say, "Nicolette, listen, we should go to the police. You can tell them whatever you want. No one's going to think you hurt Connie. Just tell them what happened. I don't know how else to keep you safe."

"*You* thought I hurt Connie, and you were into me. You *were* into me right?"

"Yes!"

"Fine, so now you're going to keep me safe. You and your brother's gun."

For a second, this gun feels like the hard metal center of the universe. This gun—which I should have left in my mother's garage, in its box on a shelf behind a bunch of engine parts for Don's shitmobile—is what defines me and Nicolette and danger and safety.

I want to grab it from her and throw it out the window; unload it, wipe it clean, and drop it through the grate on a storm drain; chuck it into a Dumpster with the chamois it was wrapped in.

I say, "How am I going to do that? I'm the dupe who let Yeager's guys follow me to El Molino. I mean, your dad's guys. Whoever they were, they knew what they were doing. I don't think waving a gun at them is going to get them to stop."

"Just drive." Then she says, "Plus, you evaded them. You grabbed me, and we got away. You didn't totally blow this."

Without thinking, when we finally get to a town with a couple of gas stations and a traffic light, I pull onto the interstate, driving in the opposite direction of El Molino.

She says, "If you think you're taking me someplace, don't."

"Where are we going, Nicolette?"

"You're not going to like this," she says. "But you're driving me to Cotter's Mill."

Part 5

65

Nicolette

Jack says, "No."

"Point the car east. Turn left at Texas."

"Have you ever been on a road trip?" he says. "That's not how it works."

Being made fun of by a guy you have a gun on (it's actually on the seat, but he has no way to know that) is kind of demoralizing.

"Do it! I want to go home! I want this to end! Do it!"

Jack's voice drops when he shouts. "Don't be stupid! Assess your target! If Mendes wants you dead, what do you gain by delivering yourself to his doorstep?"

I tell him what I have to tell him. I don't care if he likes it. "I'm just going to *talk* to him. Then I'm going to turn him in."

Jack says, "That's your whole plan? Turn left at Texas, yell at Mendes, turn him in? That's not a plan you'll survive."

"It is now. Do it!"

Jack pulls off the freeway. I really hope this isn't a wave-the-gun-to-get-my-way moment.

He pulls his phone out of his pocket—the real one, not the burner. He says, "I need directions to Cotter's Mill, Ohio."

The phone says, *"These are directions to Cotter's Mill, Ohio,"* in its friendly, robotic voice. It's the only friendly voice in the car.

"Thank you."

We drive along in more silence, which is better than listening to someone tell me I'm an idiot. Then he says he's hungry.

66

Jack

I want a burger and a fistful of Tylenol. I don't know how Nicolette plans for us to drive for thirty-seven hours and forty-three minutes—according to my phone—to get to her house, but at some point she's going to have to let me eat and sleep.

She says, "Is your headache getting worse?"

"Why?"

"I have to look this up. *Gently* drop your phone into the back."

"I'm not dropping my phone. Shoot me."

"Obviously, you've become deranged. Look up a doctor. You might have a concussion."

"You knocked me unconscious. Good call."

"Pull over. Find an urgent care on your phone. Like, in a shopping mall."

Bakersfield is crawling with urgent cares. I pick one as far out of town as possible, on the edge of the middle of nowhere. Every portion of my head has its own separate, insistent pain: throbbing here, aching there, my forehead trying to tear itself off my face.

Nicolette is walking along slightly behind me, beyond arms' reach.

"Don't look back at me like that. Come at me, and I'll seriously shoot and make up why."

"You'd really shoot me in cold blood?"

She doesn't answer.

It's probably my head, but I feel as if I'm standing outside of myself, watching the weirdest situation imaginable unfold, knowing I created it but unable to take anything like control over it.

"Don't even." The scorn coming from behind me could knock over even someone less concussed. "You thought I cut somebody's throat. How do you know what I'd do? Maybe being hunted down by a preppy jerk turned me into the very thing you thought I was. Think about that."

I would think about that, but my head hurts too much.

67

Nicolette

So great, I gave him a concussion.

He tells the doctor he's Gerry Rheingold, which he signs
so messy, you can't tell what his name is. He says he was hors-
ing around with some guys over football, and it got out of
hand. Go, Niners.

The doctor is old and dried-up and couldn't care less how
it happened. I'd be a better doctor after two weeks of online
medical school. I, at least, would know to sweep the rabbit-size
dust bunnies out of the waiting room.

I say, "Don't you have to check his blood pressure and
take his temperature and everything?" So he does, but he
doesn't like it.

When he touches Jack, bare-handed, I wonder if he washed.

If he's an old drunk who came looking for drugs and tied up the real doctor in a broom closet in back.

Bottom line, it's okay for Jack to sleep. Which is all he wants to do besides eat. I have to wake him up every two hours to make sure he can talk straight and his pupils match. If he gets worse, I have to haul him to another doctor.

Which means I have to put down the gun. Let him have the backseat. Drive the car myself. Trust him a little.

I don't mind.

It feels like the right penance for doing what I did to him. For once, I feel morally superior. I bashed him when I didn't have to, and I'm cleaning it up. Because I'm not actually scared of him. I'm more pissed off at him. Which, now that I wrecked his head, I'm calling off and driving.

Even with a concussion and no power, Jack is bossy.

"You're sure you can drive manual?"

"Guess what? Girls can drive stick. Just last week, ladies got the vote. Get in."

"The gun can't be in the car."

"Says who?"

"Hide it in the trunk," he says. "And if you play Autobahn and we get stopped, no mouthing off."

"Just so you know, that's not how girls get out of tickets. Mouthing off isn't even close to what I'd do if I got stopped."

"Never mind. I'll drive."

"That's not what the doctor said."

"Are you sure that wasn't a weed dispensary?"

I stick him in back, put my hoodie over him, and hide the gun under his gear in the trunk. Pissed off that I'm doing what he told me to do, but still doing it.

He's the one with the impulse control and the sensible advice, but I'm the one who's getting us out of this.

He's asleep before I pull away from the curb.

We drive past desolate, sad square stucco apartment buildings. Small wooden houses with falling-down porches. Fields of wilted plants I can't even identify.

If I don't get back to Cotter's Mill and take care of this, I could end up being the receptionist at that doc-in-a-box, hiding out for the rest of my life. I could make that doctor coffee on his old, sorry coffee maker and stare at his dirty fingernails every day until he dies.

I could get out of the car and lead a small tiny anonymous life right here.

Not go anywhere.

Not do anything.

If I don't get my life back, that could be my story.

That or premature death.

But (thank you, stupid inspirational poem) there's another path in Jack's stupid woods.

This better work.

68

Jack

I wake up in the parking lot of a motel outside of Primm, Nevada. You can't miss Primm: motels in the form of molded plastic castles with roller coaster scaffolding all the way around them and factory outlets as far as the eye can see.

Nicolette says, "What do you mean, 'It's too close'? Too close to what? Are you hallucinating?"

I open my eyes, and she's peering at me over the front seat, the car lit up with acid greens and pinks from the motel's looming sign. It takes me a while to register that the hallucination question isn't an insult.

"Close to Las Vegas, home sweet home." The flickering green and pink lights hurt my eyes and make my stomach lurch.

"You come from here?" she says. "Well, that explains a lot."

"If you knew me, you'd see what a solid citizen I am. I go to high school in a tie."

She pulls out a brush and starts fixing her hair. "I could check us in and you could pass out for a couple of days. They'll take cash, right?"

This motel has the neon signs but not the amusement park, and it's off the highway. "How old is Catherine Davis again?"

"Nineteen."

"Knock yourself out." I'm too dazed to be worried enough. Then a horn honks, and I start to worry. This car, for one thing, should have been ditched. And we shouldn't be here.

Nicolette comes back with a key.

The motel's sign has an eerie neon screech.

I say, "Open the door and mess up the bed, stick the key somewhere, and we've gotta go."

She shrugs. "If stopping here was *your* idea, we'd be asleep by now. You know we would."

69

Nicolette

Jack's in the backseat, retching.

I'm driving us to Utah on roads that cut through mountains I wouldn't like the look of even if this was a vacation. Even if all these 5-hour Energy shots and black coffee in cups the size of Big Gulps made me happy and energetic instead of just jumpy.

All I am is jumpy.

Saint George is where Jack's going to ditch the car and then somehow acquire another one. He isn't clear on the specifics. Whenever I look at the scenery or weave and check the rearview mirror for company, he tells me to watch the road.

Princess of Paranoia, meet Careful, Careful, Careful Boy.

I say, "See, I knew you were going to keep me safe." So he

won't succumb to total misery while throwing up into a paper bag. He says it's the chili cheese fries we bought in Primm.

I'm the one who drove through the night, pulling over and checking his iPad for car rental places that take cash. There aren't any. Then I found a nine-year-old Toyota on Craigslist. Made the call from the burner. Drove us there. Got cash out of the trunk. Handed him a wad of it and told him to go buy a car.

Jack salutes. "Anything else?"

We ditch the old car in the desert, clear everything out of it.

I say, "Shouldn't we be pushing it off a cliff or burning it or something?"

"Should we be adding pyromania to your list of talents?"

I've been up all night. My whole body is buzzing like there were locusts in it, flailing like crazy, trying to get out. I have no sense of humor left.

Jack unscrews the license plates and tosses them out the window into some actual tumbleweed.

He says, "We have to get out of here before they find us."

"I swear to God, no one was following me. Ever. I looped all over the place."

He sighs his you're-an-idiot-but-I-know-everything sigh. "Could be those guys who let me have it in El Molino put on a tracker. You wouldn't see them."

I want to smack him. I swear to God, the self-control it takes to keep my hands on the wheel and off him could keep the entire Cotter's Mill Unified dance team virgins until marriage. We're in a car in the desert with no one around. I can't keep hitting him, but I can scream all I want. "You took me in a car with a *tracker*?"

He's so out of it, he can't even shout back. "I just thought of it. But let up—even if I'd thought of it before, do you have a better alternative to offer?"

Duh.

"How about, we could have ditched the car in Bakersfield? Taken a bus. Gotten on a train. Gone camping. Rowed a boat to Canada."

He just looks confused. "Jesus, maybe this was stupid."

"You need to drive faster! We need to get away from that car! If you're going to wuss out at sixty-five, get out of the driver's seat."

He keeps going speed limit, taking the curves like he was driving a school bus.

"Jack!" I punch him on the arm. Not hard, just to get his attention. He doesn't need two arms for an automatic anyway. "Pull over. I have to drive."

Jack says, "You're like a three-year-old. Use your damn words."

"My words are *pull over!*"

"Why don't you sleep? We can alternate. Do us both a favor."

He sounds completely wasted in a sloppy drunk way even though all I've been feeding him is Coke from gas station mini-marts.

"Do you have slurred speech?"

"This isn't the concussion, doc. I just spent the night driving in the back of a Japanese mini-car with an armed toddler."

"Do I call you names? No. I'm totally nice to you. Go faster! I want to get to the other side of Utah and crash at a motel."

"We can't go to a motel."

"Why not? They don't know what car we're in anymore. For all they know, we stopped for a Big Mac and now we're having a picnic." I feel brilliant for accidentally parking at McDonald's and getting more fries while he bought this noisy piece of whatever.

"Come on, Jack. Please. You're crazed. I'm crazed. Let's find a motel and sleep. On a bed. With pillows. I want to take a two-hour shower."

70

Jack

I wish she'd talk about Mendes and what, exactly, she hopes to accomplish on this cross-country expedition, but she won't. Half the time, it feels as if she's playing Bonnie and I'm supposed to be Clyde. The other half, I wonder if I'm supposed to be her bodyguard or a family therapist when we get there.

When I bring up reasonable objections—for example, the unlikelihood of her having an enlightening conversation with a man who wants her dead—she yells. Mostly she yells about how I have to do it because Mendes has to pay.

I can't argue with her there. If Mendes is the guy who started all this, I wouldn't mind asking him what happened to Connie. I wouldn't mind making him pay. But getting Nicolette killed by playing along with the insane idea that me standing there with a gun will make her safe while she confronts the guy is a poor form of payment. Every time I try to convince her that this isn't a plan, she intones, "Said the guy who was supposed to kill me."

By the time we hit Nebraska—Nicolette, still white-knuckled from being driven back through the Colorado Rockies in the slow lane, terrified, not bothering to deny it, grabbing my arm—you'd have to be stupid to think that a rational conversation on this topic was going anywhere.

"Baby, please rethink," is my new tagline. "Think" would be more technically correct, but I don't relish the blowback—not after I called her a toddler and she's responded to half the things I've said to her since by sticking her thumb in her mouth, posing, and refusing to acknowledge me.

Nicolette says, "I know exactly what I'm doing." She seems to be channeling Wonder Woman, but without the stunt person standing by to leap from building to building for her. Apparently, her role model is Xena, Warrior Princess. "Why can't you just trust me and drive?" she says. "Just do what I say, and we'll be totally safe."

When we pull into the motel against my better judgment, she says, "Wait, Jack." She sounds like Cat, the girl who thought I was a great guy, and not like Nicolette, the disappointed, pissed-off one. "I know you don't agree with this. I get you could have taken off and left me to deal, and you didn't. Plus, there's what I did to your head. Total idiot. I'm sorry, and I *hate* apologizing. But you kind of owe me. I was fake to you and you were fake to me, but it was also real. Which makes it worse. Not that getting grabbed by a stranger would have been a trip to Disney World."

"Nick, I'm losing the thread."

"The point is, stop trying to talk me out of it," she says. "Please. It's not going to work."

"Fine."

"Don't make fun of me."

"You don't own the word 'fine.' Other people say it."

Nicolette squints and makes a face at me. "*Fine*, Jack, all right? *Fine*."

Then she takes an hour-long shower and runs the hair dryer forever, long enough to dry her hair one strand at a time.

All night, I sit there next to her watching her sleep like she's a baby quadruped, burrowing into my side, grabbing on to me with her hands and feet, her hair curling around her face and brushing against my arm. The room gets lighter, until there are shadows in the hollows of her cheeks, and she's climbed out from under the covers, lying on the bedspread, still asleep, still grabbing on.

One eye opens. "Are you guarding me?"

"No."

You can hear other travelers getting a move on, wheeling suit-cases through the parking lot, slamming shut their trunks.

Nicolette sits up and stretches her neck, shoulders, and legs, working her hamstrings on the side of the bed. "God, I wish I could run right now."

We're in a middle-of-nowhere motel on flat, empty terrain.

I say, "How come you were so careful before, no one could find you, and now you want to jog down the highway in broad daylight? If you want to get caught before we get to Cotter's Mill, I'm all over it. Let's call the FBI right now. We could end this right here."

I put the filter into the coffee maker. It's going to be a long day.

"Someone *could* find me before," she says. "You could."

"I'm not playing bodyguard while you jog."

"Don't be like that," she says. "Am I saying I'm going to do it? And I don't jog, I *run*. You should try it. I hear it's invigorating."

"Nicolette, don't. Come on. There are plenty of invigorating things we can do that don't make you a target."

"Give it a rest! I'm not giving it up in a fleabag motel room. Forget it."

"You forget it! You're the one who wanted to check into a motel in El Molino that night."

"*Any* inducement to keep you from driving us into a tree."

"Stop acting like I'm a pirate who's going to steal your virginity and plant a skull and crossbones in your navel! I don't know where you got that, but I actually *like* you—God knows why—and it's insulting."

"I'm not a virgin!"

"What?"

She sits back down on the side of the bed, turning her head so her now-black hair covers her face. "You're the only person who knows that, so shut up."

I have nothing, absolutely nothing, against girls who have sex. I'm for it. But I always thought that if they were already doing it, they didn't fight you so hard over unhooking their bras: wrong again. I try to say something less addled than *What the hell?* or *Huh?* I say, "Sorry, but you can't carry that off solo."

She's stands up, blushing to the point that her chest is mottled red. "The only person except for the *guy*, obviously. Thank you *so* much for pointing that out. Fine, so it was really idiotic. I hate him. I wish he was dead. I wish it didn't happen, and I take it back."

"Really? Because I heard it isn't physiologically possible to take that back."

"Yes, really! Shut up!" She pulls me toward the bed, and I'm not actually unbalanced, but I let her push me all the way down. "So, do you want it or not? Because this might be a one-time offer. Right now. Going, going—"

She's sitting on my thighs, her palms flat on my chest.

"Not that this isn't a great offer, but didn't you just say you weren't giving it up—"

"Damn, Jack. Damn! You've been trying for this the whole time, and now that I'm not Miss Pure and it's not your idea, you won't?"

"Baby . . ."

She's naked in three seconds. I don't have that much experience watching girls wriggle out of their underwear, but this is warp speed. There's no part of her, not a single square inch anywhere on her—with the possible exception of the paint-by-number eyebrows—that isn't beautiful.

"Now you," she says. "And if you think I'm too fat or whatever, you'd better lie."

"You're not fat. You're perfect."

"Tell that to the boys who used to toss me in the air and catch me. Why are you still dressed?"

She starts to undo my belt.

I say, "Could we slow this down for a minute?"

"Are you turning me down? Because in Girl Land, where I come from, 'Slow it down' means no. And if you think I'm so perfect, no isn't your best move."

I start to sit up; she doesn't weigh that much. "Get off. You're always going on about how impulsive you are. Are you sure you're not—"

"Do I look like I'm going to regret this? Don't I look happy? Do you need me to sing 'Girls Just Wanna Have Fun'? I lost it to a complete—don't get shocked—*shit*, and you're my do-over. I want to! Take off your clothes."

I take off my clothes and grab a condom.

71

Nicolette

The sheets are cold and slippery.

Jack's hands, fingers splayed out, sweep up my back and meet under my hair at the nape of my neck. He has fistfuls of it, pulling my head back, slowly, and I'm waiting for the kiss.

Waiting for it, but I don't get it.

His fingers trace my collarbone, then down, spiraling around my breasts, and by the time they make it to my nipples, spiraling upward, I'm begging for it. Not literally begging.

Back arched.

Mouth waiting.

Okay, begging.

"Jack!"

Big mistake. Maybe. He holds my hands over my head

while he's kissing my face. Eyes, ears, cheeks. Barely my lips. Then finally in for my whole mouth, lips, tongue, and teeth a little.

This might be what A-plus in sex looks like.

I try to raise my head to kiss him back, but he's two inches too far above me. His hair brushes my cheek.

He pulls farther away from me, looking down from above me, and swoops back in, leading with the lips again, but more intense.

He says, "Do you like that?"

"Get your mouth back there!"

"Or here?"

Yes, here. The side of my neck. The hollow at the base of my neck. Collarbone. Breasts.

I strain to kiss him, but I still can't get there with my hands pinned. I say, "If you let go of me, there might be something in it for you."

Jack cracks up and releases me. I take hold of him. His shoulders and down his back. Pull him toward me. Reach down toward his butt.

Jack says, "Slow it down, Xena."

I feel kind of criticized, but I want it so bad, I halfway don't care.

He says, "Baby?"

"Don't tease me."

"Sorry. Soon you'll be so happy, you'll forgive me."

"You are *so* master-of-the-universe!"

"Aren't you supposed to be panting or something?"

"Make me."

Which he kind of does.

Shows me what I was slowing down for. His hands between my thighs, first gentle, then not, and then the unexpected kisses.

"Jack! Oh God! *Now!*"

"Who's bossy now?"

"Now!"

He's got me in his arms. I'm going, "Do. Not. Stop."

"Who's stopping?"

You know how people say they didn't know which way was up, and you think, *Sure you didn't?* Well, I didn't.

I completely didn't.

A hand cradling my head. An arm across my back, fingers with just enough pressure curled over my shoulder that I know he means it.

It feels like forever.

In a good way.

As if I get a forever, and this is it.

Jack going, "Do you like *this*?" Every breath of me going *yes*.

But every cell of my brain is going, *Open your eyes.*

Open up and see the problematic aspects of this.

Go back to the part before you were so turned on you

didn't care. How you made sure you could reach the iron lamp. Just in case this was another spectacular failure of judgment and impulse control.

Like last time.

I try to just be there in the perfect moment.

I try not to think, but I can't help it.

I force myself up, out of the cocoon of sheets and arms and toes.

I get all flowery disentangling myself from him. Legs entwined like morning glory. Musky like morning in the woods near Green Lake, when the mist is burning off and you can hear your footsteps in the fallen leaves.

Seriously?

This is a motel room in Nebraska. It smells like insecticide.

This is sex, not Romeo and Juliet. Who ended up dead.

Get up.

Up into the air-conditioned chill. Cover myself up on the next bed over. For perspective. The literal kind, where our legs aren't entwined like anything, and his hand isn't warm against my cheek.

I just want him.

Every cell of my head is going, *You idiot. Don't go sex-brained. It was kind of perfect, but he has an arsenal in his duffel bag.*

Every cell of the rest of me—heart, nerve endings, the pit of my stomach—is going, *More, more, more. Forever. Jack, Jack, Jack.*

Brain: *Get dressed.*

Heart: *Look at that smile. That's the way a girl is supposed to be smiled at. This is it. Accept it. Take it. Cave.*

Seriously, *cave.*

But how can I?

When all I know for sure is that I have to get home and fix this or there's no forever.

For me.

Or for him.

Or for us.

72

Jack

This girl is not a virgin.

"Oh my God, Nicolette."

She's sitting on the other bed, draped in a sheet, looking at me. I've been with three girls, not counting her, but this was a different thing. I'm not a guy who gets sappy about sex. Sex is sex, but this was her giving me everything. And me giving her everything back. Nicolette being Nicolette, she wanted what she wanted, but she returned the favor in spades. This was me wanting her a hundred yards beyond happy the whole time. This was fuck-your-brains-out sex. The only words that come to mind are words that produce eye-rolls, words from the afternoon soaps I used to watch with my grandma when I stayed at my dad's: *secret passion, abandon, bliss,* the four letter *l* word. There's no cliché we didn't hit, and hit hard.

There's nothing I wouldn't do for this girl. There's a cliché I'd stake my life on. I'd slay the Nemean lion and clean out the Augean stable like Hercules. (Xena, Warrior Princess hung out with Hercules, right?) I'd wave a gun at a guy who no one in his right mind would consider waving a gun at.

I say, "That was beyond."

She opens her eyes wider. "You'd better not be slut-shaming me. Now that I know where you keep the knives."

"I'm *thanking* you. Oh God. Whoever that guy was, he should have held on to you."

She looks pissed off in her playful mode of pissed off, not her lethal one.

"That is so sexist and wrong. I was underage. He was a creep. Worse than a creep. He totally had another girlfriend. His *real* girlfriend."

She shifts the sheets she's cuddled up in, and there's a quick flash of a breast. This is a marathon of being *uncontrollably* (thank you, Grandma's soaps), capital *O*, On. Holding up my end of the conversation is an act of pure will. That's how bad it is.

I say, "Jesus, what happened?"

"It kind of blew up. One minute he's got me in the back of his car, this red Camaro, stoned out of his mind, and he's all in love with me, sure he is, and then—"

I'm so jealous of this creep, it's ridiculous. I go over to the other bed, two feet away, and grab her. "Don't tell me. I don't want to visualize it." She makes her sour-lemon face. I ask her, "Was that wrong to say?"

"So, so wrong." I think she's joking, but you can't always tell with her. "But I forgive you because now I redid it with a guy I *wanted* to give it up to."

"Happy to oblige, but do you want to stop saying 'give it up'?"

"Make me. I don't know what I want. Figure it out."

I spend the rest of the morning, until after checkout time with the maid pounding on the door, trying to figure it out.

Nick starts rolling her things into her backpack at the speed of molasses.

Then, not thinking, I slap her on the butt and tell her to hurry up.

73

Nicolette

Jack is shocked out of his mind. And also grateful. It's very sweet. Everything about it. Every second.

Sweet and fierce.

Then the maid starts banging on the door, and he freaks.

I say, "What was *that*?"

"What?" Jack looks dazed and confused, but I know he's not. "*That?* That was a pat on the ass. Sorry."

"That was more like a *swat*."

Jack sits down on the unmade bed. Buttons his cuffs. Looks insanely cute. Looks flummoxed. Then looks angry. "I would never *swat* you. That was a *pat*. *You* pummel people for fun, so you might miss the distinction."

"Laugh at me all you want. But that felt slightly like getting hit."

Jack sits there, pressing his fists into the mattress, looking like a guy who just got punched in the stomach for real.

I go, "Jack? What did I say? What just happened?"

"Let's see." He's buttoning his shirt up to his neck. "Two minutes after . . . we're together . . . like that . . . you think I'd *hit* you?"

"That's not what I said! I said that was slightly too hard of a swat—that's all I said!"

He's packing up like a crazed shirt-folding robot. "I've hit five people in my life. You're not on the list."

"Who?"

He stands up. Looks away. As if the effort of counting the five is beyond him.

"My brother." He won't even look at me. "He was all over me when we were kids. My best friend, once. The drunk in the parking lot. That asshole I downed in my apartment."

"That's four."

There's a long pause. "And my father."

"No way!"

He's still examining the headboard, talking to the wall.

I can only imagine what happened next. I mean, I saw what happened next, I'm pretty sure. On his back.

I say, "If anybody hurt my kid, I'd kill him. If you take the guy out at the first swat, he never gets to carve up anybody."

"Yet you look so much like a sane girl." Jack can be so condescending sometimes. "Did anybody ever tell you about turning the other cheek?"

"Why would I do that? I'm already going straight to hell. Why not take some scum down with me?"

"You know that's crazy, don't you? Nicolette—don't you?"

"You thought it was *fine* to get rid of me when you thought I was scum."

Jack pulls me toward him by the upper arms. Hard, so not a romantic experience. He says, "I never thought it was fine."

"I'm sorry!" I'm standing right in front of him, wedged between the two beds. "I was nicer before. But if someone was going to hurt my kid, or me, or my family, I'm not in a place where I'd turn my cheek. I'm in the place where I'd take care of it. *You* should know."

"I know I should know!" Jack shouts. "Don't you think I wanted him gone? But wanting someone gone is different from seeing him lying on the garage floor in a pool of blood because you fingered him."

"That's not what I meant!"

His head is in his hands. I try to hold him, but he leans away from me. I say, "Even if you're the one who put him there, he deserved it."

I mean this. It's completely all right with me if he flat-out killed him. That's how much I hate the man who did this to him.

I say, "Like you didn't actually *do* it, right?"

"Jesus Christ, who do you think I am?" He's rolling his head around like it's too heavy for his neck. "But I might as well have. The guy in the Hawaiian shirt says, 'Where did Art run off to?' and I say, 'He's in the garage, getting more char-coal.' I *pointed*."

"That's not the same as killing him. Jack, it's *not*."

He looks straight at me. "I've already thought of every excuse there is. People in that line of work make enemies, it's inevitable. But if I hadn't pointed . . ."

"You were a *kid*."

"I was fourteen. Old enough."

"It's not your fault."

"Yes, it is! If I didn't know how bad it was, I would have owned up to it before now."

"Oh, for Pete's sake! What is it with guys owning up and confessing and being a man and taking responsibility? What's the point of telling people, 'By the way, I might have gotten my dad killed'?"

This makes him cringe. Good going, Nicolette.

"Maybe if I did that, I'd get what I deserve."

Oh God, he's so completely effed up for a smart person.

I say, "I spent my life being totally bad, Jack. I swear. I ignored five or six rules a day. Sneaking around. Taking my clothes off for a college boy who was totally into someone else and completely depraved. I mean, I'm a good person. I'm like the *opposite* of a mean girl. But I'm close to being the daughter from hell. And Steve never even acted like he wanted to hurt me. Not once."

Apart from the time he said he was going to get rid of me (and I believed him), but this wouldn't help my argument.

I say, "I wish your mom had taken him out. I truly do. Then he never would have gotten a chance to slice you up."

Weakly, Jack says, "She wasn't in a position where she could call the police."

"She could have stopped him and plead self-defense when they got there."

He says, "You're locked and loaded, aren't you?"

"I didn't used to be. I told you. I used to be nice."

"The nice daughter from hell? What are you now, the scourge of God?"

I climb onto the other bed and take his hand. I wait for him to look at me, his face that rigid mask he has sometimes. I say, "One of us has to be."

Jack puts his arms around me, his face in my hair. "Sometimes you make my blood run cold."

But I know he likes the way I am, or why is he leaning back into me? Why is he cupping his hands on my head like a bulletproof hat? Why is he holding me like this, like I was blowing past him in a tornado and he has to hold on tight to pull me out of the vortex and into his shelter?

74

Jack

I'm a very persuasive guy. In Model UN, whatever country they gave me took over the world. But the closer we get to Ohio, the harder it is to persuade Nicolette of anything. By now, you'd think she would have figured out how into her I am and how I'm trying to look out for her.

"Could you at least lay out what I'm supposed to do?"

"You're supposed to have my back," she says. "That's it. You don't like it when the girl makes the plan, do you?"

"Give it a rest. I wasn't ecstatic when my brother made the plan either."

"That was a *bad* plan. This is a *good* plan."

"Will you at least entertain the possibility that having me wave a gun at Mendes could escalate the situation?"

"For *you*. What about for me? How does sending a guy to throw me off a cliff get escalated? Just because you're reformed, you think the next guy he sends after me is going to think I'm adorable? Because I don't."

The problem isn't that she's wrong about how bleak her situation is, it's that she doesn't see how storming the stronghold of the man who made it bleak—her stepfather, the deadly force behind Don's errand—could get us killed.

Nicolette puts her hand over my hand. "All I want is for you to do this one thing for me. You know how to work that gun, right? If you have to."

I look over at her, and she's dead serious. "Yeah, but it's not like I've been in combat."

"Or hunted. Or shot skeet. Or a moving target."

I don't let myself blow up. I say, "That's all the more reason we shouldn't be doing this."

She's tiny, but she got the gun away from me, held it on me, and humiliated me completely. What's Mendes going to do, fold his hands in his lap?

"You just have to stand there and look scary," she says, as if showing up armed were an everyday occurrence, like getting the mail and putting on your pants.

I'm gone. I shout, "Do you not see that invading the place with a gun makes it likelier someone gets shot?"

She has complete, steely focus and equally complete irrational determination. "It's my house! And he says *I'm next*? Think again. I live in that house, and nobody gets to make me scared to be there."

"Nick! If someone in there wants you dead, you're supposed to be scared."

75

Nicolette

We park by the lake and walk into the woods. The sun is starting to set, the sky lavender and orange, the path dappled with shafts of dying light.

Home.

I touch the moss on the trunks of the beech trees, hear the water lap against the shore as we hike toward Green Lake. Smell the almost moldy, loamy aroma of the place. The remnants of a campfire.

I live here.

I'm not hiding out in a converted garage in California ever again. Or wherever. No one is driving me out of here. My life is my life.

I want it back.

If everything goes right, this ends tonight.

Nicolette, one. Challengers, zero.

If it goes wrong, God help us. Literally, that's what it would take.

Jack says, "Slow down."

He's the one loaded for bear this time, prepared to break into a fortress. He has ropes and knives and, for some reason, an Allen wrench. Weighted down by instruments of mayhem.

I tell Jack, "I've been sneaking in and out of here since I was thirteen. You can offload a bunch of that stuff."

I know where the spare key is and which door you can open with a credit card. How to run across the dark part of the yard to slip back in at night. Which windows squeak and which don't.

"You really weren't a very good girl, were you?" Jack says. "You said, 'Night, Pops,' and cut out through the back door?"

"I said, 'Night, Papa.'"

"You called Mendes *'Papa'*?"

"What was I supposed to call him? Plus, who doesn't sneak out occasionally?"

"Try sneaking out past my mother," Jack says.

I'm trying to stay strictly focused on what we're doing. To avoid consideration of what God or anybody else would think about it.

To avoid thinking about the Steve who was my mostly nice dad and focus on the one who helped bury a body and *said* he was going to kill me.

To blot out the memory of him buying me pink summer dresses or signing off on notes that said I talked in class.

To avoid thoughts that might lead to crying. Anything that could keep me from getting this done.

But when I think about going in through the French windows (which I've done a thousand times), seeing his back at the desk in his office, I feel mushy. Thinking about how much I missed home, and him, and being in a family. How much I wish I didn't have to put him through this.

Then I think about the dead girl and how she got that way.

When we get in there and things go even worse than Jack imagines, I can't be that mushy girl.

When things go bad, I have to be on top of it.

This is what Jack is for.

He's so pissed at his scumbag brother and everyone who had anything to do with this thing, he's good to go.

He can talk up peace and love and backing down all he wants. But bottom line, if some guy threatens me, he'll take him out. I think.

Jack says, "Anytime before he sees us, you can bail. We don't have to do this."

I'm literally pulling him toward my personal horror show. "Let's just do this. I want to hear him admit it to my face. Then I can die happy."

Jack says, "You're not dying tonight."

It's all on me.

I can't let anything go wrong.

I picture Steve clammy and corpselike, and I start to shake. I hear the words, *It's not my kid*, echoing in my ears. *It. Useless. Whore. It.*

Tear my insides out through my eardrums, why don't you?

What was I supposed to think?

I'm glad that I'm in front of Jack because my face is crumpling. Tears are streaming down my cheeks.

This better go just right.

At the edge of the woods, the trees thin out at the clearing where our house stands in the middle of a lit-up lawn.

Jack says, "Odd to say this when we're in a reasonable facsimile of a yellow wood, but you could still take another road. You could still walk away. But if I use this gun on Steve . . . no matter what he did . . . Just think about it, okay?"

Oh God!

I think about it.

Jack says, "Now what?"

Between the coiled rope and the holster, there's a space against his chest I can fit into. His hands find the small of my back.

One hot failed assassin who gets to retire in a couple of hours.

But first, I have to make this whole thing stop.

76

Jack

She's lost it. It's as if she feels omnipotent when she's on the trigger side of flying bullets. When I mention that geese don't shoot back, she won't listen.

If Mendes wants to bury her, shoving Don's gun in his face isn't going to defuse things. If he wants to bury his kid, he's a monster who could do anything.

I'm holding her so close in the darkening woods behind her house. I've tried to talk her out of this a dozen different ways—reasonably, soothingly, threateningly—but if I were facing her down in Model UN, there'd be thermonuclear war.

I say, "What about if Mendes is armed?"

Nicolette sniffs. "He *hunts*. It's not like he carries a Winchester around the house. Come on!"

She bounds through the woods with cheerleader enthusiasm. I can barely see the path in the twilight. She thinks we can just walk up to the house and use her Catherine Davis prepaid Visa Buxx card to unlock the door and get in, that if we trip the alarm, Mendes will think it's a raccoon because it's always a raccoon.

I don't know what she plans to say to him because she won't tell me. If her plan is to provoke him so he strikes, provoking me to do something to stop him, it's a bad plan. I'll try. But why would she think she could disarm me, but a guy with decades on me couldn't?

Being this humbled this recently doesn't make for a shit ton of self-confidence.

77

Nicolette

The French doors in Steve's office open with the credit card.

The doors creak slightly, but it's a creaky house. The motion detector isn't on, no beams of light. Great, because I don't have to sprint into the kitchen to turn it off. Bad, because it means Steve is home, walking around.

I wanted to get here first.

But it's home. It's Steve. It's what I'm used to.

For a second, I relax. As if it's safe.

But this is the opposite of safe. This is the lion's den. Not the nice lion that likes the mouse for pulling a thorn out of his paw. The hungry kind that drags his prey through the woods. And stabs it eleven times.

There's a light on in the hall.

We creep toward it.

I turn to lift the rope off Jack, motioning for him to put down all his stuff. It's not like Steve is going to call the police on us, incensed homeowner pointing to a bunch of abandoned burgling tools.

Jack shakes his head.

This is what Jack looks like when he stops breathing.

He holds up his hand and points.

There's a guy in a white shirt, sitting in the kitchen, texting.

Perfect.

You don't forget the guy who hits you with the shovel he's using to bury a girl. You don't forget his profile when the flashlight lit him up, or his voice, or what you want to do to him.

Jack puts his hand on my shoulder. He actually thinks he can hold me back.

Well, he can't.

Then Gertie comes charging out of nowhere. A tiny brown fur ball, barking her head off.

The guy stirs.

Starts to turn.

Starts to ruin everything.

I grab the white china pitcher that has orange roses in it. Always. In memory of my mom.

Bring it down on the guy's head.

It's not like TV. The vase doesn't shatter. The guy doesn't

make a sound. Slumps forward over the table. His phone hits the floor.

Roses strewn.

Jack mutters, "Jesus. Are you sure you didn't cut Connie Marino?"

I punch him in the side. He grabs my wrist. I'm wrestling to get my hand back when Steve walks in. Comes toward me.

Followed by Alex Yeager.

A guy I've known since his dad, Karl, brought him up here to play in the lake while the fathers talked business.

And who is the scum of the earth.

I thought I knew how Jack sounded when crazy angry.

I didn't.

He jerks around and yells, "Stop! Now!"

Steve stops dead. He's sock-footed, like he was just taking his shoes off. Changing out of his suit. Just reaching for his jeans when he heard the vase bouncing off the guy's head. Holding out his arm to keep Alex back.

Alex is glaring at me like his eyes could burn holes through me.

I'm glaring back. Like bullets could burn holes through him.

78

Jack

This isn't looking too good for Mendes, one guy down, his other guy taking cover behind him.

He reaches out toward Nicolette as if she were an apparition. "Nicky, you came back. Did this boy hurt you?"

I reach for the gun.

Nicolette yells, "*Shit,* Steve! You better *duck*!"

"Nicolette!" Like he's the stern dad, having missed the facts that I'm aiming Don's gun at him and that once your kid figures out you're going after her, you don't get to rein in her language.

Mendes says to me, "Whatever you want, you can have it. But why don't you put that down on the table? I'll stay back here. No problem."

"No problem!" Nicolette says. "What would be a problem to

you? Your kid sees you *burying* someone and then you say she's not even your kid and you're getting rid of her?"

"How could you think I meant that?"

The young guy half-crouched behind Mendes says, "What is this, fucking *Family Feud*? Why am I even here?"

Nicolette screams, "You said I was *next*—are you kidding me? How could you *say* that? *Hey, Nicolette, I love you, just kidding, now I want you DEAD!* How could you hire someone to kill me?"

"What are you talking about?" Mendes is getting unhappier by the minute.

"He wasn't stalking me for fun!" Nicolette nods in my direction. "Somebody made him. Someone has to pay."

Mendes is moving almost infinitesimally toward her, saying, "Nicky, come over here and stand behind me," as if he missed what she just said, missed her face when she said it, and missed the fact that there's already a chickenshit bozo right behind him.

I tell Nicolette, "Don't!" with a lot of conviction.

Nicolette gives me a withering look. "Right, I'm an idiot. I want to be a human shield."

Mendes keeps coming. "He's lying. I wanted to find you and bring you home. I sent people to find you."

I say, "Nobody said anything about bringing her home."

"You look exactly like Art Manx. You're Art's boy," Mendes says. "Do you think he'd be proud of you, menacing a sixteen-year-old girl?" Mendes fixes his gaze on Nicolette. "Nicky, I love you. I didn't hire this boy."

But the fact that he has one guy slumped over his kitchen table and his second guy trailing him like a puppy, and the smooth way he's trying to deal with me, snuffs out hope that he's just an accountant with a couple of rough clients, in over his head. He's way too comfortable with this.

Nicolette puts her hands over her ears. "I *heard* you! How could you say those things about me?"

"What do you think you heard?"

She starts to sob, leaning against the chair that holds the comatose guy, who hasn't budged since she beaned him.

Mendes keeps inching toward her, his minion behind him like a mime playing a shadow. The minion's a good-looking guy, his mouth hanging open, a little confused. I'm not that worried about him, but Mendes is another story.

I bark, "Stay back!"

My arm is extended; the gun is extended.

Nicolette yells, "Don't!"

At first, I think she's yelling at Mendes.

"Jack, don't! This is a mistake! Don't hurt my dad!"

My grip tightens, and my finger is tense around the trigger. The younger guy has started creeping closer too, reaching for a kitchen drawer on his way, sliding it open, and I don't like it.

Mendes keeps coming. He's so close, I could get him through the eye with a peashooter.

Then Nicolette screams, "Knife! He's got a knife!"

It's the younger guy pulling a long kitchen knife out of a drawer as Mendes moves toward Nicolette.

"Knife! Knife! Knife!"

Nicolette has all but jumped on my right arm with all her weight, forcing the barrel of the gun away from Mendes; Mendes is reaching for it; and this muscular guy with the knife—who's no use guarding Mendes, if that's what he's supposed to be doing—is coming at her, or me, or both of us, blade first.

Screw Mendes, I have to stop the guy with the knife. Assess your target: he's it.

I'm pulling back, taking aim, not giving up the gun, when Mendes tackles Nicolette from the side. A chair pitches toward me. The bodyguard—or whoever he is with the knife—charges. And there's a blast like we just broke the sound barrier.

Blast after blast after blast.

Everything explodes. There's a spatter of blood.

It could be anyone's.

It could be mine.

79

Nicolette

Blood everywhere.

Steve's blood and Alex Yeager's blood.

Jack's pressing on Steve's arm with a dish towel.

There's no point in trying to help Alex Yeager. He's gone.

Nobody is saying anything.

Gertie is cuddled next to me, wagging her tail. Licking me with a dripping, bloodred snout.

I'm calling 9-1-1 over and over, but they keep putting me on hold.

Then men start racing in, weapons unholstered.

Jack says, "Crap, he has an army."

But it's the Cotter's Mill–Kerwin Township P.D. All these

men I recognize in flak jackets, tracking through blood to get to Steve.

Someone's on his phone confirming that the caller who said he heard a bunch of shots fired heard shots fired and they need three ambulances. Yes, three.

Jack keeps pressing down on the shattered arm, two-handed, kneeling across Steve's chest.

Steve is turning white, and then kind of gray.

I'm chanting, "I'm sorry," as if it could make him open his eyes and believe me.

I can't even think about Alex, lying on the kitchen floor in more blood than you'd think a person could lose that fast.

He's done hurting people.

I'm home. It's like I've returned to some form of sanity, where Steve spurting blood like a human fountain is just wrong.

Please, please, don't let anything happen to Steve.

Steve's touching my leg. He says, "No matter what, you go with the police."

Then everything gets fast and loud.

Steve and the guy I bashed on the head are on stretchers, paramedics shining lights into their eyes. Racing them through the house toward the sirens outside.

Jack's gun is in an evidence box. Jack is under arrest.

I'm under arrest.

I say, "How can you arrest me? You know me!"

Jack says, "Jackson Arthur Manx . . . Summerlin, Nevada . . . yeah, Arthur Manx was my dad . . ."

Before he turns completely pale, Steve says, "Not one word. To anyone."

Our hands are bound behind us with the kind of plastic fasteners you use on giant garbage bags. They hurt.

A guy in a Kevlar vest asks me, "Do you know who they are?"

Alex and his stupid friend I knocked out with the vase.

"The dead one with the knife. His dad knows my dad. And I saw the other one, too. That once in the woods by the lake. Digging the hole."

Jack, as they're leading him away, says, "Nicolette, stop talking."

The huge guy who's got him by the arms shoves him. "Are you *threatening* her?"

"I'm telling her to listen to her dad! You can't ask her questions without her parent there."

"If she's a suspect." This guy does not like Jack.

Jack says, "You arrested her. That would make her a suspect."

The guy in the Kevlar vest says, "It's the Manx kid. What do you expect?"

"Do we know who knocked out this one?" He waves his arms at the cracked vase.

"I did."

Jack says, "Nicolette, shut up!" Then he says, "Look at her. It isn't physically possible. I did."

At which point Rosalba, who can sleep through almost anything—except this, apparently—comes roaring out of her room in a bathrobe, calling out, "Nicky!" She hugs me, and then she starts yelling at people.

I end up in my room. A deputy from Kerwin is sitting on a dining room chair outside my door, waiting for the Ohio Bureau of Criminal Investigation to show up.

I could go out the window, but there are guys outside, shouting. About the perimeter and hard targets and soft targets and attempted murder and murder. About Steve and the guy that I knocked out and Alex.

Alex Yeager.

I wish I could forgive him and pray for his immortal soul and mourn his loss and be a good person.

But I can't.

I'm not.

Even Steve told me to keep quiet so the police wouldn't figure that out.

I stick my head around the door. I ask the guy, "What happens now?"

He says, "Cool your jets."

What does that even mean?

I try texting Jack, but either he's someplace without reception or he's more under arrest than I am.

I call over to St. Francis again and again to find out how Steve is. They tell me there's nobody there by that name. I ask the guy outside my door if we can go over to the hospital, and he tells me I have to sit tight.

"I don't want to sit tight. I want to go to the hospital."

"You were supposed to stay with the police, remember? I'm the police. Sit tight."

"Is Steve all right?"

"After your boyfriend shot him?"

"He's not my boyfriend! And he was trying to protect me from the guy with the knife. Please. The hospital won't tell me anything."

The marshal smacks his forehead with the palm of his hand. "Listen, honey, in the morning, you're going to have a lawyer. Your dad had someone call her. Until then, I need your phone."

"Why can't I have a phone?"

"This is for your own protection."

"Where's Jack?"

80

Jack

A man is dead.

His blood splattered in plumes. He was dead before he hit the floor. He's turning to gray blue as Mendes goes white, his eyes staring straight up but seeing nothing. I'm bombarded with weird, fragmentary thoughts. How many coats of primer will they need to paint over the kitchen? How many times did I shoot him?

The shots reverberated like a rocket catapulting past the sound barrier, breaking it, blasting through eardrums as if they were tissue paper: the first blast, then the second, the third, and again, and again, and again.

I'm bent over Mendes, my hands sticky with blood. The corpse is maybe two, not even three feet away. There's a scream coming out of Nicolette that won't stop. Her dog is licking blood.

I can't wrap my head around what just happened.

What I know is, I could have stopped it all—but I didn't.

Nicolette got the gun away from me when I was on the ground in the Sierras, concussed, lying facedown in pinecones. But who am I kidding? I'm twice as big as she is and in better shape. I could have dragged her into any sheriff station between Primm, Nevada, and Podunk, Ohio. But I didn't.

Instead: this. I marched along, not resisting, allowing myself to turn into the man I've known I was all along. Everything I wanted to believe about myself, it all disappeared into this murderer I've become.

There's a dead guy I could reach out and touch with the same hand that held the gun that felled him.

I'm a killer.

It wasn't the DNA or the sinister dad with his boxes of bullets, or the mother who sat there while he trained me to "think," or the orders of my sociopath shit brother, that brought me here. It was my decision after my decision after my decision.

I'm tracking blood down the hall, tracking Mendes's and his goon's blood all along his carpet to the front door of Nicolette's house. The cop protects my head, pushes me into the back of the black-and-white, and we drive away past a line of cars with government plates and, where the driveway meets the street, a red Camaro.

I say, "My name is Jackson Manx, and I want to make a statement."

81

Nicolette

When all else fails, I pitch a fit. When I finish breathing into a paper bag, it's one in the morning and they take me to see Steve.

There are tubes running in and out of him. A heart monitor beeping a rhythm just behind him. And his skin's still the wrong color.

I am so sorry.

A security guard with a vintage crew cut and a *Men in Black* suit stands rigid just inside the doorway.

Steve opens his eyes. "What? Are you protecting me from my daughter? Go."

Steve tells me, "Sit." As if I were a dog. Or a girl who likes to be ordered around. The security guy looks back over his shoulder, checking to make sure I heel.

I sit in an olive-green plastic chair that squeaks whenever I move.

Very softly, Steve says, "Tell me what you did."

Not the first time I've heard this particular instruction.

"I'm really, really, really sorry!" I bend over the hospital bed to hug him. He smells medicinal and unfamiliar. "This was *not* supposed to happen to you. Please believe me."

"*Tell me what you did.* I can't make it go away if I don't know what it is."

I sit back down in the chair. I fold my hands in my lap. "Starting when?"

"That girl in the woods."

"That was totally Alex Yeager!"

"Nicky, come here." He holds out his functional arm.

It's like God is making me stand and look at my own evil handiwork. "I'm so sorry! You weren't supposed to get shot! I swear!"

Steve says, "How could you think I would harm you?"

"You *said* I wasn't even your kid. And you were going to get rid of me. And I was nothing but trouble to you."

Which, given that I got him shot, might not have been that far off base.

"Sweet girl, I would have lied on my mother's soul to get those boys away from you. I would have said anything."

"You said—"

"*I know what I said!* They bring me a corpse to bury . . .

this young girl. They're in my shed, looking for shovels. I go downstairs to see what's going on, and they think I work for Karl so that means I'm going to help them." He starts to shake his head, but winces. "I crunch *numbers* for Karl. Then you show up on the trail out of nowhere."

"I'm sorry."

"When they came back, and you were gone . . . My God. I didn't know if I would get you back."

"I'm so sorry!"

"Don't cry." He's patting my shoulder, squeezing my hand, calling me *mi'ja*. I am so the daughter from hell. "Nicolette, what were that Yeager boy and his lackey doing at my house again?"

Truly, I'm waiting for lightning and the wrath of God to strike me as I sit there and lie. "I don't know! I'm so sorry!"

"And that Manx boy who found you? What were you doing with that one?"

"Nothing! He was trying to protect me. His mother was going to get killed if he didn't find me. Don't do anything to him!"

"Don't you believe a word he says. Not one word."

"But, Papa—"

"He stays out of my way, he stays out of your way. Do you understand me?"

"But—"

"No 'buts,' Nicolette. No maybe, no nothing, no anything

but you being a good girl who stays in the house until this is over."

"But it *is* over, right? They found that girl's body; they know who did it; they know why I ran away; they know Jack was trying to protect me. What's left?"

"If it's over, it's because I'm Karl Yeager's accountant," Steve whispers as if someone was manning a stethoscope on the other side of the wall. "I know where Karl Yeager's money goes. Because Karl doesn't think like a normal person." He looks straight into my eyes. "Karl might think you set up his kid."

All of a sudden, I understand what Jack meant when he said that thing about me making his blood run cold. Only this time it's *my* blood. The sensation of ice chips in my veins. My heart trying to beat with an icicle through it.

"Please, you have to make him think it was an accident! Can't you make him see that?"

Steve shifts position so his face is inches from my face. "An accident? Two people are dead. This isn't like giggling too loud during assembly. I can't write you a note. And now it's a *Manx*?"

"He didn't mean it! He's nice! It was totally my fault! I'm sorry. Can't you please, please make this go away?"

He sighs and squeezes my hand so hard, it almost hurts.

"You're a little girl who had a knife coming at her head in her own kitchen. What kind of a boy does that? Karl knows something wasn't right with that boy. We'll talk, and we'll end it."

"Not just me! I *made* Jack come with me. None of this was his fault."

Steve looks over the giant cast on his left arm and shakes his head. "Fine, but he's out of your life. This happens my way or it doesn't happen. Understood?"

When he gets like this, all you can say is yes.

I say, "I'll do whatever you say. I just want my life back."

He sighs. "All right, Nicolette. Show me your hands so I know you're not crossing your fingers, and tell me this Manx boy is not in your life."

"Please."

"It's over."

I tell him, "Whatever you say, Steve," but I don't look him in the angry, angry eyes.

82

Jack

I can feel where my fingers were curled around the trigger, my palm against metal. My forearm is caked in dried blood. I lean back in the metal chair, trying to get comfortable, but comfort is out of the question.

This is a shit show. There's no way around it, just through it.

I wanted to be the guy who pulled out of the swamp, stepped up, and lived with the consequences—but it's not working out.

The interrogation room buzzes with an almost-spent fluorescent light bulb. We've been here for hours. They keep dragging me back through the story as if they think they're going to trip me up. But I've already incriminated myself, Don, Karl Yeager, Esteban Mendes, the guys who beat me up in my apartment, the anonymous drunk guy I beat up—everyone but Nicolette and her ice pick.

By the time I get to the part with the biker bar confession, no matter how bad a picture I paint of myself, they think I'm worse. They think that without reason or provocation, I attacked a biker and dumped him somewhere. I don't want to give them the idea that Nicolette helped me do this thing that never happened.

"Would your story change if you knew Esteban Mendes has been cooperating since he was forced to help bury the girl? We've been tracking those boys in the kitchen like flies on a carcass until we could secure Miss Holland—which leads us straight to you. Quite a coincidence, no?"

"No! And how do you know Mendes was forced? Are you taking his word for it? And the girl has a name: Connie Marino."

"You seem to know a lot about that," Agent Birdwell says, looking put out, while Agent Garrity sits there. "You were there, weren't you?"

"I was in Nevada! Check the attendance records at my school." I imagine how much the ladies in the front office at El Pueblo will enjoy police inquiries about me.

"Yet you know when it happened and who it happened to." Agent Birdwell keeps spouting irrelevant truths.

"I didn't know Connie was dead until my brother told me."

"You're sticking to that? Your brother told you Nicolette Holland did it? And she knew things about Karl Yeager?" This is a game of cat and mouse where the only rule is, the mouse loses.

"The way we see it, maybe you were there," he says. "Maybe

you dragged Miss Holland away with you, and maybe you came back to get rid of the witnesses."

I can't predict the plot of the story they're making up. I have to keep controlling waves of anger, grabbing on to the seat of the chair, wadding my hands into fists and sitting on them as a last resort.

I say, "What witnesses was I trying to get rid of?"

It wasn't supposed to go like this. I was supposed to confess to what I actually did, and in return, they were supposed to believe me and lock me up somewhere I couldn't do any more damage— not this.

"How did you get involved with Alexander Yeager?" Birdwell demands. "Dead at *twenty-one years old*. Ten degrees to the right, and you'd have had Mendes, too. Two witnesses blown away. One minute Alexander Yeager is burying Connie Marino, the next minute you shoot him."

"*Wait!* The dead guy in the kitchen was a *Yeager*?"

Garrity presses his lips together as if he wants his mouth to disappear, a tell. Never play poker face with a guy from Las Vegas.

"Come on! I shot Karl Yeager's kid? *He* buried Connie? Don't you get this? Of course Karl Yeager wanted Nicolette dead! She saw his kid bury Connie—with Mendes. I was the guy they sent to do it."

"You've had a long time to think this up, haven't you?" Birdwell says. "Was one of those shots meant for Miss Holland?"

"No!" Jesus, this guy only believes his own stories. "Why would I drag her to Ohio to shoot her?"

The back of the chair is digging into me. I start to stretch, but

Birdwell pushes me down with such relish, the fact that I've put myself at this asshole's mercy starts eating at me.

"We're not done here," he says.

I try to turn to get out from under his hands, but the only way to shake him would be to come up punching. My fingernails are pressed into my palms. I'm saying to myself, *Think, Jack. This would be a colossal mistake. Don't do this.*

I lace my fingers behind my neck and squash my head between my arms.

Garrity says, "Kid, do you want some water?" Birdwell looks as if he might bite him. His hands linger, but they come off me.

It's late, and my mind is Swiss cheese, but I can still recognize his provocation for what it was. I wouldn't give him what he wanted, so he issued an invitation to assault a cop. Thanks, but no thanks.

My ability to control myself for much longer is doubtful if I don't get somewhere I can punch something other than Birdwell's face. I want to land it right in his smug mouth right now, when he's reveling in how much power he has over me.

I'm not going to prison for something a blowhard who likes pushing me around claims I did, a confabulated tall tale that ends with me trying to kill Nicolette. I didn't. I want to *be* with Nicolette. I want to wash the blood off my hands and go to sleep and wake up to her—not this.

"I want a lawyer. I invoke my right to counsel."

Birdwell doesn't make a move out of his chair, but Garrity yawns. "He's invoked, Bill. Let's call it a night."

Birdwell looks as if he'd like to make it Garrity's last night on earth.

I say, "If you haven't contacted my mother, I want to make my phone call. On the off chance I'm telling the truth, she needs more security."

Garrity says, "On the off chance, yeah, we did—about three hours ago."

"Thank you."

Birdwell is so pissed at Garrity for giving me this, he half-throws a chair.

83

Nicolette

The car they use to drive me back and forth to the hospital has dark tinted windows and door locks the passenger can't control. They hustle me into the house through the back door. It's somewhat weird to be there with police nannies and not Steve.

At the hospital, Steve said, "Are you all right over there? I could sell that house in a week, move to the south shore, get more land."

"Then I'd have to go to Jefferson! Please! I have to be in school with Liv! I just want things to be *exactly* like they were."

Steve was so doped up, he couldn't control his face. How sorry for me he looked. How amazed at my cluelessness.

I said, "Except for the kitchen."

He looked relieved I wasn't in a total state of (sick) denial.

He paid a counselor big bucks to get me to stop that before. When the therapist thought I was substituting sparkly nail polish for a mother.

"Sweet girl, I'll tear it out. I'll gut the whole room."

I pictured him hacking away at the bloodied cabinets with a sledgehammer, tearing up his left arm even worse. "No! I'll do it!"

He laughed. "Nicky, I don't need you pulling out the stove. You pick the colors."

I don't want to think about it in color.

Bloodred.

Meanwhile, my guards don't want me having visitors. No point asking them why. They don't answer questions. They say to sit tight. Buck up. Ratchet it back.

Meaning shut up.

They have semi-control of me. I get it. But Olivia's in the front hall, yelling. "Is she here or not? People saw her at St. Francis. What did you do with her? Where is she? Niiiiick!!!"

I want to make a break for it and squeeze her so hard, no one can pry us apart.

She yells, "I'm not ratcheting anything back! It's a free country!"

I yell, "Olivia!"

Two guys block like I'm the QB, and Liv is a blitzing linebacker.

They want everything but her birth certificate.

Steve doesn't get out of the hospital for three more days. *He'll* let me see my friends. Even if they don't bring two forms of government-issued photo ID. In three days, maybe he'll forget he ever said Jack Manx can't live in the same universe as I do.

Olivia keeps craning her neck, looking past the crime scene tape on the kitchen door, down the hall to where I'm blocked by guys trying to protect me.

She calls, "Niiiiick! Hey! It's not like she's invisible. She's *right there.*"

I start chanting "please" while she yells at them. They think this is hilarious, but they let her come upstairs.

We close the door to my room and hug for a half hour while she cries into my hair.

Everything we want to say is so cheesy, we can't actually say it. I missed you. I love you. Thank you.

Promise you'll still be my best friend when we get old.

Promise you won't get shot.

Promise Summer's not your new best friend.

"Promise you didn't do any idiotic thing with that Jack."

Uh.

"Oh sweet Lord, promise you didn't!"

I nod and try to look as not-guilty as possible about the fact that I did. It's not that challenging given that I don't feel at all guilty. At least not about that.

"Don't get snot in my part."

"Shut up. Did you see that girl get stabbed? You could have told me."

"Does everyone know?"

"No murders in Cotter's Mill for twenty years, then *two* murders. What do you think?" She's walking around me. "You want me to help put your hair back?"

"It has *layers*. It's going to take years to grow back."

"We could make it really short, like Keira Knightley in that commercial."

"I'll look like a nine-year-old boy."

Liv shakes her head. "Not anymore. You going to keep it?"

"Is there a way a person can keep the T but not the A?"

"It's not a bad A."

"That's what Jack thought."

This is what I wanted. My friend who'd do anything for me, who'd risk having thugs track down her burner phone but still cares if my hair looks good. Being (quasi-secretly) less than the purest girl in cheer. Having a family. Living where I belong.

I would have done anything to get this back.

I did.

84

Jack

I've spent the night in what might be solitary confinement. There's no one else around, and the lights don't go all the way out. They still think I killed Karl Yeager's kid, Alex, on purpose, that I was gunning for Mendes, and that Nicolette was next.

Yet again, I'm scared shitless.

Then I get to the interview room on no sleep, and there's my mother in a black suit and a look on her face that says that she's about to blow.

"Where's my lawyer?"

She says, "I'm on a leave of absence from work. *I'm* one of your lawyers. Do you understand what that means?"

"I don't think you should be my lawyer."

"It means you can talk to me, and I can't testify against you."

I don't understand where she's going with this.

I say, "Is Mendes all right?"

She reaches into her briefcase for a yellow legal pad, which she holds up like a shield. "What were you thinking? Do you value your freedom this little?"

Don't ask someone who just spent his first night in prison if he values freedom.

"I was thinking that if I didn't make Nicolette Holland disappear, I could visit you in the Manx crypt." It comes out as a snarl, but at least I don't call her a name.

The pad drops to the metal table. "We might be talking about two different things," she says slowly, back in overly calm control. "Was someone threatening me?"

"Your laundry room went up in flames, someone tripped the alarm inside the house when the security cameras weren't working, and then they messed with the brakes on your car. You do the math."

"Watch your tone, Jackson!"

I'm sitting in lockup, and my mom wants me to watch my tone.

"Sorry."

Then I tell her what Don said I had to do; what I thought I had to do; what I thought I had a plan to get out of doing—only everything backfired, and I ended up in Cotter's Mill, Ohio, holding what turned out to be a murder weapon.

She's clutching me and sobbing hard, despite all the signs prohibiting physical contact, and no one's doing anything about it.

85

Nicolette

If they'd just laid it out sooner, I could have fixed it sooner.

"Jack didn't kidnap me. Why would I say he didn't if he did?"

My lawyer, the good cop who thinks I'm a porcelain teacup, and the bad cop who thinks I'm the devil, don't believe a word I say.

They're talking among themselves about Stockholm syndrome. This is when a hostage starts thinking her captor is Mr. Dreamy. It's caused by mental collapse due to the stress of being a hostage.

Not me.

I'd act like he was Mr. Dreamy. I'd peer into his eyes with pseudo-adoration. Then I'd cut his heart out with my nail file.

I say, "I can't have Stockholm syndrome. *Nobody kidnapped me. I was nobody's hostage.*"

Bad Cop says, "Where did he hold you?"

Clearly, this is bad.

They don't believe the truth.

Not that I plan to tell them that much of it. But there are critical bits of the truth that should (if there's any fairness in the world) keep Jack out of jail.

I mean, Alex was coming at me with a knife. Isn't that classic self-defense? (I looked it up.)

I'm not letting Jack go to jail. The whole point was for us to be safe. Not dead and *not* in prison.

My lawyer hooks her hand onto my arm, all boney and tight. She says, "Could we take a break?"

Bad Cop won't stop glaring at me.

I say, "I know I screwed up." My lawyer's hand tightens like a vise. I say, "I believed the wrong thing. I'm sorry."

My lawyer's hand is cutting off the circulation to my arm. I don't know if this is maximum sympathy or another signal to shut up.

Good Cop says, "Nobody thinks what happened is your fault."

I've watched enough *Law & Order* reruns to know they mostly say this when they're trying to get killers to confess.

I'm not confessing. I'm assessing my target. Like Jack kept saying to do.

"It *is* my fault. Kind of. I thought Steve was going to kill me! So stupid. But he *said*."

Bad Cop says, "Is that why your boyfriend shot him?"

I have to fix this.

I have to fix this fast.

My lawyer says, "We're leaving, Nicolette."

I'm done with leaving.

"He isn't my boyfriend! I'm not even allowed to talk to him. I said I was running straight into the house to get Gertie. Jack kept going, 'No, Mendes is going to kill you! Don't do it!'"

Blankness and incredulity.

I say, "Gertie is my *dog*. I just wanted to get my dog back and not be killed. Why don't you get it? Jack was there just in case. The gun was totally my afterthought."

Even Good Cop isn't buying this. "Um, that's not what Mr. Manx says. Miss Holland, if you could walk us through it."

"Of course that's not what he says! Like he wants people to know he's in jail over a cockapoo? He was trying to save me. I was going in to get Gertie, and then he was going to help me leave the country. He had the cash in his trunk."

"That's where you found the gun?"

"I told you! It was wrapped up in his fishing gear." I look up. Three blank faces. I can't tell which one of them snorted. "I mean, it was a gun. I wasn't going to leave it lying there. Somebody could get hurt."

My lawyer sighs.

"So I stuck it in my bag."

Bad Cop mashes his pen into his notebook.

"Out of the country where?"

"I didn't care where. It was some kind of a plantation. Somewhere like Costa Rica? Does that sound right? Argentina, maybe."

The stupider I sound, the more they like it.

86

Jack

I'm bailed out, cleaned up, and living in a hotel in Cincinnati, a cop posted at my door. He makes a big show of frisking the room service waitress every time she brings a burger. We're waiting on Don. Everybody knows he's going to finger everyone in sight, after which he'll get a deal and I can get out of here.

I've gone from being criminal conspirator to being the clean-cut dupe, according to everyone but Agent Birdwell. I'm back to being trusted with Wi-Fi, my phone, and sharp objects.

Calvin, who gets that the phone (which my lawyer says to use with caution) might not be entirely private, clears his throat. "My only question would be, who else is bankrolling your lawyer? Because obviously *you're* not going to be giving him any more business."

I've got the same lawyer who represented my dad the time he

got indicted for selling something to someone in Angola. My mom gave Mr. Ferro to me and not to Don presumably because I'm the horse to bet on if you want one kid who's not behind bars.

"Have you no respect for organized crime?"

Calvin says, "Don't dick around. This isn't funny."

"Calm down. I'm on the bus straight back to Boy Scout camp as soon as Don testifies."

There's a long pause. "Nobody's so stupid that they think you did anything, are they? They know you were just trying to warn her?"

It occurs to me that if this goes much further, I could be turning him into an accomplice. I say, "Have fun with your Mermaid Ninjas," and hang up while he's still groaning.

My attorney says, "Talk to your lawyer and only your lawyer," but he acts pained when I do.

I say, "To be honest, there were times when I didn't know what I was going to do. It was like being on autopilot, but you don't know where you're going to land."

"You won't be sharing that unless somebody asks you under oath."

"Asks me what, specifically?"

"If trying to save your *mother* was like being on autopilot and not knowing where you were going to land. In those words," Mr. Ferro says. "Then you can say yes."

"Got it."

Mr. Ferro paces around the hotel room, adjusting his tie. "I don't think you've got it. You're a lucky kid. Don't screw it up."

I'm the lucky kid whose brother wanted to become the Yeager

clan's right-hand man by doing Alex Yeager a favor: getting me to kill Nicolette. This would prove how useful Don could be to the Yeagers, a chip off the old block—except that Karl Yeager had no idea what his kid, Alex, was up to, and Alex Yeager wanted to keep it that way.

When they asked Don to explain how it was that his mother got threatened in three different ways, he whined that it was Alex Yeager's fault so many times, he sounded like a parrot with a limited supply of sentences. And Alex Yeager was such a piece of work, even if he could tell his side of the story from the grave, it would be a case of dueling liars.

I'm left not knowing the magnitude of what Don put over on me or how much I get to hate him—if I hunted down America's sweetheart to save my mom and Don and myself from Alex Yeager's machinations, or if the whole thing was a Donald Manx production. It's like having a scab you can never tear off completely.

Damn fucking Don.

What I do know is I shot down a man in cold blood.

Mr. Ferro says, "That man was charging a sixteen-year-old girl with a knife."

"A bread knife."

"Did you have time to process that fact? *No you did not!* Two experts say so. And who knows what Alex Yeager would have done with that knife? His girlfriend was close to decapitated when he got done with her."

This image starts to bring up lunch.

"Wait. Was Alex Yeager *seeing* Connie?"

Mr. Ferro rolls his eyes. "Alex Yeager was a buffoon. Who goes running to his father's accountant with his girlfriend's body?"

"Accountant to thugs, right? Mendes must have loved my father's spreadsheets."

"Your father was a legitimate businessman!" Mr. Ferro roars at me. "Esteban Mendes is a legitimate accountant!" He stops to catch his breath. "Anybody asks about your father, you wait for me to object. Then you stop speaking."

"It would be a lot easier if someone would tell me what's happening. Why can't I talk to Nicolette?"

With the hundreds of dollars an hour of Manx money he's getting for defending me, it would be nice if Mr. Ferro could disguise his annoyance. "Nicolette Holland is sixteen years old. She's got a stepfather who doesn't want her talking to you. Ergo, no conversation."

"She's not the most obedient daughter on earth."

"She is now. And I don't want you pissing her off. She's told her story, and we don't want it to change."

"What story?"

"I'm telling you this, and all you do is nod and listen. Can you do that?"

"Yes, sir."

He smiles. "Cute girl. She says you got to California, frantic to warn her that people were after her. That was her word, 'frantic.' To quote her"—he digs around in the files he wheeled in here—"'Like I didn't already know people were after me? Why did he think I was hiding, for fun?

"'Jack was all, *Hello, Nicolette, I was sent here to off you, but never fear, I'm Dudley Do-Right.*

"'Then *I* explain it was *Steve* behind the whole thing, and Jack's all, *Oh no, it was Karl Yeager; my brother said it was Karl Yeager; your dad would never do that.* And I say, *Really, do you know Steve? Did you hear what he said?*

"'I'm such an idiot.

"'Jack's whole thing was, he didn't want me to go into my house. After I convinced him it was Steve who was after me. But I made him take the gun. To protect me from Steve. Turns out he was lucky to have that gun because Alex Yeager would have killed us, right? That was a really big knife.'"

I look Mr. Ferro dead in the eyes. "That isn't how it happened."

"It is now. You tried to give her, and I quote, 'a bunch of money.' And you offered to buy her, wait, this gets good, 'a rubber plantation' in Argentina."

I start to speak but Mr. Ferro puts a finger to his lips. "That's what she says happened. No one believes her. But if she keeps saying it, they can't prosecute you."

I say, "But the guy in the parking lot—"

"What guy in what parking park? There's no police report. She says she stabbed a would-be rapist, but her psychologist thinks it's the pressure of captivity speaking."

"They think she was my *captive*?"

Mr. Ferro massages the bridge of his nose and scans the transcript. "She says not. The party line is you're a misguided saint who had her stashed away to save her, and she's a spitfire who thought she was in mortal danger."

"She *was* in mortal danger."

"Not," Mr. Ferro says, "from you."

I shrug.

"Look, Jackson—"

"Jack."

"I know you're not as stupid as she's making you out to be, and I know it wasn't this clear-cut. But this girl is your fairy godmother. Don't mess this up." Ferro shakes his head. "And Jack, no guns. Your name is Manx. You can't go near a gun."

This is the one thing he doesn't have to worry about, and not because of what my name is.

87

Nicolette

I beg Steve to let me call up Jack, but it's a no.

Steve says, "These people aren't joking. That one with the squinty eyes who asked you why you told your boyfriend to shoot me, he has handcuffs and keys to the jailhouse. Do you understand me?"

"Yes."

"Are you crossing your fingers?"

"No! You know I would never, ever, ever do something like that to you. You know that, right?"

Steve puts the arm I didn't wreck around me. "He's not a great shot. But I know the difference between an accident and a target. I was the accident."

"And there's no way—?"

"Ask fifty times, it's still no. Ask a hundred times, no. Cry and breathe into a grocery bag, no. And forget about the French doors. Welded shut for all the good they're going to do you."

"Who's waving the keys to the jailhouse now?"

"You're not throwing your life away on a *Manx* boy. One of them blackmails the other to kill my little girl? They're scum. I'm sending you back to the counselor. Don't say no, it's yes. Say yes."

I say yes.

I want my life back. This is how to get it.

88

Jack

It's over.

Don says everything he has to say to save his ass, as expected. For the purpose of Don's hearing, the Feds—who showed up hoping Don would reveal a vast interstate criminal conspiracy—love me. When it's all over, the police, in the form of Agent Birdwell, keep coming at me, looking for contradictions I don't provide. When I come out of Interrogation Room A, I've been in there for five hours straight.

My mother's in the hall thanking Mr. Ferro when Nicolette comes out of Interrogation Room D with her lawyer, who looks like she eats alligators for breakfast. Nicolette looks like she just crawled out of an avalanche, white and traumatized. Esteban Mendes is standing half an inch from her, holding a little pink case with her dog, Gertie, in it.

I want to wrap my arms around Nicolette. I want to take her hand and run out the emergency exit and into the street.

"Nick, are you all right? Can we talk for a minute?"

Mendes says the most definitive no I've ever heard.

Ferro tries to steer me to the opposite side of the hall.

Birdwell, just behind us, close enough to grab me in case someone tells him in his earpiece that he gets to arrest me, says, "I would advise against that."

Mr. Ferro loves getting under this guy's skin. "You dropped all the charges. You can't stop them from talking."

Mendes extends his arm in front of Nicolette, as if they're in a car that's about to make a sudden stop, and he won't let her lurch forward when he hits the brakes. But there's something about not being allowed to do pretty much anything that galls her. She says, "Steve, don't. Let me. Just this once. Please."

He says, "You want to cross me on this?"

"Fifteen minutes. Please."

Mendes says, "Fifteen minutes is right."

Her lawyer reaches back and opens the door of the room they just came out of. It's a lot nicer than the room I just came out of, upholstered chairs, wooden table.

Ferro says, "The recorder still switched on in here? No, thanks," and pulls open the door to an adjoining break room with a coffee maker and a microwave.

Our lawyers follow us in.

Nicolette says, "I can take care of myself."

They don't seem so sure about this, but they leave us alone.

Nicolette stares out the window across the skyline to the steel grey river.

"I'm so sorry," I say to the back of her head. "If you could forgive me, ever—"

"Stop it!" She turns, and I'm looking at her real eyebrows, pale brown, and her hair bleached back to the blond it's supposed to be. She looks like a badly disillusioned angel. "You've more than paid."

I say, "I told the truth."

"I know," she says. Then she whispers in my ear, "God will probably smite me for lying to the police, but I'm not putting you in prison."

I hold her while she cries. I'm surprised she lets me, but maybe it's an any-port-in-a-storm kind of thing. Her body is still so warm, still the only girl I can imagine wanting. And it's not just lust-wanting. I'm capable of lust-wanting anyone. I could probably lust after her scary lawyer stripped down if you dared me. I want Nicolette like wanting to be in the same room with her forever, wanting to take care of her even though she can take better care of herself than I ever did.

But even in the middle of her narrative, which is saving me; and Mr. Ferro's narrative, which has kept me ten paces ahead of the law; and Birdwell's narrative, which has me as a cold-blooded killer who heartlessly fucked his victim before kidnapping her and dragging her off to be murdered, I have to know what really happened in Esteban Mendes's kitchen.

I open the door to a balcony that runs along the outside of the room. We stand in the far corner, facing into the noise of the traffic below.

I say, "Baby, how well did you know Alex Yeager?"

89

Nicolette

As if it's nothing, as if it's just something to say between bites of burger, Jack says, "Is Alex-the-creep-from-Ann-Arbor Alex Yeager?"

I know how to do, *Yikes, busted!* I do. I'm the reigning princess of the cute confession. If cute confession was classified as an official talent, I'd be Miss Ohio Teen USA.

But I don't know how to do *this*.

"How . . . ?"

"Your friend Olivia. She thought I might be him in Cotter's Mill, when I was looking for you." He pauses, waiting for something I don't give him. "And there was the car. There was a red Camaro at the end of your driveway."

I start to cry, which is a key element of cute confession, but it's completely real. Real and unstoppable.

Plus, I have a headache. I don't even get headaches. But this is like an ax hacking off the top of my head.

"Don't be mad at me."

"Is there some reason I'd be mad at you?" It's like he's torturing me, and I haven't even told him the things he should be torturing me with yet.

"You know there is, or you wouldn't be asking! You know the answer." Shouting makes my head ache more. It's like the mother of being hungover.

"I suspect the answer."

"Jack, come on. Please."

He closes his eyes. "I'm going to sit here in complete control while you tell me if I shot your boyfriend."

"*You're* my boyfriend! Is it that he touched me first?"

"Not even close."

"Please, please, please, let's not go there. You don't want to hear it. I don't want to say it." At which point, it occurs to me I could have just answered the first question with, *Alex who? Huh?* and this wouldn't be happening. I'd still be a terrible person. I'd be lying through my teeth. But at least he wouldn't *know*.

I say, "You first. Tell me something terrible about yourself. The absolute worst thing."

"Apart from shooting someone?"

"That was kill or be killed. It doesn't count. Some other worst thing."

"You know the worst thing after that. It's what I did to you when I was J and you were Cat—and what I thought about doing."

Jack is so earnest, like the face on an *earnest* vocabulary flash card.

Earnest with a dark side.

Human.

"Worse than that."

His jaw moves around like he's trying to decide whether to open it or not. "I liked holding that gun, in the kitchen. I knew what I was doing was stupid shit, but I felt like God."

I'm not confessing to a guy whose worst thing is something he *felt*. "Oh no, a boy who likes guns. I heard there's a club with, like, forty million of you in it. Come on, something you're *ashamed* of."

Jack looks like he wants to throw me but not catch me. Not the look a girl wants to inspire.

"Besides what happened to my father? Isn't that enough?"

"Stop yelling."

Jack retakes control of himself. I'm pretty sure he can change his pulse, heart rate, and body temp at will like ancient yogis.

Oh God, I really didn't want to make him go there.

I say, "*Fine,* I'll tell you. I went to a lot of parties last summer. U of M college parties. I made out a lot, are you happy?" I'm halfway between you-asked-for-it and wanting to jump off the balcony. "I was all, 'Eff you, Connor, you think you can sleep your way through the dance team and I won't notice? *I'm with college guys, ha!*' I was *fifteen*."

"Right, and now you're *sixteen*. I don't care if you did every guy in Sigma Nu—"

Why would he say something like that? I halfway want to tell him just because it'll make his stomach hurt.

Jack says, "I didn't mean that. I'm sorry. Nick? Sorry."

"Like you never went to parties or drank or hooked up?"

"I'm sorry. I never should have said that. But, Nicolette: Alex Yeager. *Was Alex Yeager your boyfriend?* It's a yes-no question."

"He was not my boyfriend! He was *cheating* with me." It just falls out of my mouth when I didn't mean it to. "He had this other girlfriend. Only he says they broke up. Except they didn't. Then he says he loves me. Only he didn't. And I totally didn't love him—I was getting back at Connor. I was being an idiot. I was having an adventure."

Jack is over being sorry.

You can see it in his face. In the way he tilts his head, waiting for me to tell him the rest. And it's not that I don't want to tell him. It's that I want to tell him and for him to still like me.

What are the odds?

Jack won't even look at me. "Get to the part with Connie."

"*Stop judging me.* I completely blame myself for that, I do. If I'd broken up with him when I figured out there was this other girl. Or if I'd figured out that the reason he wanted us to be a big secret was *so* not because I was so underage. If I'd done one thing differently . . ."

My ears are ringing so much, it feels like my head is going to shatter like a wineglass when a show-offy soprano belts a high note.

"This isn't recounting your life to Saint Peter to get into heaven," Jack says. "I hunted you down. My good-guy credentials were canceled, ask a cop."

"Fine. So he tells me he broke up with her, but she's, like, a stalker. I can sort of tell he's a creep, but he keeps saying he loves me. And he's in college. And he comes out for the weekend sometimes. We go to the drive-in in Kerwin."

Jack looks up. "Esteban Mendes let you go to the movies with this twenty-one-year-old sleaze son of a mob boss? Try again."

"I'm not making this up! I didn't *tell* Steve! Are you kidding me? I mean, this guy drives his Camaro out from Michigan to go on a *date*. It's not like I wanted him in jail for statutory rape. Which is what Steve would have done to him. He would have skinned him and hung his head over the fireplace."

"But I graciously did it for him."

"Please, that wasn't supposed to happen!"

Jack is stone-faced.

"If you don't even believe me, can I stop? Even though this is no end of fun."

"No."

It's the no you don't want to poke with a stick. That no.

"Fine. So life is going along fine. Alex supposedly loves me. Everybody still thinks I'm all that. Then his girlfriend shows up."

"Connie Marino just happened to be taking a walk across your property?"

"I told you, she was a stalker. Who follows her boyfriend to the next state? You figure out he's a dog, and you dump him. But she *follows him*! She *shows up*. She's parked down the street from my *house*. And God, Jack, the minute I saw her, she was so pretty and in love with him, plus she wanted to make him hurt as bad as he hurt her. Which I totally get. Only she thought it was my fault. *My* fault! She won't stop screaming at me."

Jack is looking at me like I'm a piece of stinky cheese.

"Jack! She was going to tell everyone I was a *slut*. Everyone was going to *believe* her. She was going to tell my dad and *everyone*. I felt bad for her. I didn't even want to *look* at Alex again. I wanted her to get in her car and take him back to Michigan and *shut up*. I didn't want her *dead*, I just wanted her to be quiet.

"So I'm telling him to make her be quiet. Steve's going to hear. I'm going, 'Make her shut up!' and Alex is going, 'What am I supposed to do?' and I'm going, 'You're freaking Alex Yeager. Think of something!'"

Jack says, "Shit, no."

"Oh God, Jack. There's so much screaming. I run into the trees to make him stop, but he's waving his knife at me. He's covered in blood, like, he's *dripping*! Then he's on the phone to some guy to come help him, and he tells me to go inside and stay in my room and don't come out and don't say anything to Steve or anybody or *I'm next. I'm next!* And she's *dead*."

Jack's head is in his hands. He says, "It's not your fault. It's *not* your fault."

"I'm on the edge of the woods yelling, 'Do something! Make her shut up!' at Alex freaking Yeager—how is it not my fault?"

90

Jack

When she pulls herself together, she says, "I can't see you. You understand that, right?"

"We could at least communicate, couldn't we?"

"I was *in love* with you when you were there to *kill* me."

She was in love with me? I start to say her name, but she says, "Don't you want your life back? Talk about something else."

How do you talk about something else? We go inside and sit in two upholstered chairs facing the window, me stealing glances at her, her not looking back.

I say, "Mendes wants my head, right?"

"Of course he does. But not everyone's dad kills people, all right? Just don't show up at my house."

"I won't. I'm sorry."

She brushes against me as she heads for the door, her skin against my skin. I still want her. Maybe she's not a candidate for sainthood, but what did she do that was anywhere close to what I did? I want to buy that plantation on an island somewhere and take her there.

She says, "It's going to be fine. You'll see."

And then she's gone.

Jack Says

So here I am in college, spring semester. My life is supposed to be rolling along down the same path as usual, with a minor interruption between the end of high school and now.

I spent fall semester doing a gap thing, built an orphanage in Oaxaca, learned carpentry, went to bed exhausted, and not with anybody. The girls were great, very dedicated, very cute. But they weren't Nicolette.

I did months of heavy labor. I told my mom I was exhausted and she wrote back, *Be grateful you're not in prison. Stop complaining and plaster some walls.*

I wasn't complaining, it was a statement of fact. Not only am I grateful I'm not in jail, I'm grateful for all the other things I deserved but I got out of.

Agent Birdwell kept saying, "We have our eye on you," as if there were a big, disembodied eye that the Ohio Bureau of Criminal Investigation could program to follow me around while I ate refried beans in Oaxaca and beam pictures of my fork scraping across my plate back to headquarters.

But I'm not even on any kind of probation, thanks to Nicolette lying like a rug on my behalf.

My mom keeps dabbing her eyes and saying, "I don't understand," about everything she doesn't want to understand.

"It's not just Don who grew up in that house," I say.

She says, "I don't care if you're eighteen. You're on a six-inch leash."

"One more Manx requiring *careful* supervision or who knows what he'll pull."

"Jackson, stop!" She shakes her head, shakes herself (temporarily) out of mourning the loss of her delusional take on Don, looking more furious than I've seen her for a while—even at me. "You got exploited because of your last name. Assumptions were made. . . . But listen up." She's right in my face. There's no way to avoid listening up. "You were trying to save me, and Don, and yourself, and this poor little girl. Are you hearing this, Jack? I spent seventeen years with Art, and you're not like him."

I wish I believed her.

"I have your future in an iron grip," she says. This I believe. "Don't try to throw it out again."

Thus the heavy labor to pay for my sins. But there's no way to make up for what I did to Nicolette. Stuck in my head forever is the image of her giving me that heartbroken last look.

Then Esteban Mendes, who had his arm around her, said, "You come near her, you're dead. You call her, dead. You text, you get a sock puppet to send her a text—dead."

He said this within the hearing of the police, his lawyer, Nicolette's lawyer, my lawyer, and my mom. They kept looking at the little pink case he was carrying, the one holding Nicolette's dog, Gertie, and they didn't take him seriously. As for me, by the third time the man got to the word *dead*, I believed him.

Don isn't even in much trouble—for him. He'll be in Witness Protection prison before being released into the world someday with a new identity. Years from now, my mom and I can meet up with him at a secure, secret location. My mom will go. I won't.

College is weird but good. I live in the Mercer freshman dorm with a roommate and a resident advisor named Bonnie we're supposed to take our troubles to. My roommate paints his face for basketball games and puts a sock over the doorknob when his girlfriend is there. As far as I can tell, they go at it with face paint on.

I walked on to the crew team. The coach was pissed I hadn't shown up in the fall, but he wasn't going to turn me away. I train harder than anyone. I'm still programmed to go for the fastest time, the highest A, the most outstanding honors.

I might have to get an apartment pretty soon, though, before I bang my head against the dorm room wall so hard, I end up staring down the guys in the next room over and then having to go work through my aggression with Bonnie the RA.

I don't hold out much hope that I'm getting Nicolette back. She got her real life back, and I was never in it. I keep trying to think of ways to show her I'm a different guy. That now I'm the guy who, when his brother tries to dupe him into killing her, says, *Are you fucking insane?* and calls the FBI—not the guy the police want to sic a big, hovering eye on.

But why would she believe this? How would I prove it?

Hey, Nick, look at me. I'm through the first three months of my first semester of college with a 3.8, and I haven't once tried to kill anybody? I've returned from the dark side, and now I'm into college sports?

Why should she trust me? I don't trust me.

But I'm planning to get there.

I'm planning to get there, risk my life to walk past her dad and, if I survive that, talk to her: *I get what I did to you. I'm sorry. I love you.*

Nicolette Says

Now that it's officially behind me, I can breathe. The untrue story of what happened is such old news, nobody even wonders anymore.

Anytime I get slightly upset, people think I have PTSD. They make me sit down, and they get me a glass of water and a doughnut.

(I say, "Oh no, it's a frosted doughnut from my hideous past. I'm having a flashback."

Jack says, "Shut up and eat your frosted doughnut."

Jack so gets me.

Almost.)

I was a perfect, pure girl for six months.

No infractions.

No detention.

No back talk.

I sent the real Catherine Davis a thank-you card. (Plus her license and four hundred dollars.) For Luna, eight honest words. "I'm safe. Thank you for taking me in."

Steve finally relented about Jack. It took a while, but how could he miss that Jack was trying to save me? And that I would never give up.

Five seconds later, I'm on the green burner. I'm pretty sure Jack's crying. God knows, I am.

Jack says, "Before you say anything, I love you."

I say, "You better. I'm not loving some guy who doesn't love me back."

I'm safe.

Jack's safe—he doesn't even know how safe.

We're all safe, and it's all kind of over.

Steve says I ought to thank my lawyer for the story of what happened. The one that got me back into Cotter's Mill Unified High School and straight onto homecoming court. Treated like I was a kitten that got rescued from a drainpipe.

The fake yet useful story.

Which is, Jack Manx has self-control and I don't.

Which is, I was a total victim and therefore can't be blamed for anything.

(The part where I was good at hiding, jumped on a flatbed truck, took cross-country buses, hitched, changed my name repeatedly, got jobs, gained thirteen pounds, stole things, disarmed Jack, had a plan—not in the story. *Nothing* that makes me sound like Xena, Warrior Princess made it into the story.)

My part of the action is screaming, *"Knife, knife, knife!"* like an out-of-control wind-up toy. Reaching for the gun because I was scared that Jack would hurt my daddy. That's what my lawyer keeps calling Steve. My daddy. It makes me sound like a crazed, blameless little kid.

I'm nobody's crazed, blameless kid.

As soon as I figured out Jack wasn't lying to me anymore, in the mountains, in California, I knew what had to happen.

Here's the thing:

When Jack said it was Yeager who wanted me dead, I knew he was right.

It wasn't Steve sending Jack after me at all. This made me almost happy it was Yeager.

And I knew *which* Yeager.

The one with the reason to want me dead.

Alex.

Not Karl Yeager. *Alex.*

"The whole Yeager clan is rabid pit bulls," Jack said.

"They won't stop until they stop breathing," he said. "As long as they're breathing, they keep coming at you."

Alex Yeager wouldn't have quit coming after me until I was dead.

And after Alex disposed of me, he would have found Jack. On Jack's secret eggplant plantation in Paraguay or wherever.

And Alex's guys would have killed Jack too for not doing the job. For not tossing me off a cliff.

But with Alex Yeager *gone*, there would be no reason to get rid of me or Jack.

Jack, in his effort to show me how illogical I am, demonstrated how syllogisms work.

Bob is a crow. All crows are black. Therefore Bob must be black.

Alexis Yeager was going to keep coming at me until he stopped breathing. Alex Yeager had to be stopped. Therefore?

Alex Yeager had to die.

And I had to take care of it.

I mean, Jack wasn't going to—at least not on purpose. Try going, *Hey, Jack, let's go kill someone who's really bad on purpose.*

His big brother already tried telling him to do that to me, and look what happened. Look at me. Not dead.

I just needed Jack to think it was *Steve* he had to protect me from for as long as it took to get from that ugly California forest to Cotter's Mill. I thought it was Steve who was after me for so long. Why wouldn't Jack believe it for a couple of days?

And so I called up Alex. When Jack and I were halfway to Ohio, and I was supposed to be taking an extra-long shower in a motel bathroom. Several extra-long showers.

I said, "It's me."

"Nicky?"

"*Zandy*, why are you hounding me? Don't you know I'd do anything for you—just like what you did for me? You're *amazing*. I want to *be* with you. Which won't work if I'm planning my funeral. Don't you want me?"

"It isn't me who's after you," he says.

Liar.

"It's my dad," he says.

Double liar. I heard you whine, "Don't tell my dad," so many times while you were digging the hole. Over and over.

"Oh God, Nicky, can I see you?" Alex says.

Bingo.

Come into my kitchen, said the spider to the guy who stabbed Connie Marino eleven times. When, where, and unarmed because if Steve is there, he'll take your gun and your stupid SOG SEAL knife right off you. He keeps a pistol loaded in the drawer under the toaster in the kitchen if you need one.

Not.

Steve keeps his guns locked up, not rattling around with bread knives.

Guns versus knives? Guns take it.

Steve's arm was collateral damage. I'm truly sorry. That was *not* supposed to happen.

Jack was supposed to shoot *just* Alex in defense of me.

Steve was right there. He saw me pitch a fit over a dull knife. He knows his arm getting shot was my fault.

But how could he blame me?

Alex Yeager was going to kill me. And if I turned him in, his dad was going to kill me. *Anyone. Anywhere. Anytime.* Just like Jack said.

But if Alex turned a knife on a five-foot-two-inch high school cheerleader in her own house, how could anybody call out me or Jack or Steve for stopping him?

If all else failed, I would have done it myself.

Terrified teen girl clutches gun, fires wildly, fatally wounds assailant. Followed by a lot of prayer that nobody who ever saw me shoot the bull's-eye right out of a target would ask too many questions.

But Alex took the knife.

I screamed.

Jack shot.

Alex went down.

What happened afterward was improv. But all those first responders running around? It was kind of ideal. A great big free-for-all. *Terrible* tragedy. Look around. Arrest everybody in sight. Interrogate us right and left. Call it self-defense and file it. They already knew Alex Yeager was a very bad guy.

I wanted my life back.

The outcome couldn't have been better. Except for messing up Jack.

Jack feels guilty as hell. Jack thinks that civilization rises and falls on whether he personally follows the rules. He's going to feel bad about what he thinks he did forever. He's going to go through life believing he killed someone when it could have been avoided. The exact opposite of what he wanted. He takes this as proof that any minute he could morph into his dick dad.

He keeps telling me he's going to reform. He's going to be a stand-up guy I can count on.

I tell him he has nothing to reform from. He's the most stand-up guy I've ever met. Plus, I already count on him.

He doesn't buy it.

Jack judges himself so hard.

As for me not having self-control: wrong. I'll never tell him what actually happened. Him or anyone else.

What good would it do? Alex would still be dead, and Jack would still have gunshot residue all over him. He'd just hate himself that much more.

Plus, he'd leave me.

When I told him how Connie Marino ended up dead by Green Lake (what I did, what I shouldn't have done, what I knew I shouldn't have done but did anyway), he said the right words. *Not your fault. There, there. So not your fault.*

But his eyes.

Different story.

The way he saw me. The way there was an *anyway* in the middle of his liking me. He liked me *anyway*.

This time he wouldn't like me.

I swear to God, if I could think of some way I could tell him and not crush him and not lose him, I'd do it. This guy *so* deserves not to suffer.

But it beats being dead.

I saved him.

I saved his life. I got rid of the asshat who tried to make him kill me and threatened his mother and would have killed him, too.

But he'd still blame me. And he'd blame himself worse. If he knew.

He'll never know.

I saved us.

Ask me if I'm sorry.

Or not.

You know the answer.

Acknowledgments

First, thanks to my agent, Brenda Bowen, without whom this book (not to mention my life as a novelist) would not exist.

The team at Simon Pulse has been stellar. Thanks to editors Patrick Price, who acquired *How to Disappear*; Sara Sargent, who inherited it, but embraced, nurtured, and shaped it as her own; and Sarah McCabe, who has run with it, energetically and brilliantly, toward release. Thanks also to Mara Anastas, Jodie Hockensmith, Carolyn Swerdloff, Tara Grieco, Mary Marotta, Lucille Rettino, Kayley Hoffman, Sara Berko, Michael Rosamilia, Michelle Leo and her team, my sales rep Kelly Stidham and the entire S&S sales force, and jacket artist Regina Flath.

As for the team at JKS—Marissa DeCuir, Chelsea Apple, Caroline Davidson, Jenna Smith, and Angelle Barbazon—magic!!!

To my primary beta reader, Rick, who goes through every word of every draft; to Laura, whose close reading and notes have been spectacular; and to Michael, who gets story structure so well it's scary, more thanks than can fit in this space.

I am so fortunate to have Alexis O'Neill, Carolyn Arnold, Gretchen Woelfle, and Nina Kidd as my critique group, not only because of their expertise and their constant encouragement, but because it's a pleasure to know them.

I came close to fan-girling when Sarah Aronson offered to trade manuscripts. Her strong, fresh perspective moved me forward when I was stuck. And having writers whose work I so admire—Carrie Mesrobian, Gretchen [McNeil, and Martina Boone—take time from their own work and deadlines to blurb this book put me on the giddy side of grateful.

As for the generous and incisive April Henry, who started off as a blurber and ended up as a forensic expert/plot wrangler/editor/hand holder/and general thriller writer's best friend and resource, thank you!

The experts who've helped me with this book have been extraordinary in the depth of their knowledge and their ability to convey it to a novice in their fields. Special thanks to Robin Burcell in equal measures for her forensic expertise and creativity, and to Jason Scott, whose insights into technology and privacy (or lack thereof) on electronic devices was indispensible. Any technical errors in this book are entirely my fault, not theirs.

Alethea Allarey has made it possible for me to hold my head up online, and Lissa Price has been my voice of sanity throughout this process. (And to the secret FB group that's been so enlightening, helpful, and just generally wonderful . . . you know who you are, and thanks!)

Finally, thanks Mom!!! You started cheerleading for my writing when I could barely hold a pencil, and you're still going strong. Alethea Allarey has made it possible for me to hold my head up online, and Lissa Price has been my voice of sanity throughout this process. (And to the secret FB group that's been so enlightening, helpful, and just generally wonderful . . . you know who you are, and thanks!)

Finally, thanks, Mom!!! You started cheerleading for my writing when I could barely hold a pencil, and you're still going strong.

Don't miss Ann Redisch Stampler's
Where It Began.

"Unputdownable!"

—JENNY HAN, bestselling author of *To All the Boys I've Loved Before* and the Summer I Turned Pretty trilogy

I

THIS IS HOW IT STARTS: SOME HAPLESS GIRL IN A
skanky little tank top lying on her back in the wet grass somewhere in Hidden Hills. She is gazing at the stars through the
leaves of a eucalyptus tree. The trunk of the eucalyptus tree is
wrapped in Billy Nash's blue BMW. Midnight-blue. The girl
is trying to figure out what's going on, beyond the more obvious facts: a mouth lined with a sick combination of beer and
stale vodka, a crunched-up car with black smoke pouring out
of it, a night sky filled with glassy constellations and a big
white moon.

There are certain unavoidable conclusions.

Even so, the girl is trying to remember the particulars. The
keg, maybe. The crash. She is trying to remember who she is
and what happened to whoever that person might be.

She is trying to remember she is *me*.

When I wake up, I am wired to machines. Everything looks somewhat gray. I check to see if my toes can wiggle and I start counting my fingers, which proves to be more challenging than you'd expect. I'm pretty sure they're all there, but I keep having to start over around finger number six.

Someone speaks, but it doesn't make sense, pieces of words and random syllables. It occurs to me that I might be on some fairly serious drugs. Then I go back to counting my six fingers.

Just after this, or maybe way later, it is hard to tell, someone else says, "Good morning, Sunshine."

I start to say, "Good morning," but I end up throwing up instead. Which is evidently a good thing. I am surrounded by happy, blurry, celebrating people in scrubs.

Someone grabs my hand and yells "Good morning!" again, enunciating all the consonants in case I'm deaf or speak Serbo-Croatian. My name remains a mystery of life, but I do remember this horrible story about a gray-haired old lady discovered locked up in a mental hospital in Chicago or someplace, where she'd been stuck since she was sixteen years old when a policeman found her wandering the streets speaking Serbo-Croatian. Only nobody knew it was Serbo-Croatian so they decided that she must be crazy and locked her up basically forever.

Whoever I am, I'm pretty sure that I'm not her.

Then it occurs to me that all these greenish-gray, blurry-looking figures I've been thinking of as people might actually be space aliens doing a bad job of pretending to be human. I try to go back to counting the fingers, but this is hard with the big happy alien clutching my hand as if she is afraid that I might make a break for it and cut out of the mother ship if she let go.

I try to get my hand back, which is cause for further celebration.

The hand-grabbing alien is wearing a V-neck scrub shirt with bunnies all over it. "Can you tell us your *naaaaame*?" she yells over and over.

I am still trying to reclaim the hand.

I hear myself saying, "Bunnies."

They all echo me and someone writes it down, or writes down something. I can hear the ballpoint scratch against the paper, harsh and loud.

"That's very *goooooood!*" someone else says. I have made the space clones ecstatic. "You've been in a *car accident*, Bunny," she shouts cheerfully.

The car. I sort of remember the car.

"You probably feel a little sick, but you're going to be *fine*. Dear? We need to know your last name too. What's your last name, Bunny?"

By now I am overwhelmed by the mystery of the situation. Although, I am in command of several key facts:

1. My name is not Bunny.

2. I have ten fingers, or at least I have six, and none of them actually seems to be missing.

3. I might or might not be in a hospital somewhere.

Ideas float through my head like big, goofy cartoons. Elephants and bunny shirts and bags.

"My ID," I say.

"Heidi!" they say. "That's great! Are you Heidi?"

"ID," I say. "Look in my bag. Give me my wallet."

All right, so I have no idea who I am, but at least I'm not stupid. This is something of a relief.

"I'm afraid the paramedics didn't find it, honey," Bunny Shirt says. "Let's see if you can tell me what day it is today."

This seems like an exceptionally stupid, random question under the circumstances.

"Calendar," I say.

They seem to be missing a lot of important items around here, such as calendars, and where is my bag? I remember my bag. It is the small, black fabric Prada bag, the kind with the leather strap and not the woven cloth one. The kind you can buy somewhat cheaply on the Internet and look somewhat richer than you really are. Unlike Louis Vuitton bags, which are always fake on the Internet and everyone can tell you bought some cheap, fake bag and you just look like a poseur.

There: car accident, toes and fingers, no name, no ID, and an encyclopedic knowledge of bags. I try to think about bags. What else do I know about them? I know I want mine back. Did they leave it in the car?

"Look in the car," I say.

The aliens chirp and huddle, letting go of the hand. I think about escaping, but I don't seem to be able to move. Also, there are tubes coming out of the back of my hand and the crook of my elbow. There are wires glued to my chest.

"Okay, Heidi," Bunny Shirt says, turning back with a great big toothy smile that makes her look like she might want to suck blood out of my neck. "The car you were driving is registered to Agnes and William B. Nash. Could you be *Agnes*?"

"Billy!" I say.

I remember Billy. Billy Nash. William B-for-Barnsdale Nash. I remember him in glorious and perfect detail, his hair and his shoulders and the salty smell of him.

"Is Billy all right?"

The nurse-like creature strokes my arm. "You were the only person by the car, dear," she says.

All right. So just after I was in some car crash that I don't remember, I was kidnapped by helpful aliens. The first part makes about as much sense as the second part. And oh, right, I did all this without my bag, which I ditched somewhere just before losing my mind.

"Can you tell me your whole name now?" the nurse asks, still stroking my arm. "Can you remember who you are?"

How could she know that the second I remembered Billy, I knew who I was too?

So I tell them my name and they all go scurrying off someplace to celebrate without me.

THESE GIRLS DON'T MESS AROUND.